the cocaine chronicles

the cocaine chronicles

edited by
gary phillips & jervey tervalon

Akashic Books
New York

This collection is a work of fiction. All names, characters, places, and inci-
dents are the product of the authors' imaginations. Any resemblance to real
events or persons, living or dead, is entirely coincidental.

Published by Akashic Books
©2005 Gary Phillips & Jervey Tervalon

ISBN-13: 978-1-888451-75-7
ISBN-10: 1-888451-75-0
Library of Congress Control Number: 2004115619
First printing
Printed in Canada

Akashic Books
PO Box 1456
New York, NY 10009
Akashic7@aol.com
www.akashicbooks.com

For all our brothers and sisters who now only get high on life

table of contents

10   introduction
gary phillips & jervey tervalon

part I: touched by death

16   ten keys
lee child

26   the crack cocaine diet
laura lippman

40   white irish
ken bruen

48   beneficent diversions from the crackdkins diet
donnell alexander

part II: fiending

58   poinciana
susan straight

74   the screenwriter
james brown

92   twilight of the stooges
jerry stahl

100   chemistry
robert ward

part III: the corruption

126   shame
kerry e. west

138   viki, flash, and the pied-piper of shoebies
deborah vankin

152   golden pacific
nina revoyr

168   sentimental value
manuel ramos

178   just surviving another day
detrice jones

part IV: gangsters & monsters

188   a.k.a., moises rockafella
emory holmes II

208   camaro blue
bill moody

224   serving monster
jervey tervalon

252   disco zombies
gary phillips

Cocaine made me feel like a new man. And he wanted some too.

—Richard Pryor

I went right home and I went to bed
I stuck that lovin' .44 beneath my head
Got up next mornin' and I grabbed that gun
Took a shot of cocaine and away I run.

—Johnny Cash

But consider! . . . Count the cost! Your brain may, as you say, be roused and
excited, but it is a pathological and morbid process which involves increased
tissue-change and may at least leave a permanent weakness. You know, too,
what a black reaction comes upon you. Surely the game is hardly worth the
candle. Why should you, for a mere passing pleasure, risk the loss of those
great powers with which you have been endowed? Remember that I speak
not only as one comrade to another but as a medical man to one for whose
constitution he is to some extent answerable.

—Dr. John Watson to his friend Sherlock Holmes in *Sign of the Four* by
Arthur Conan Doyle

Ibarionex R. Perello

JERVEY TERVALON & GARY PHILLIPS

introduction
by gary phillips & jervey tervalon

So, Jervey, how about it? Did you ever partake?

No, G, I've never smoked cocaine, never hit the pipe, didn't tempt
me in the least, because I had been inoculated against it with a
healthy dose of junior high school ass-kicking. I assumed the push-
erman would just as soon poison me as get me high. It never
occurred to me that it would be a way to live, but it's always fasci-
nated me, how folks fall into it, plunge headlong into the depths of
human tragedy through the pursuit of the pipe. I've written about
murderous crack addicts, about dope fiends, the true zombies of
the streets *because.*

 If you lived through the '80s anywhere near an urban core,
you'd have to be stone-cold stupid not to notice them. And you'd
have to be dull-witted not to know that these drug zombies were
fictionally interesting and shouldn't be consigned to the lower
rungs of pulp fiction or ghetto literature. Certainly cocaine has had
a long-lasting appeal in popular culture, from Cab Calloway's
"Minnie the Moocher" to Public Enemy's "Night of the Living
Baseheads." But it's not just about popular appeal, it's also about an
inclusive literary landscape.

What about you, G?

For me, blow serves as two clear demarcations in my life. The first
was the summer of '73, when I was home from my first year of college at San Francisco State. That summer there were sartorial rip-

ples in the ghetto culture caused by the film *Superfly*. That flick laid down some serious iconographic shit in the brains of my friends from high school like crack would grip fools in the years to come. Cats were stylin' in long quilted coats, wide-brim hats, and flared slacks. Everybody was sporting ornamental coke spoons around their necks when they hit the club, trying to keep their balance in those silly-ass platform shoes while rapping to a fox in fake leather thigh-high boots and a velvet mini.

I didn't sport a coat like the anti-hero drug dealer Priest in *Superfly*, with a style and attitude that would influence other movies and TV shows like *Starsky and Hutch* and *Baretta*— Antonio Fargas as Huggie Bear in the former, and Michael D. Roberts as Rooster in the latter. But I do remember going to a hat store on Manchester and purchasing a gray gangster brim and wearing that bad boy to parties, driving my dad's yellow '65 Galaxie 500 with the black Landau top and blasting Curtis Mayfield's too-cold *Superfly* sounds and Isaac Hayes's "Theme from Shaft" on the 8-track. There was a lot of weed at those parties but I don't recall much blow—though there was a lot of talk about somebody knew a dude who knows a dude and we can get some—but sure as hell, if there was some getting, nobody offered me any that summer. This was before crack became synonymous with the inner city, and powder the suburbs.

Drugs are class-driven like everything else, and stories about crack cocaine aren't for the mainstream readers of fiction; not the polite subject for drug literature or its crasser little brother, *heroin fiction*. Lithium is cool, antidepressants are too, but don't mention crack or freebase . . . those low-class drugs for self-medication.

Which brings me to the second incursion of coke into my life, Jervey. This was a few years later when I met this older woman—I mean, she was in her thirties and I was in my twenties—and we started going around together. She introduced me to the wonders of the toot. Now, given my wife might be reading this, or my teenage kids, I shall eschew graphic reportage of intimate encounters enhanced by the 'caine. But as Hendrix would say, I did, indeed, kiss the sky.

As to how this book came about, we'd been invited to the *Los Angeles Times* Festival of Books to participate on a panel commemorating the tenth anniversary of the Los Angeles riots of 1992.

Jervey had edited *Geography of Rage*, a collection of essays about the civil unrest published in 2002, and Gary had a piece in it.

Later we talked about how weird it was that with all the anthologies, from the erotic to the criminal, we hadn't come across any inspired by cocaine, the scourge of our times. We both thought it would be a good idea, but good ideas get lost with bad ones.

So we met a few weeks after the panel, kicked the idea around some more, and came up with an outline, but didn't get too far beyond that. We went our separate ways assuming it wouldn't get done.

Then along came Akashic Books publisher Johnny Temple, who, fresh from the success of *Brooklyn Noir*, an ambitious collection of crime-fiction stories, asked us about the cocaine idea months after we'd mentioned it to him in passing. Soon the concept was cranking, and not long after we began inviting submissions, excellent stories started blowing in.

The stories we ultimately selected for this collection reflect what interests us as observers of the human condition in its various physical and psychological permutations. The four sections of the book are used as a rough breakdown of the effects cocaine has on the participants in a given story, no matter what side of the tracks it occurs on—though some relate tales of those who actually *cross* those tracks in their hunt for the flake, the rock . . . or in their attempt to escape its grip.

Here are some samples:

Detrice Jones's powerful vignette of a young girl living with addicted parents who spend their days trying to gank their daughter's lunch money; National Book Award—nominee Susan Straight's hard-ass story of an aging crackwhore; Jerry Stahl's absurd, ribald portrayal of a debased coke fiend; and Bill Moody's low notes about the nature of caring and waste. There's also Bob Ward's tale of love gone strange, Nina Revoyr's harrowing piece revealing how things do not always go better with coke, and Laura Lippman's hilariously twisted slice of the underbelly.

These are some of the scary charms found in *The Cocaine Chronicles*. We hope you find value in them.

Every contributor to this anthology stepped up and delivered. We are very grateful to each of them for coming through on relatively short notice and relatively minimal pay. They were truly inspired by the subject matter.

For as the late, great superfreak Rick James once said, *"Cocaine, it's a hell of a drug!"*

part i
touched by death

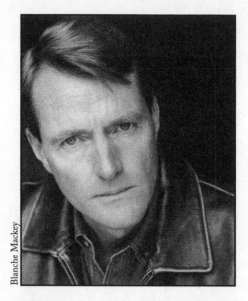

Blanche Mackey

LEE CHILD is the author of the Jack Reacher thrillers, published worldwide in thirty-nine countries. A native of England and a former television producer, he lives in New York City. The ninth Reacher novel, *One Shot*, is due soon, and Child is currently at work on the tenth in the series, *The Hard Way*. His debut, *Killing Floor*, won both the Anthony and Barry Awards for Best First Mystery. For more information, visit www.LeeChild.com.

ten keys
by lee child

Mostly shit happens, but sometimes things fall in your lap, not often, but enough times to drop a rock on despair. But you can't start in with thoughts of redemption. That would be inappropriate. Such events are not about you. Things fall in your lap not because you're good, but because other people are bad. And stupid.

This guy walked into a bar—which sounds like the start of a joke, which was what it was, really, in every way. The bar was a no-name dive with a peeled-paint door and no sign outside. As such, it was familiar to me and the guy and people like us. I was already inside, at a table I had used before. I saw the guy come in. I knew him in the sense that I had seen him around a few times and therefore he knew me, too, because as long as we assume a certain amount of reciprocity in the universe, he had seen me around the exact same number of times. I see him, he sees me. We weren't friends. I didn't know his name. Which I wouldn't expect to. A guy like that, any name he gives you is sure to be bullshit. And certainly any name I would have given him would have been bullshit. So what were we to each other? Vague acquaintances, I guess. Both close enough and distant enough that given the trouble he was in, I was the sort of guy he was ready to talk to. Like two Americans trapped in a foreign airport. You assume an intimacy that isn't really there, and it makes it easier to spill your guts. You say things you wouldn't say in normal circumstances. This guy certainly did. He sat down at my table and started in on a whole long story. Not immediately, of course. I had to prompt him.

I asked, "You okay?"

He didn't reply. I didn't press. It was like starting a car that had been parked for a month. You don't just hammer the key. You give it time to settle, so you don't flood the carburetor or whatever cars have now. You're patient. In my line of work, patience is a big virtue.

I asked, "You want a drink?"

"Heineken," the guy said.

Right away I knew he was distracted. A guy like that, you offer him a drink, he should ask for something expensive and amber in a squat glass. Not a beer. He wasn't thinking. He wasn't calculating. But I was.

An old girl in a short skirt brought two bottles of beer, one for him and one for me. He picked his up and took a long pull and set it back down, and I saw him feel the first complex shift of our new social dynamic. I had bought him a drink, so he owed me conversation. He had accepted charity, so he owed himself a chance to re-up his status. I saw him rehearse his opening statement, which was going to tell me what a hell of a big player he was.

"It never gets any easier," he said.

He was a white guy, thin, maybe thirty-five years old, a little squinty, the product of too many generations of inbred hardscrabble hill people, his DNA baked down to nothing more than the essential components, arms, legs, eyes, mouth. He was an atom, adequate, but entirely interchangeable with ten thousand just like him.

"Tell me about it," I said, ruefully, like I understood his struggle.

"A man takes a chance," he said. "Tries to get ahead. Sometimes it works, sometimes it don't."

I said nothing.

"I started out muling," he said. "Way back. You know that?"

I nodded. No surprise. We were four miles from I-95, and everyone started out muling, hauling keys of coke up from Miami or Jax, all the way north to New York and Boston. Anyone with a

plausible face and an inconspicuous automobile started out muling, a single key in the trunk the first time, then two, then five, then
ten. Trust was earned and success was rewarded, especially if you
could make the length of the New Jersey Turnpike unmolested.
The Jersey State Troopers were the big bottleneck back then.

"Clean and clear every time," the guy said. "No trouble, ever."

"So you moved up," I said.

"Selling," he said.

I nodded again. It was the logical next step. He would have
been told to take his plausible face and his inconspicuous automobile deep into certain destination neighborhoods and meet with
certain local distributors directly. The chain would have become
one link shorter. Fewer hands on the product, fewer hands on the
cash, more speed, more velocity, a better vector, less uncertainty.

"Who for?" I asked.

"The Martinez brothers."

"I'm impressed," I said, and he brightened a little.

"I got to where I was dealing ten keys pure at a time," he said.

My beer was getting warm, but I drank a little anyway. I knew
what was coming next.

"I was hauling the coke north and the money south," he said.

I said nothing.

"You ever seen that much cash?" he asked. "I mean, really *seen*
it?"

"No," I said.

"You can barely even lift it. You could get a hernia, a box like
that."

I said nothing.

"I was doing two trips a week," he said. "I was never off the
road. I wore grooves in the pavement. And there were dozens of
us."

"Altogether a lot of cash," I said, because he needed me to open
the door to the next revelation. He needed me to understand. He
needed my permission to proceed.

"Like a river," he said.

I said nothing.

"Well, hell," he said. "There was so much it meant nothing to them. How could it? They were drowning in it."

"A man takes a chance," I said.

The guy didn't reply. Not at first. I held up two fingers to the old girl in the short skirt and watched her put two new bottles of Heineken on a cork tray.

"I took some of it," the guy said.

The old girl gave us our new bottles and took our old ones away. I said *four imports* to myself, so I could check my tab at the end of the night. Everyone's a rip-off artist now.

"How much of it did you take?" I asked the guy.

"Well, all of it. All of what they get for ten keys."

"And how much was that?"

"A million bucks. In cash."

"Okay," I said, enthusiastically, deferentially, like, *Wow, you're the man.*

"And I kept the product, too," he said.

I just stared at him.

"From Boston," he said. "Dudes up there are paranoid. They keep the cash and the coke in separate places. And the city's all dug up. The way the roads are laid out now it's easier to get paid first and deliver second. They trusted me to do that, after a time."

"But this time you picked up the cash and disappeared before you delivered the product."

He nodded.

"Sweet," I said.

"I told the Martinez boys I got robbed."

"Did they believe you?"

"Maybe not," he said.

"Problem," I said.

"But I don't see why," he said. "Not really. Like, how much cash have you got in your pocket, right now?"

"Two hundred and change," I said. "I was just at the ATM."

"So how would you feel if you dropped a penny and it rolled down the storm drain? A single lousy cent?"

"I wouldn't really give a shit," I said.

"Exactly. This is like a guy with two hundred in his pocket who loses a penny under the sofa cushion. How uptight is anyone going to be?"

"With these guys, it's not about the money," I said.

"I know," he said.

We went quiet and drank our beers. Mine felt gassy against my teeth. I don't know how his felt to him. He probably wasn't tasting it at all.

"They've got this other guy," he said. "Dude called Octavian. He's their investigator. And their enforcer. He's going to come for me."

"People get robbed," I said. "Shit happens."

"Octavian is supposed to be real scary. I've heard bad things."

"You were robbed. What can he do?"

"He can make sure I'm telling the truth, is what he can do. I've heard he has a way of asking questions that makes you want to answer."

"You stand firm, he can't get blood out of a rock."

"They showed me a guy in a wheelchair. Story was that Octavian had him walking on his knees up and down a gravel patch for a week. Walking on the beach, he calls it. The pain is supposed to be terrible. And the guy got gangrene afterward, lost his legs."

"Who is this Octavian guy?"

"I've never seen him."

"Is he another Colombian?"

"I don't know."

"Didn't the guy in the wheelchair say?"

"He had no tongue. Story is Octavian cut it out."

"You need a plan," I said.

"He could walk in here right now. And I wouldn't know."

"So you need a plan fast."

"I could go to L.A."

"Could you?"

"Not really," the guy said. "Octavian would find me. I don't want to be looking over my shoulder the whole rest of my life."

I paused. Took a breath.

"People get robbed, right?" I said.

"It happens," he said. "It's not unknown."

"So you could pin it on the Boston people. Start a war up there. Take the heat off yourself. You could come out of this like an innocent victim. The first casualty. Nearly a hero."

"If I can convince this guy Octavian."

"There are ways."

"Like what?"

"Just convince yourself first. You were the victim here. If you really believe it, in your mind, this guy Octavian will believe it, too. Like acting a part."

"It won't go easy."

"A million bucks is worth the trouble. Two million, assuming you're going to sell the ten keys."

"I don't know."

"Just stick to a script. You know nothing. It was the Boston guys. Whoever he is, Octavian's job is to get results, not to waste his time down a blind alley. You stand firm, and he'll tell the Martinez boys you're clean and they'll move on."

"Maybe."

"Just learn a story and stick to it. *Be* it. Method acting, like that fat guy who died."

"Marlon Brando?"

"That's the one. Do like him. You'll be okay."

"Maybe."

"But Octavian will search your crib."

"That's for damn sure," the guy said. "He'll tear it apart."

"So the stuff can't be there."

"It *isn't* there."

"That's good," I said, and then I lapsed into silence.

"What?" he asked.

"Where is it?" I asked.

"I'm not going to tell you," he said.

"That's okay," I said. "I don't want to know. Why the hell would I? But the thing is, you can't afford to know either."

"How can I not know?"

"That's the exact problem," I said. "This guy Octavian's going to see it in your eyes. He's going to see you *knowing*. He's going to be beating up on you or whatever and he needs to see a blankness in your eyes. Like you don't have a clue. That's what he needs to see. But he isn't going to see that."

"What's he going to see?"

"He's going to see you holding out and thinking, *Hey, tomorrow this will be over and I'll be back at my cabin or my storage locker or wherever and then I'll be okay*. He's going to *know*."

"So what should I do?"

I finished the last of my beer. Warm and flat. I considered ordering two more but I didn't. I figured we were near the end. I figured I didn't need any more of an investment.

"Maybe you should go to L.A.," I said.

"No," he said.

"So you should let me hold the stuff for you. Then you genuinely won't know where it is. You're going to need that edge."

"I'd be nuts. Why should I trust you?"

"You shouldn't. You don't have to."

"You could disappear with my two million."

"I could, but I won't. Because if I did, you'd call Octavian and tell him that a face just came back to you. You'd describe me, and then your problem would become my problem. And if Octavian is as bad as you say, that's a problem I don't want."

"You better believe it."

"I do believe it."

"Where would I find you afterward?"

"Right here," I said. "You know I use this place. You've seen me in here before."

"Method acting," he said.

"You can't betray what you don't know," I said.

He went quiet for a long time. I sat still and thought about putting one million dollars in cash and ten keys of uncut cocaine in the trunk of my car.

"Okay," he said.

"There would be a fee," I said, to be plausible.

"How much?" he asked.

"Fifty grand," I said.

He smiled.

"Okay," he said again.

"Like a penny under the sofa cushion," I said.

"You got that right."

"We're all winners."

The bar door opened and a guy walked in on a blast of warm air. Hispanic, small and wide, big hands, an ugly scar high on his cheek.

"You know him?" my new best friend asked.

"Never saw him before," I said.

The new guy walked to the bar and sat on a stool.

"We should do this thing right now," my new best friend said.

Sometimes, things just fall in your lap.

"Where's the stuff?" I asked.

"In an old trailer in the woods," he said.

"Is it big?" I asked. "I'm new to this."

"Ten kilos is twenty-two pounds," the guy said. "About the same for the money. Two duffles, is all."

"So let's go," I said.

I drove him in my car west and then south, and he directed me down a fire road and onto a dirt track that led to a clearing. I guessed once it had been neat, but now it was overgrown with all kinds of stuff and it stank of animal piss and the trailer had degenerated from a viable vacation home to a rotted hulk. It was all covered with mold and mildew and the windows were dark with organic scum. He wrestled with the door and went inside. I opened the trunk lid and waited. He came back out with a duffle in each hand. Carried them over to me.

"Which is which?" I asked.

He squatted down and unzipped them. One had bricks of used money, the other had bricks of dense white powder packed hard and smooth under clear plastic wrap.

"Okay," I said.

He stood up again and heaved the bags into the trunk, and I stepped to the side and shot him twice in the head. Birds rose up from everywhere and cawed and cackled and settled back into the branches. I put the gun back in my pocket and took out my cell phone. Dialed a number.

"Yes?" the Martinez brothers asked together. They always used the speakerphone. They were too afraid of each other's betrayal to allow private calls.

"This is Octavian," I said. "I'm through here. I got the money back and I took care of the guy."

"Already?"

"I got lucky," I said. "It fell in my lap."

"What about the ten keys?"

"In the wind," I said. "Long gone."

Jim Burger

LAURA LIPPMAN is a Baltimore writer best known for her series about Baltimore-based P.I. Tess Monaghan. She also has written two stand-alone novels, *Every Secret Thing* and *To the Power of Three*. A *Baltimore Sun* reporter for twelve years, she also has written for the *New York Times*, the *Washington Post*, and Slate.com. Her work has won virtually all the major prizes given to U.S. crime writers, including the Edgar, Anthony, Agatha, Shamus, and Nero Wolfe.

the crack cocaine diet
(or: how to lose a lot of weight and change your life in just one weekend)
by laura lippman

I had just broken up with Brandon and Molly had just broken up with Keith, so we needed new dresses to go to this party where we knew they were going to be. But before we could buy the dresses, we needed to lose weight because we had to look fabulous, kiss-my-ass-fuck-you fabulous. Kiss-my-ass-fuck-you-and-your-dick-is-really-tiny fabulous. Because, after all, Brandon and Keith were going to be at this party, and if we couldn't get new boyfriends in less than eight days, we could at least go down a dress size and look so good that Brandon and Keith and everybody else in the immediate vicinity would wonder how they ever let us go. I mean, yes, technically, *they* broke up with *us*, but we had been thinking about it, weighing the pros and cons. (Pro: They spent money on us. Con: They were childish. Pro: We had them. Con: Tiny dicks, see above.) See, we were being methodical and they were just all impulsive, the way guys are. That would be another con—poor impulse control. Me, I never do anything without thinking it through very carefully. Anyway, I'm not sure what went down with Molly and Keith, but Brandon said if he wanted to be nagged all the time, he'd move back in with his mother, and I said, "Well, given that she still does your laundry and makes you food, it's not as if you really moved out," and that was that. No big loss.

Still, we had to look so great that other guys would be punching our exes in the arms and saying, "What, are you crazy?" Everything is about spin, even dating. It's always better to be the dumper instead of the dumpee, and if you have to be the loser, then you need to find a way to be superior. And that was going to take about seven pounds for me, as many as ten for Molly, who doesn't have my discipline and had been doing some serious break-up eating for the past three weeks. She went face down in the Ding Dongs, danced with the Devil Dogs, became a Ho Ho ho. As for myself, I'm a salty girl, and I admit I had the Pringles Light can upended in my mouth for a couple of days.

So anyway, Molly said Atkins and I said not fast enough, and then I said a fast-fast and Molly said she saw little lights in front of her eyes the last time she tried to go no food, and she said cabbage soup and I said it gives me gas, and then she said pills and I said all the doctors we knew were too tight with their 'scrips, even her dentist boss since she stopped blowing him. Finally, Molly had a good idea and said: "Cocaine!"

This merited consideration. Molly and I had never done more than a little recreational coke, always provided by boyfriends who were trying to impress us, but even my short-term experience indicated it would probably do the trick. The tiniest bit revved you up for hours and you raced around and around, and it wasn't that you weren't hungry, more like you had never even heard of food; it was just some quaint custom from the olden days, like square dancing.

"Okay," I said. "Only, where do we get it?" After all, we're girls, *girly* girls. I had been drinking and smoking pot since I was sixteen, but I certainly didn't buy it. That's what boyfriends were for. Pro: Brandon bought my drinks, and if you don't have to lay out cash for alcohol, you can buy a lot more shoes.

Molly thought hard, and Molly thinking was like a fat guy running—there was a lot of visible effort.

"Well, like, the city."

"But where in the city?"

"On, like, a corner."

"Right, Molly. I watch HBO, too. But I mean, what corner?

It's not like they list them in that crap Weekender Guide in the paper—movies, music, clubs, where to buy drugs."

So Molly asked a guy who asked a guy who talked to a guy, and it turned out there was a place just inside the city line, not too far from the interstate. Easy on, easy off, then easy off again. Get it? After a quick consultation on what to wear—jeans and T-shirts and sandals, although I changed into running shoes after I saw the condition of my pedicure—we were off. Very hush-hush because, as I explained to Molly, that was part of the adventure. I phoned my mom and said I was going for a run. Molly told her mom she was going into the city to shop for a dress.

The friend of Molly's friend's friend had given us directions to what turned out to be an apartment complex, which was kind of disappointing. I mean, we were expecting row houses, slumping picturesquely next to each other, but this was just a dirtier, more run-down version of where we lived—little clusters of two-story town houses built around an interior courtyard. We drove around and around and around, trying to seem very savvy and willing, and it looked like any apartment complex on a hot July afternoon. Finally, on our third turn around the complex, a guy ambled over to the car.

"What you want?"

"What you got?" I asked, which I thought was pretty good. I mean, I sounded casual but kind of hip, and if he turned out to be a cop, I hadn't implicated myself. See, *I* was always thinking, unlike some people I could name.

"Got American Idol and Survivor. The first one will make you sing so pretty that Simon will be speechless. The second one will make you feel as if you've got immunity for life."

"O-*kay*." Molly reached over me with a fistful of bills, but the guy backed away from the car.

"Pay the guy up there. Then someone will bring you your package."

"Shouldn't you give us the, um, stuff first and then get paid?"

The guy gave Molly the kind of look that a schoolteacher gives you when you say something exceptionally stupid. We drove up to the next guy, gave him forty dollars, then drove to a spot he pointed out to wait.

"It's like McDonald's!" Molly said. "Drive-through!"

"Shit, don't say McDonald's. I haven't eaten all day. I would kill for a Big Mac."

"Have you ever had the Big N' Tasty? It totally rocks."

"What is it?"

"It's a cheeseburger, but with, like, a special sauce."

"Like a Big Mac."

"Only the sauce is different."

"I liked the fries better when they made them in beef fat."

A third boy—it's okay to say boy, because he was, like, thirteen, so I'm not being racist or anything—handed us a package, and we drove away. But Molly immediately pulled into a convenience store parking lot. It wasn't a real convenience store, though, not a 7-Eleven or a Royal Farm.

"What are you doing?"

"Pre-diet binge," Molly said. "If I'm not going to eat for the next week, I want to enjoy myself now."

I had planned to be pure starting that morning, but it sounded like a good idea. I did a little math. An ounce of Pringles has, like, 120 calories, so I could eat an entire can and not gain even half a pound, and a half pound doesn't even register on a scale, so it wouldn't count. Molly bought a pound of Peanut M&Ms, and let me tell you, the girl was not overachieving. I'd seen her eat that much on many an occasion. Molly has big appetites. We had a picnic right there in the parking lot, washing down our food with diet cream soda. Then Molly began to open our "package."

"Not here!" I warned her, looking around.

"What if it's no good? What if they cut it with, like, something, so it's weak?"

Molly was beginning to piss me off a little, but maybe it was just all the salt, which was making my fingers swell and my head pound a little. "How are you going to know if it's any good?"

"You put it on your gums." She opened the package. It didn't look quite right. It was more off-white than I remembered, not as finely cut. But Molly dove right in, licking her finger, sticking it in, and then spreading it around her gum line.

"Shit," she said. "I don't feel a thing."

"Well, you don't feel it right away."

"No, they, like, totally robbed us. It's bullshit. I'm going back."

"Molly, I don't think they do exchanges. It's not like Nordstrom, where you can con them into taking the shoes back even after you wore them once. You stuck your wet finger in it."

"We were ripped off. They think just because we're white suburban girls they can sell us this weak-ass shit." She was beginning to sound more and more like someone on HBO, although I'd have to say the effect was closer to *Ali G* than *Sopranos*. "I'm going to demand a refund."

This was my first inkling that things might go a little wrong.

So Molly went storming back to the parking lot and found our guy, and she began bitching and moaning, but he didn't seem that upset. He seemed kind of, I don't know, amused by her. He let her rant and rave, just nodding his head, and when she finally ran out of steam, he said, "Honey, darling, you bought heroin. Not cocaine. That's why you didn't get a jolt. It's not supposed to jolt you. It's supposed to slow you down, not that it seems to be doing that, either."

Molly had worked up so much outrage that she still saw herself as the wronged party. "Well, how was I supposed to know that?"

"Because we sell cocaine by vial color. Red tops, blue tops, yellow tops. I just had you girls figured for heroin girls. You looked like you knew your way around, got tired of OxyContin, wanted the real thing."

Molly preened a little, as if she had been complimented. It's interesting about Molly. Objectively, I'm prettier, but she has always done better with guys. I think it's because she has this kind of sexy vibe, by which I mean she manages to communicate that she'll pretty much do anyone.

"Two pretty girls like you, just this once, I'll make an exception. You go hand that package back to my man Gordy, and he'll give you some nice blue tops."

We did, and he did, but this time Molly made a big show of driving only a few feet away and inspecting our purchase, holding the blue-capped vial up to the light.

"It's, like, rock candy."

It did look like a piece of rock candy, which made me think of the divinity my grandmother used to make, which made me think of all the other treats from childhood that I couldn't imagine eating now—Pixy Stix and Now and Laters and Mary Janes and Dots and Black Crows and Necco Wafers and those pastel buttons that came on sheets of wax paper. Chocolate never did it for me, but I loved sugary treats when I was young.

And now Molly was out of the car and on her feet, steaming toward our guy, who looked around, very nervous, as if this five-foot-five, size-ten dental hygienist—size-eight when she's being good—could do some serious damage. And I wanted to say, "Dude, don't worry! All she can do is scrape your gums until they bleed." (I go to Molly's dentist and Molly cleans my teeth, and she is seriously rough. I think she gets a little kick out of it, truthfully.)

"What the fuck is this?" she yelled, getting all gangster on his ass—I think I'm saying that right—holding the vial up to the guy's face, while he looked around nervously. Finally, he grabbed her wrist and said: "Look, just shut up or you're going to bring some serious trouble to bear. You smoke it. I'll show you how . . . Don't you know anything? Trust me, you'll like it."

Molly motioned to me and I got out of the car, although a little reluctantly. It was, like, you know, that scene in *Star Wars* where the little red eyes are watching from the caves and suddenly those

weird sand people just up and attack. I'm not being racist, just saying we were outsiders and I definitely had a feeling all sorts of eyes
were on us, taking note.

"We'll go to my place," the guy said, all super suave, like he was
some international man of mystery inviting us to see his etchings.

"A shooting gallery?" Molly squealed, all excited. "Ohmigod!"

He seemed a little offended. "I don't let dope fiends in my
house."

He led us to one of the town houses, and I don't know what I
expected, but certainly not some place with doilies and old over-
stuffed furniture and pictures of Jesus and some black guy on the
wall. (Dr. Martin Luther King, Jr., I figured out later, but I was
really distracted at the time, and thought it was the guy's dad or
something.) But the most surprising thing was this little old lady
sitting in the middle of the sofa, hands folded in her lap. She had a
short, all-white Afro, and wore a pink T-shirt and flowery ski
pants, which bagged on her stick-thin legs. Ski pants. I hadn't seen
them in, like, forever.

"Antone?" she said. "Did you come to fix my lunch?"

"In a minute, Grandma. I have guests."

"Are they nice people, Antone?"

"Very nice people," he said, winking at us, and it was only then
that I realized the old lady was blind. You see, her eyes weren't milky
or odd in any way, they were brown and clear, as if she was staring
right at us. You had to look closely to realize that she couldn't really
see, that the gaze, steady as it was, didn't focus on anything.

Antone went to the kitchen, an alcove off the dining room, and
fixed a tray with a sandwich, some potato chips, a glass of soda, and
an array of medications. How could you not like a guy like that? So
sweet, with broad shoulders and close-cropped hair like his
granny's, only dark. Then, very quietly, with another wink, he
showed us how to smoke.

"Antone, are you smoking in here? You know I don't approve
of tobacco."

"Just clove cigarettes, Grandma. Clove never hurt anybody."

He helped each of us with the pipe, getting closer than was strictly necessary. He smelled like clove, like clove and ginger and cinnamon. Antone the spice cookie. When he took the pipe from Molly's mouth, he replaced it with his lips. I didn't really want him to kiss me, but I'm so much prettier than Molly. Not to mention thinner. But then, I hear black guys like girls with big behinds, and Molly certainly qualified. You could put a can of beer on her ass and have her walk around the room and it wouldn't fall off. Not being catty, just telling the literal truth. I did it once, at a party, when I was bored, and then Molly swished around with a can of Bud Light on her ass, showing off, like she was proud to have so much baggage.

Weird, but I was hungrier than ever after smoking, which was so not the point. I mean, I wasn't hungry in my stomach, I was hungry in my mouth. And what I wanted, more than anything in the world, were those potato chips on the blind lady's tray. They were Utz Salt 'n Vinegar; I had seen Antone take them out of the green-and-yellow bag. I loooooooooooooooooooooooooooooove Utz Salt 'n Vinegar, but they don't come in a light version, so I almost never let myself have any. So I snagged one, just one, quiet as a cat. But, like they say, you can't eat just one. Okay, so they say that about Lays, but it's even more true about Utz, in my personal opinion. I kept stealing them, one at a time.

"Antone? Are you taking food off my tray?"

I looked to Antone for backup, but Molly's tongue was so far in his mouth that she might have been flossing him. When he finally managed to detach himself, he said: "Um, Grandma? I'm going to take a little lie-down."

"What about your guests?"

"They're going," he said, walking over to the door with a heavy tread and closing it.

"It's time for *Judge Judy!*" his granny said, which made me wonder, because how does a blind person know what time it is?

Antone used the remote control to turn on the television. It was a black-and-white, total Smithsonian. After all, she was blind, so I guess it didn't matter.

Next thing I knew, I was alone in the room with the blind woman, who was fixated on *Judge Judy* as if she was going to be tested on the outcome, and I was eyeing her potato chips, while Antone and Molly started making the kind of noises that you make when you're trying so hard not to make noise that you can't help making noise.

"Antone?" the old lady called out. "Is the dishwasher running? Because I think a piece of cutlery might have gotten caught in the machinery."

I was so knocked out that she knew the word "cutlery." How cool is that?

But I couldn't answer, of course. I wasn't supposed to be there.

"It's—okay—Granny," Antone grunted from the other room. "It's—all—going—to—be—*Jesus Christ*—okay."

The noises started up again. Granny was right. It did sound like a piece of cutlery caught in the dishwasher. But then it stopped—Antone's breathing, the mattress springs, Molly's little muffled grunts—they just stopped, and they didn't stop naturally, if you know what I mean. I'm not trying to be cruel, but Molly's a bit of a slut, and I've listened to her have sex more times than I can count, and I know how it ends, even when she's faking it, even when she has to be quiet, and it just didn't sound like the usual Molly finish at all. Antone yelped, but she was silent as a grave.

"Antone, what are you doing?" his granny asked. Antone didn't answer. Several minutes went by, and then there was a hoarse whisper from the bedroom.

"Um, Kelley? Could you come here a minute?"

"What was that?" his granny asked.

I used the remote to turn up the volume on *Judge Judy*. "DO I LOOK STUPID TO YOU?" the judge was yelling. "REMEMBER THAT PRETTY FADES BUT STUPID IS

FOREVER. I ASKED IF YOU HAD IT IN WRITING, I DON'T WANT TO HEAR ALL THIS FOLDEROL ABOUT ORAL AGREEMENTS."

When I went into the bedroom, Molly was under Antone, and I remember thinking—I was a little high, remember—that he made her look really thin because he covered up her torso, and Molly does have good legs and decent arms. He had a handsome back, too, broad and muscled, and a great ass. Brandon had no ass (con), but he had nice legs (pro).

It took me a moment to notice that he had a pair of scissors stuck in the middle of his beautiful back.

"I told him no," Molly whispered, although the volume on the television was so loud that the entire apartment was practically reverberating. "No means no."

There was a lot of blood, I noticed. A lot.

"I didn't hear you," I said. "I mean, I didn't hear you say any *words*."

"I mouthed it. He told me to keep silent because his grand-mother is here. Still, I mouthed it. 'No.' 'No.'" She made this incredibly unattractive fish mouth to show me.

"Is he dead?"

"I mean, I was totally up for giving him a blow job, especially after he said he'd give me a little extra, but he was, like, uncircum-cised. I just couldn't, Kelley, I couldn't. I've never been with a guy like that. I offered him a hand job instead, but he got totally peeved and tried to force me."

The story wasn't tracking. High as I was, I could see there were some holes. *How did you get naked?* I wanted to ask. *Why didn't you shout? If Grandma knew you were here, Antone wouldn't have dared misbehaved.* He had clearly been more scared of Granny than he was into Molly.

"This is the stash house," Molly said. "Antone showed me."

"What?"

"The drugs. They're here. All of it. We could just help ourselves.

I mean, he's a rapist, Kelley. He's a criminal. He sells drugs to people. Help me, Kelley. Get him off me."

But when I rolled him off, I saw there was a condom. Molly saw it, too.

"We should, like, so get rid of that. It would only complicate things. When I saw he was going to rape me, I told him he should at least be courteous."

I nodded, as if agreeing. I flushed the condom down the toilet, helped Molly clean the blood off her, and then used my purse to pack up what we could find, as she was carrying this little bitty Kate Spade knockoff that wasn't much good for anything. We found some cash, too, about $2,000, and helped ourselves to that, on the rationale that it would be more suspicious if we didn't. On the way out, I shook a few more potato chips on Granny's plate.

"Antone?" she said. "Are you going out again?"

Molly grunted low, and that seemed to appease Granny. We walked out slowly, as if we had all the time in the world, but again I had that feeling of a thousand pairs of eyes on us. We were in some serious trouble. There would have to be some sort of retribution for what we had done. What Molly had done. All I did was steal a few potato chips.

"Take Quarry Road home instead of the interstate," I told Molly.

"Why?" she asked. "It takes so much longer."

"But we know it, know all the ins and outs. If someone follows us, we can give them the slip."

About two miles from home, I told her I had to pee so bad that I couldn't wait and asked her to stand watch for me, a longtime practice with us. We were at that point, high above the old limestone quarry, where we had parked a thousand times as teenagers. A place where Molly had never said "No" to my knowledge.

"Finished?" she asked, when I emerged from behind the screen of trees.

"Almost," I said, pushing her hard, sending her tumbling over the precipice. She wouldn't be the first kid in our class to break her neck at the highest point on Quarry Road. My high school boyfriend did, in fact, right after we broke up. It was a horrible accident. I didn't eat for weeks and got down to a size four. Everyone felt bad for me—breaking up with Eddie only to have him commit suicide that way. There didn't seem to be any reason for me to explain that Eddie was the one who wanted to break up. Unnecessary information.

I crossed the hillside to the highway, a distance of about a mile, then jogged the rest of the way. After all, as my mother would be the first to tell you, I went for a run that afternoon, while Molly was off shopping, according to her mom. I assumed the police would tie Antone's dead body to Molly's murder, and figure it for a revenge killing, but I was giving the cops too much credit. Antone rated a paragraph in the morning paper. Molly, who turned out to be pregnant, although not even she knew it—probably wouldn't even have known who the father was—is still on the front page all these weeks later. (The fact that they didn't find her for three days heightened the interest, I guess. I mean, she was just an overweight dental hygienist from the suburbs—and a bit of a slut, as I told you. But the media got all excited about it.) The general consensus seems to be that Keith did it, and I don't see any reason to let him off the hook, not yet. He's an asshole. Plus, almost no one in this state gets the death penalty.

Meanwhile, he's telling people just how many men Molly had sex with in the past month, including Brandon, and police are still trying to figure out who had sex with her right before she died. (That's why you're supposed to get the condom on as early as possible, girls. Penises *drip*. Just fyi.) I pretended to be shocked, but I already knew about Brandon, having seen Molly's car outside his apartment when I cruised his place at 2 a.m. a few nights after Brandon told me he wanted to see other people. My ex-boyfriend and my best friend, running around behind my back. Everyone feels so bad for me, but I'm being brave, although I eat so little that

I'm down to a size two. I just bought a Versace dress and Manolos for a date this weekend with my new boyfriend, Robert. I've never spent so much money on an outfit before. But then, I've never had $2,000 in cash to spend as I please.

Dieter Auner

KEN BRUEN is the author of many novels, including *The Guards*, winner of the 2004 Shamus Award, and is currently editing *Dublin Noir* (forthcoming from Akashic). His novels have been published in many languages around the world. He lives in Galway, Ireland, and also calls New York home.

white irish
by ken bruen

Man, I'm between that fuckin' rock and the proverbial hard place. Hurtin'?

Whoa . . . so bad.

My septum's burned out. Kiddin', I ain't. There's a small mountain of snow on the table. Soon as the bleed stops, I'm burying myself in there, just tunneling in. The blood ran into my mouth about an hour ago, and fuck, made the mistake of checking in the mirror.

Nearly had a coronary. A dude staring back, blood all down his chin, splattered on the white T-shirt, the treasured Guns n' Roses one, heard a whimper of . . .

Terror.

Horror.

Anguish.

A heartbeat till I realized I was the one doing the whimpering. How surprising is that?

The Sig Sauer is by the stash, ready to kick ass. Say it loud, Lock 'n' fuckin' load. Is it an echo here, or does that come back as *rock 'n' roll*?

I'm losing it.

Yeah, yeah, like I don't fuckin' know? Gimme a break, I know. All right?

Earth to muthahfuckah, HELLO . . . I am, like . . . receiving this.

The devil's in the details. My mom used to say that. God bless her Irish heart. And I sing, *"If you ever go across the sea to Ireland . . . It may be at the closing of your day . . ."*

Got that right.

A Galway girl, she got lost in the nightmare of the American Dream and never got home again. If she could see me now.

Buried her three years ago, buried her cheap. I was short on the green, no pun intended. A pine box, 300 bucks was the most I could hustle. I still owe 150 on it.

A cold morning in February, we put her in the colder ground.

Huge crowd and a lone piper playing "Carrickfergus."

I wish . . . There was me, Me and Bobby McGee.

Sure.

One gravedigger, a sullen fuck, and me, walking point. For the ceremony, a half-assed preacher. Him I found in a bar, out of it on shots of dollar whiskey and Shiner.

Bought him a bottle of Maker's Mark to perform the rites.

Perform he did and fast, as he wasn't getting the Mark till the deal was done.

Galloped through the dying words. "Man, full of misery, has but a short time."

Like that.

Even the gravedigger gaped at the rapidity, the words, tripping, spilling over each other.

"Ashes to ashes."

I was thinking David Bowie. The first pound of clay was shoveled, and I went, "Wait up."

Didn't have a rose to throw, so what the hell, took my wedding band, a claddagh, bounced it off the lid, the gold glinting against the dirt.

Caught the greed in the digger's eyes and let him see mine— the message: *Don't even think about it.*

I get back down that way, he's wearing the ring, he's meat.

My current situation, fuck, it just, like, got the hell away from me, one of those heists, should have been a piece of cake.

Cake with shredded glass.

Take down a Mex named Raoul. A medium mover of high-grade powder. Me and Jimmy, my jail buddy, my main man.

Simple score, simple plan. Go in roaring, put the Sig in Raoul's face, take the coke, the cash, and *sayonara* sucker.

No frills.

Went to hell in a bucket.

Raoul had backup. Two moonlighting Angels. We never thought to check the rear, where the hogs were parked. Jimmy had sworn Raoul would be alone, save for some trailer trash named Lori.

And so it had seemed.

We blazed in, I bitch-slapped Raoul, Jimmy hit Lori on the upside of her skull—then the bikers came out of the back room. Carrying. Sawed-offs.

The smoke finally cleared and I was in Custer's Last Stand. Everyone else was splattered on the floor, across the carpet, against the walls. Improved the shitty décor no end, gave that splash of color.

Jimmy was slumped against a sofa, his entrails hanging out. I went, "You stupid fuck, you never mentioned Angels. This is way bigger than us."

The coke, too, more than he'd known. I needed two sacks to haul it out of there, and a bin liner for the cash.

Shot Jimmy in the face. Did him a favor. Gut shot? You're fucked.

So, bikers, cops, and some stone-cold suppliers from way south of Tijuana on my tail. I covered my tracks pretty good, I think, only made a few pit stops. A bad moment when I saw a dude give me the hard look, but I'm fairly sure I shook him.

I'm holed up in the Houston Airport Marriott. Who's gonna look there?

Checked in two days ago, leastways I figure it. Living on room service and the marching powder, thinking I'd have one hit, but it kinda sneaks up on you and you're doing a whole stream without realizing. Got me a bad dose of the jitters, real bad.

The first day, if that's the day it was, I was nervous as a rat, pacing the room, taking hits offa the coke, chugging from the Jack D. Had made the pit stop for essentials, loaded up on hooch and a carton of Luckies, oh, and on impulse, a Zippo—had a logo if not the edge.

Yankees, World Champions, 1999. Like that.

Made me smile, a good year for the roses. The year I almost made first base. McKennit, met her in a bar, I'd been drinking Lone Star, nothing heavy, and building a buzz, almost mellow. Hadn't even noticed her.

Me and the ladies, not a whole lot of history there, leastways none of it good.

She'd leaned over, asked, "Got a light?"

Sure. Got a boner, too.

Bought her a drink, figuring, a fox like she was, gotta be a working girl. I could go a couple of bills, have me a time.

I was wrong, she wasn't a hooker.

Things got better, I took her home and, hell, I didn't make a move, hung back, kissed her on the cheek, and she asked, "So, Jake, wanna go on, like, a . . . date?"

Two months it lasted. Had me some fun, almost citizen shit, even bought her flowers and, oh god, Hershey's Kisses, yeah, like, how lame is that?

Got me laid.

I'd a cushy number going, a neat line in credit card scams, pulling down some medium change. I was on the verge . . . fuck . . . I dunno. Asking her something. Telling her I'd like to set us up a place . . . Jesus, what was I thinking?

We were sitting in a flash joint, finishing plates of linguini, sipping a decent Chianti, her knee brushing mine.

I can still see how she looked, the candle throwing a soft blush on her cheek, her eyes brown, wide, and soft.

Before I could get my rap going, the layout, the proposal, two bulls charged in, hauled me out of the chair, slammed me across the table, the wine spilling into her lap.

The cuffs on my wrists, then pulling me upright, the first going, "Game's up, wise guy, you're toast."

The second leered at her, spittle at the corner of his mouth, asked, "The fuck a looker like you doing with this loser?"

And her body shaking, she stammered, "There must be some mistake."

The bulls laughing, one went, "Nickle-and-dime con man, penny-ante shit, never worked a day in his goddamn life, he's going down, honey, hard. You wanna spread your legs, baby, least get some return."

They weren't kidding about the hard bit. I got two years on that deal, fuckin' credit cards. They call it white-collar crime, meaning they do not like you to fuck with their money.

Did the max, the whole jolt. Never saw McKennit again, used my one phone call to try and reach her, heard, "This number is no longer in use."

Sent a letter, got *"Return to sender."* Like the bloody song.

So, so fuck her.

The two years, in maximum-security penitentiary, trying to sidestep the gangs, the Crips, the neo-militia, the Brothers, the Mexs—motherfuckahs, would put a shiv in you for two bits or a pack of Camels.

How I met Jimmy. Hooked up the first week, walking the yard, my hands in the pockets of the light denim jacket, a north-easterly howling across the stone, freezing my nuts off.

Wasn't one of those movie deals. He didn't, like, save me from the white supremacists or prevent some buck from turning me out.

Slow burn.

A favor here, a nod there, a gathering of little moves, till we had the buddy system cooking.

Guy could make me laugh, and on the block there wasn't a whole lot of . . . what's the word I want . . . heard it on *Regis* . . . or *Leno* . . . yeah, *frivolity*.

He got early release, and when I finally got out, he was waiting in a Pinto, some speed, a six of Miller (ice cold), and a wedge, said, "Some walking 'round bills."

A buddy. Am I right or am I right? We had one album in the joint, belonged to Jimmy, Patti Smith's *Horses*. Fuck, goes back thirty years. How old is that?

Thing is, I flat out loved it, still do. The reason why, in this tomb hotel room, I have the new one, *Trampin*.

Fuckin' blinder.

Dunno is it cos Jimmy's dead, or the whole screwed-up mess, but the goddamn songs speak to me.

You're on the zillionth floor of the Airport Marriott, with the sole view being the runways, planes moving 24/7, you better have something talk to you. I'm chugging Jack D., singing along to "Mother Rose."

And is this weird or what, I sound like Roy Orbison. My mom, when she wasn't whining along to Irish rebel ballads, would play Roy endlessly.

Man, I don't know politics from Shinola, but Radio Baghdad, hearing that, watching CNN and the body count, I'm weeping like a baby. Like what? Some kind of loser?

Loser? Me?

Hey, shithead, look in the corner, see that hill of coke, the bag of Franklins? Who's losing?

My mom, her wish was to get back to Ireland, walk the streets of Galway, have oysters near the Spanish Arch, do a last jig in the Quays, but money, yeah, never put it together. So I'm, like, gonna make the pilgrimage for her—why I'm at the airport, got the documents, ticket, the whole nine.

Only worry is the beer isn't cold there. How weird is that? But hey, I'll drink Jameson. A few of those suckers, I might dance a jig my own self.

I rang a guy to offload the coke. Can't really bring that shit to Ireland, and I'm worried he might sell me out, but we've done business before so had to tell him where I'm at, thinking maybe that was stupid, but I wasn't focusing real hard when I dropped the dime.

Gotta get my shit together.

So I jump in the shower, blasting in the scald position, and I freeze. A knock at the door.

The Sig is where?

Think, fuck.

Another knock. Louder. Insistent.

And I'm stumbling outta the shower, hit my knee against the sink, that mother hurts, hobble to the bed, grab the Sig from under the pillow, shout, "With you in a sec."

Slide the rack, my voice coming out croaked, sounding like, "Wiv y'all." Texas, right?

I look through the peephole, and it's the maid, fuckin' room service. I shout, "I'm good, *muchas gracias*."

Hear, *"De nada."*

And the trolley moving on, oil those goddamn wheels. My body is leaking sweat, rivulets down my chest, back, thinking, *Gotta . . . get . . . straight.*

Rest of the day is purple haze, must have ordered some food as I came to on the floor. It's dark, the only light coming from the runway, throwing an off/on flicker across the wall.

Half a turkey hero is on the floor, close to my mouth, smothered in mayo. The Sig is in my right hand and, yeah, my nose is pumping blood again.

The carpet is, like, fucked.

I have clothes on, 501's, and, naturally, a white T with the bloodstained logo.

Redemption Road.

Almost illegible, it's stuck to my chest.

I get to my feet, stagger a bit, so do a quick hit of the snow to straighten out, no biggie. I'm sitting on the bed, waiting for the rush, the phone rings, I pick up, figuring reception.

A voice goes, "You're dead, sucker."

Things to do in Houston when you're dead.

I slam it down, hurting the palm of my hand.

I'm waiting. Let 'em come. I'm, like, ready . . . ready-ish. I'd play Patti but I'm listening to every sound, for every sound . . . a 747 about to take off . . .

Wonder where that's bound?

DONNELL ALEXANDER smoked crack for about six weeks in 1985, before the drug's warning labels were printed. When his buddies started pawning their shit just to get another hit, dude figured that scene was not his. In 2003, Crown published his memoir, *Ghetto Celebrity*.

beneficent diversions
from the crackdkins diet
by donnell alexander

She was the most accomplished person in Jerome's life. Something central to her, he could not trust. Down and out, Jerome couldn't fathom the chasm between Elaine's refined lust and his own hunger.

His lover held a doctorate in sociology and an undergrad minor in statistics. Daughter of a minor painter mom and a documentary editor old boy, the woman's sense of applied visual art was not something he could argue with—even as an artist, one of almost feral ambition.

That animal appetite would ultimately win out, Elaine told him time and again. It would save him from the insinuating downward tug. "Follow *that* urge," she said, "and you'll be free in no time . . . It will feel like nothing."

Usually she had just swallowed his semen, and before that demanded "baptism of the throat"—her words. Then she forecast. Elaine also offered her most explicit descriptions of the fashion in which he would recover.

She would wipe her chin clean of—again, her words—the "gravy," his silver, silky gravy.

And next she'd rise and take Jerome by the shoulders, tap his chin up so that their eyes met, and swiftly paint a picture with words, numbers, and theory. Taken as a whole, they said, "It's going to be all right. I swear it will be all right."

He hardly ever ate because Jerome was on what he called the Crackdkins Diet. The habit had brought about an effortless— necessary, frankly—yet undesired weight loss. For Jerome's first date with Elaine—downtown, off Ludlow Street—he forced himself to consume four pieces of sushi.

Although they were hardly acquainted, Elaine at that time seemed peculiarly invested in his becoming nourished. "I really get off on turning people on to new things," she said, voicing an urgency not often associated with high-end Eastern cuisine. "Don't you find it sexy when someone enjoys an experience you introduce them to?"

It had become difficult for Jerome to bask in the reflection of another's pleasure. His joys were now too dualistic, illumination and malevolence twinned. By the time of this dinner, he had taken two or three casual acquaintances into the Tenderloin's remaining unoccupied buildings for smoking and communion. Recalling those scenes while sitting in this Lower East Side restaurant made him lick his lips.

Jerome thought of hits taken 3,000 miles away.

Those friends were like Elaine—good, adventurous souls looking for the next vivid sensation. Jerome knew the address of every cool rockhouse in SF, Oakland, and Richmond, but he was never clear on how solidly his buddies had stepped into their tango with the rock. For sure, he saw them afterward in the workplace and at openings and award ceremonies. There were no references to crack-fueled rocket rides with tenements for launch pads and homeless junkies as audience. Bic lanterns bright, not spotlight. Jerome's casual acquaintances kept it quiet.

The blind date, promising as she was, turned into a reminder. As would Elaine, these slumming kids from Generation X had tongued their lips upon swallowing, and he now saw those other lips thin and almost begging, all but squirming now that the caressing was through.

She said, "It's like when your photographs are published, I'd imagine. Do you ever happen upon readers glimpsing them? Does it turn you on?"

"I almost never see people see my pictures. They're at home in their pajamas, drinking coffee. Or taking a poop. Generally, it's a gloss, the way they look. People are mad busy. They pass through the horror. I can't get there, to the turn-on, so much."

Jerome picked over his California roll. Mashed into wasabi, the food lost its artfulness and seemed a bit primordial. The Japanese eatery disguised its elegance aurally, through a soundtrack of outer-borough hip-hop and obscure European soul tracks. The DJ, tucked away in anteroom shadows, wore his knit, brimmed Triple Five Soul cap low on his brow and played fewer than ninety seconds of each song.

Cool scene, Jerome thought, but nobody's gonna face death. And in that, this place struck him as deprived.

The last time he had been drug-free was in Fallujah.

That San Diego soldier, the one who had dropped 150 pounds between enlisting and being sent out, died horribly.

Jerome had seen viscera before. He had even seen that of other youngsters eager to strike up friendships with a black war photographer. Insides out, yes, he'd seen that, but Jerome hadn't seen the insides of someone with such exquisite back story.

Josephine Six-Pack has got to witness Dude.

And he began clicking away—auto-drive, auto-focus—at the boy's boots and his gear. From a variety of angles Jerome photographed an iPod clutched in the SoCal corpse's stiff, newly thin, chalky fingers. Wedged as it was between belt buckle and sand, the iPod would make subscribers wonder what the boy was listening to when death hit. A candid shot might make them ponder the concerns of his parents back home.

This documentarian of deadly conflict thought, *They will be so trippin' on the train.*

And Jerome felt kinda high.

He resented that his favorite rhetorical device for preparing for war no longer provided.

The freaks come out at night . . .
The freaks come out at niiight . . .

Because they attacked during the day now. And they were not freaks. These were not the coca-crazed rebels and U.S.-worshipping zealots he'd gotten used to in Central American insurgencies. In this war, they were the faithful. They prayed all the time. Or they blindly followed scripture favored by that other land, the one whose bounty earned its minions' trust.

They came out during the brightest times. Bombing in a fashion that appeared on the surface to be indiscriminate, the locals calculated with the personal specificity of a high-level computer-code creator. Yet their rationale unearthed the truth in terror, robbing light of meaning and upsetting Jerome's metaphor.

On a return flight to Berlin, surfing the Web via wireless modem, he grasped exactly how untethered his worldview had become. A pop-up for an international restaurant had tweaked Jerome's sensibility. He'd pushed away a prefab meal he'd pushed away 500 times before. This time he pushed away the food with feeling.

And the faithful came out all day. Maiming their own. They invoked the name of Allah and the other God, and they grabbed hold of their weapons and refused to let go.

While on a brief break from his legal theater of pain, Jerome had dallied with the girl who got excited by sharing what turned her on. He had bracketed the episode by ingesting rock cocaine in San Francisco. Next thing, the most real place on earth was where Jerome set. He huddled with Air Force officers, saw some death, took some pictures. And now the shooter was on his way to the Baghdad airport.

That reporter he hung with, the Aussie who had ended his career in the States by announcing that the war in Iraq wasn't going so well, was done and so was Jerome. This was his shortest fling yet. He caught a ride with an American newspaper columnist and a documentary photographer he knew only from textbooks and lore.

The reporter talked nonstop about the American mission. The iconic shooter stared impassively into the sand.

Five miles outside town a shell hit, about 150 yards off the bumpy path that passed for a road. The writer insisted the car be diverted.

No one argued, so the Jordanian hired to drive took the next left he could find.

The explosions only got closer. And louder.

The car stopped completely just outside Baghdad. The gunshots started, bullets arriving from every angle, first strafing the top of their Hummer, then piercing its metal and glass. Jerome took cover, pulling his flak jacket over his head. He dug himself as deep as he could into the space between the driver's side backseat and the floor.

When an acidic explosion blew apart the passenger side, Jerome was surprised to see the documentary photographer still moving, albeit slowly and with more than a little pain. The man's arm had nothing beyond its wrist. No more bullets hit the vehicle. Careening slightly, the Hummer ambled off the road in low gear.

A degree of same-old, same-old cut in on Jerome's reaction to the sight of both that writer's destroyed body and the utter health of their driver. The Jordanian gestured to the roadside man in a skull-cap who dropped his Russian rifle and fled. Jerome rose and rammed the length of his telephoto lens into the Jordanian's ear. As the Hummer commenced to spinning, he again buried himself in the space beneath his seat.

Jerome was on the roof, then back on the seat, and back on the floor. His door turned to the floor. His backseat partner fell onto Jerome, drenching him with blood, touching him with gore.

As minutes passed, both photographers became soaked in the absolute desert quiet.

Jerome tied a tourniquet on his photographic hero. He called his agency's Baghdad bureau, then picked up a camera and climbed out.

As he captured images of the blown-apart reporter in front of the vehicle, Jerome thought of Elaine. This new thing needed no introduction, even where the afterlife holds so much sway. Death can be a kind of baptism. The reporter's back story, familiar enough to Jerome, seemed canned and uninteresting. He'd tell it easily enough. But for the folks back home and in Europe and even here, the hit wouldn't be much stronger than the name that accompanied the man's newspaper column. No one would be turned on.

And that was fine for once. Not every hit could be truly killer. In fact, each hit seemed to be diminishing in its potency.

Jerome looked at his stoic comrade and, just past him, spotted sandwiches—hints of turkey, cheese, and wheat—sticking out of the man's Nikon bag.

Lactose-intolerant or not, Jerome wanted—nay, needed—to consume what he saw.

"Can I have some of that?"

His colleague reached with a limb that could not perform the task. He laughed and began to cry and Jerome documented every emotion.

When he finally got hold of the sandwich, Jerome devoured it in half a dozen bites. Perhaps the worst thing about the Crackdkins Diet is that it only satisfies its adherents' appetites for destruction. And what he really wanted was life.

part ii
fiending

SUSAN STRAIGHT was born in 1960 in Riverside, California, where she lives with her three daughters. She has published five novels, all set in fictional Rio Seco; she is currently working on a new story collection featuring Glorette and other Rio Seco women. Her new novel, *A Million Nightingales*, is forthcoming from Pantheon.

poinciana
by susan straight

W hy you waste your money here?" she asked Sisia. The smell of the chemicals at the nail salon went through Glorette's eyes and into her brain. Passed right through the tears and the eyeballs. *Through the irises,* she thought.

"Not a waste," Lynn Win said, moving around Sisia's hand like a hummingbird checking flowers. Like the hummingbird that came to the hibiscus in front of Western Motel. Mrs. Tajinder Patel's hibiscus. "Only to you," Lynn Win said.

"Please." Glorette walked into the doorway to breathe and looked at the cars roaming past the strip mall. Every strip mall in Rio Seco, in California, in the world, probably, was like this. Nail salon, pizza place, video store, doughnut shop, liquor store, Launderland, and taqueria. All the smells hovering in their own doorways, like the owners did in the early morning and late at night, waiting.

Like she and Sisia hovered in their own route: Sundown first, Launderland in winter when it was cold in the alley, taqueria when the cops cruised by. All the standing and waiting between jobs. They were just jobs. Like clean the counter at the taqueria. Take out the trash. Uncrate the liquor. Wash the sheets. All up and down the street. Lean against the chain-link fence, against the bus stop but you can't sit on the bench, shove your shoulder into the cinder-block wall outside Launderland and sleep for a minute, if the fog settled in like a quilt, like the opposite of an electric blanket, and cooled off the night.

The nail polish vapors stung her eyes. Why you couldn't get high off these fumes? So convenient. 7-Eleven was a convenience store. Easy. She could sit here and close her eyes, and Lynn Win would paint her like a statue and the vapors would rise up into her mouth and nose and make the inside of her forehead turn to snow. She would pay Lynn Win. Instead of paying for the rock to turn into fumes.

The plant to a powder to a chunk the size of a cocklebur in your hand. Then it turned red and glowed, like a rat's eye in the palm tree when you looked up just as headlights caught the pupils. Did rats have pupils?

Then you breathed in. And behind your eyes, it was like someone took a Wite-Out pen and erased everything. Your whole head turned into a milk shake. Sweet and grainy and sliding down the back of your skull.

Look at all these nail salons. She turned the pages of the advertisements in Vietnamese, the flyer on the coffee table. Massage pedicure chairs. Swirling water. The women with perfect eyebrows and lips and hair. Every other name Nguyen.

Linh Nguyen. She remembered what Lynn Win had said when she changed her name: "Win like money I get."

Glorette breathed again at the open salon door. "Sisia. Please. Tell me you ever heard a man say, 'Girl, I love those nails. That color perfect with your clothes. The decals are fresh.'"

"Shut up, Glorette. You just cheap."

Lynn Win glanced up at her and frowned, her perfect Vietnamese face sheened with makeup, her eyes encircled by a wash of pale green, her lips pink as watermelon Jell-O. On the left side of her neck was a scar. A healed gash that must have gaped, against tight neck skin.

No one had loose neck skin until forty. *She must be about thirty-five*, Glorette thought. *Just like us.*

Sisia had a scar on her neck, too, a keloid caterpillar, shiny as satin. Curling iron. Fifteen. They'd been getting ready for some high school dance. Back when Sisia still hot-combed her hair and then curled it back like Farrah Fawcett and Jayne Kennedy. Hell.

What did the DJ play at that dance? Cameo? She'd have to ask Chess when she saw him next time. Funkadelic?

The hot air at the door mixed with the cold air and nail polish fog.

No scars. She had never done anything with her hair other than wash it, comb in some Luster Pink or coconut oil, and let it hang loose in long, black ripples. Back then. Now she wore it in a high bun every night, unless a man requested that she unpin it.

Now this new woman cruising Palm in the brown van had poked her finger into the bun a few nights ago and then pulled. "Man, I know that shit ain't real," the woman had said, her voice New York like rappers in a video, her words all pushed up to the front of her lips. People from New York kept their words there, just at their teeth, never deep in their throats like Louisiana people. Like her mother and father.

Then the new woman had said, "I-on't-even-care you think you the shit around here. Just cause you light. Cause you got all that hair. Anybody get hair. Bald man get hair he want to. You need to move your ass off this block. Cause I'm parked here."

She couldn't have been more than twenty, twenty-two. Short, thick-thighed in her miniskirt, her hair in marcelled waves close to her forehead. Her words moved behind her lips and her lips moved like a camel's, while her eyes stayed still.

"Sound like she said she some pork," Sisia said, hands on her hips.

Glorette just shrugged and looked back over her shoulder at the woman near her van. That's where she worked the men. She had a CD player in there and some silk sheets, she said. And her man stood in the doorway of the liquor store for a long time, talking with Chess and Casper and the others who were just biding their time.

"I ain't no crack ho," the girl called, and Sisia laughed.

"I ain't either," she said. "I'm somethin else."

"This ain't the eighties." The girl shot them the finger.

"And I ain't Donna Summer."

Glorette watched Sisia move her head on her neck like a turtle and stalk away, and she followed.

Glorette thought, *1980? Was I fifteen?*

Damn.

Gil Scott-Heron said the "Revolution Will Not Be Televised," brother. You will not be able to turn on or tune out. But they did. That's what Sere always said. Brothers tuned out. *Green Acres* and *Beverly Hillbillies* will not be so important, Gil Scott-Heron said— but they were. The revolution will not be televised, brothers, the revolution will be live.

One night Glorette had run into Marie-Therese at Rite Aid. Marie-Therese used to be with Chess, back then when they were girls in the darkness of the club called Romeo's. 1981? Only two clubs in Rio Seco back then—Romeo's for jazz and funk, and Oscar's Place for nasty old blues and knife fights and homebrew.

That was where she met Sere. A brother with a flute. Didn't nobody in Rio Seco have a flute.

Gil Scott-Heron's band had a flute. Yusuf Lateef had a flute. War had a flute. Herbie Mann had a flute. Sere had loved that Mann song—"Push Push." She could still remember it. Sere's band was called Dakar. His last name.

Called himself Sere Dakar.

Where the hell was Sere playing his damn flute now? For Jay-Z or 50 Cent? For Ludacris? What else did this girl from New York always have blastin out her CD player when she was waiting?

Nobody said *hey, brotha.* Nobody but the old ones. Her age. Chess and Octavious and them. That Sidney, the one ran into her at Sundown. He used to work at the hospital. Chess and them said he burned the body parts after the doctors cut them off. Said he burned up Mr. Archuleta's leg, and Glorette always wondered how heavy that piece of meat would have been. She ran her shoulders up under her ears with the shivers. Piece. *Give me a lil piece, sugar. Just a lil piece.* What the hell was that? What they wanted wasn't no size. You couldn't give anybody just a lil bit of anything.

Sisia handed the money to Lynn Win. Sisia's skin was so thin over her facial bones that her temples looked stretched from the tight cornrows.

They had been smoking for so long. Chess gave her the pipe first but then he got done with it. He said he didn't need it.

He had his weed and Olde English.

How was the skin distributed over the bones? How did her buttocks stay in the right place? When did men decide they wanted buttocks and cheekbones and hair instead of something else? Like a big nose or huge forehead or belly? Some caveman picked.

Sisia stood up with her nails purple as grape juice and rings winking. But could a woman kill someone with her nails? Because this new woman from New York looked like she wanted to kill Glorette.

The man stopped in his old Camaro. Moved his chin to tell her *come on*. Glorette knew he wanted head. That's all. He parked in the lot behind the taqueria. Five minutes. A little piece of her lip and her tooth banged on his zipper when he jerked around.

Her piece. Twenty dollars. She walked back toward Launderland where Jazen and his boys kept their stash in a dryer.

The rock was so small. Not even a piece. A BB. A spider egg. A grasshopper eye. But not perfectly round. Jagged-edged.

A white freckle, she thought, and started laughing, waiting for the screen like a windshield in front of her eyes when she breathed in hard. Like someone had soaped up her brain. Store was closed.

Headphones. Al B. Sure—"Nite and Day." Switch—"I Call Your Name." All those sweet-voiced men from when she was first walking out here. Not jazz. Jazz was Sere. "Poinciana." "April in Paris." And funk. Mandrill and Soul Makossa and Roy Ayers.

But somebody always stole the headphones. And she wanted Victor to have headphones, and they kept stealing his, too. So he slept in them, with a chair against his bedroom door. She tried to make sure only Chess or someone she knew came home with her, but sometimes Sisia begged to let her use the couch or the floor with a man and then sometimes he stole.

Her son Victor knew everything about music.

"New York rappers, man, I have to listen real careful to understand," he always said. "Oakland and L.A. are easy. St. Louis is crazy—I mean, they mess with the actual words."

Victor analyzed everything. Sometimes Glorette stared at his forehead while he was talking, at the place where his shorn hair met his temples. He kept it cut very short, and the hairline curved like a cove on a map. She had been to a cove once. To the ocean. With Victor's father. Sere.

He'd seen her in the club. He thought she was twenty. He got her address. He'd borrowed a car, pulled up in front of her father's house and leaned his chin on the crook of his elbow like a little kid. A little boy with an arm turtleneck. He told her, "I'm fixin to see this place California's supposed to be. What they all talk about in Detroit."

"What you think you gon see?" Glorette had watched the freeway signs above them, the white dots like big pearls in the headlights.

"Remember Stevie singing 'Livin for the City'? Skyscrapers and everythang. I'ma see waves and sand and everythang. Surfers."

"At night?"

"They probably surf at night." He'd turned to her in the passenger seat. That car belonged to Chess. It was a Nova and someone had spilled Olde English in the backseat and the smell rose from the carpet sharp like cane syrup. "It's an hour to the ocean and you never been there?"

Glorette had shrugged. She had felt her shoulders go up and down, felt her collarbone in the halter top graze the cloth. He had left a love bruise on her collarbone. He'd said her bones made her look like a Fulani queen. "I bet them sorry brothas call you a Nubian or Egyptian. Cause they don't know the specifics. Huh?"

She'd touched cheekbone and collarbone and the point of her chin. But after all that it was the soft part they wanted.

No bones.

Sere took out the Cameo cassette from the old stereo and slid in an unmarked one. "Poinciana," he said. Piano hush-hush and cymbals. Like rain on a porch roof and swirling water.

"It's a hour I ain't never had free," she said.

Then, after they'd driven to the ocean and sat in the car looking at the blackness that was one with the horizon, a cold purple-blue blackness like charcoal, with the waves the only sound and then a splash of white in a long line as if someone were washing bleach clothes in too much detergent, Sere turned to her and he only wanted the same things as the rest of them.

Why have buttocks? What good were they? And hair? If Glorette's great-great-whoever had been Fulani and had gotten with some Frenchman in Louisiana, why all this hair down her back? How was that supposed to keep her warm? Hair was fur. Nails were claws. Sisia was ready to kill some damn lion now that they were done with Lynn Win's place. Glorette had gotten high off the fumes anyway, waiting for Sisia's toenails to dry. Who the hell was she gon kill with them toenails? Lynn Win's mother sat in front of the spa chair waiting for the next pedicure. The mother looked old but probably wasn't. She wore knit pants like an old woman, and her hair was in a bun on her head. Black hair with gray threads shot through like moss.

All the blood moving through the pieces of their bodies. When she woke up at noon or so, the already-hot light streaming through the blinds like X-rays on her legs where she lay on the couch, she would see the tops of her feet smooth and golden, her toes dirty from the walking, but her skin still sleeping.

Sometimes Sisia spent the eighteen dollars on a pedicure so she could sit down for an hour, she said.

But Glorette didn't want decals on her toes. She saved twenty dollars a day for Victor. For CDs and ramen.

The store was open. She went to the older mall with the Rite Aid and auto parts store. The lipsticks stacked in the bin like firewood. Hair color boxes always started with blond. Blond as dental floss and then about thirty more yellows. Saffron and Sunflower. Gingercake and Nutmeg. Black always last. Midnight.

Black hair ain't nothin you could eat.

There were flowering plants in front of the drugstore. Her father always shook his head and said, "Anybody buy plant when they buy cough syrup don't grow nothin. Put that tomato in the ground and throw water on it and wonder why it die, *oui*."

She walked past the window of the auto parts store. When she was with Chess, she'd wander the aisles touching the oil filters like paper queen's collars and fan belts like rubber bands for a giant's ponytail. Chess fixed cars all day and loved her all night. But he had to love Marie-Therese and Niecy, too, and she told him, "Only me," and he shrugged and said, "Only always too small. Only one dollar. Only one rib. See? I ain't livin only."

She saw the boxes and boxes of fuel filters near the window. Same size as hair color. A lil piece. Only a lil piece.

Ramen was ten for a dollar. Beef.

Now, when she looked at her hands on the counter, they were smooth and gold. She slid the dollar across. But by midnight, when she sat in the taqueria just before it closed, she would study her hands, the veins jagged like blue lightning. Her feet—it looked like someone had inserted flattened branches of coral under her skin. The skin so thin by midnight, at hands and feet and throat and eyelids.

She imagined she was swimming down the sidewalk. The pepper trees in the vacant lot after the strip mall, where the old men used to play dominoes on orange crates, where the city had put a chain-link fence, trying to keep "undesirables" from loitering. She didn't loiter. The streetlights shone through the pepper branches. She was under the ocean. Sere had brought a flashlight that night they went to the ocean, and he'd found tidal pools where the water only swayed in the depressions of the rocks, and the flashlight beam showed her a forest of seaweed and snails clinging to the leaves—were they leaves, underwater? stems?—and the whole world under the surface swayed.

Like now, when the evening wind moved the whole street. The pepper branches swayed delicate and all at once, the palm fronds rustled and glinted above her, and the tumbleweeds along the fence trembled like anemones.

She'd gotten a book, a child's book, after that night at the ocean and learned the names of every animal in the tidal pool. She had waited a year for him to take her back there, but he disappeared when she was eight months pregnant, veins like fishnet stockings all stretched out along her sides.

She swam along the sidewalk now, wondering where Sisia had gone, waiting to see who was looking for her. Maybe Chess. Maybe the brown van, with New York City in the back pissed at Glorette because she'd shrugged and said in front of the woman, "Ain't hot to me. Long as my hair up and my soda cold."

"Pop."

"What?"

"You mean pop."

"I'ma pop you," Sisia came up behind the woman and said. "Don't nobody care if you from New York or New Mexico. Time for you to step. Don't nobody want to get in no nasty van. Fleas and lice and shit."

The woman spat a cloud onto the sidewalk near Sisia's sandals. "Then why I had five already tonight? Make more in one night than you make all week. This the way in New York. Mens want some convenience. And it's the shit up in there. I got incense and candles and curtains. So you take your raggedy country ass back to the alley." But all this time she was looking at Glorette. "And your high yella giraffe, too."

The custodian at the junior high said, "Just a lil minute, now. Just stand still. I ain't even gon touch you. But it ain't my fault. Look at you. The Lord intended you for love. Look at you. Hold still. See. See. Lord. See."

The mop was damp like a fresh-washed wig at the back of her neck. "Pretend that's me." He stood close enough that she smelled Hai Karate, and then the bleach smell of what left his body and he caught in a rag.

"See." His voice was high and tight. His white name tag was small as a Chiclet when she crossed her eyes and didn't focus at all.

She wanted some chicharrones. Explosions of fat and chile on her molars.

When she turned down Palm to head toward Sundown, seeing Chess and two other men, thinking the chicharrones would give her enough time to let Chess see the backs of her thighs and her shoulder blades, her miniskirt and halter top better than what New York had, better than curtains or candles, it was like her thoughts brought the brown van cruising down Palm slowly, stopping at the liquor store. The woman got out and folded her arms, cocked her head to the side, the tails of her bandanna like a parrot's long feathers curling around her neck.

Glorette turned down the alley and headed toward the taqueria instead.

"Look here," the custodian said. Mr. Charles. But he was not old. His fade was not gray at the edges. "Look here." He held out money rolled tight as a cigarette. "I ain't gon bother you no more."

The five dollar bill was a twig in her sock all day.

She sat at the table in the taqueria for a few minutes, feeling the blood move and growl in her feet. No socks. Sandals. Heels. The money not in her cleavage. No money yet tonight. When she got money she put it inside the thick hair at the back of her head, just before the bun.

Chess would give her money. But most of the men just slid a rock into her palm.

The custodian didn't have to touch her after that. He didn't give her money ever again. He watched her walk in the hallway, and she knew he went into his broom closet and stood there and saw her when he moved his hands. Free. A lil piece. He stood facing the mop. The string hair. Then he was gone.

They were all gone.

At the taqueria, the woman behind the counter watched her, waiting patiently. Her mop was already wet. It stood up behind her, at the back door. Her night was almost over. The carne asada was dry and stringy in the warming pan.

Just a lil piece of meat. And a warm tortilla.

She still had the bag of ramen but Victor would be asleep now. He was seventeen. He was about to graduate. He stayed up late studying and fell asleep on the couch, even though he knew she might bring someone home if she had to. The only one who always insisted on coming to her apartment was Chess. He liked to sit on the couch and drink a beer and pretend they were married. She knew it. He would watch TV like that was all he came for, laughing at Steve Harvey, like this living room was TV, too, and there were sleeping kids in the bedrooms and a wife.

"Look at your feet," he would say, like she'd been working at 7-Eleven all day. Convenience. "You should get your feet done like Sisia. Look like they hurt. And get your toes did. Ain't that how y'all say? 'I done got my toes *did*.'"

Glorette smiled.

* * *

Victor was afraid of fingernails. He'd cried when he was little when Sisia came over and Glorette didn't know why. Sisia wasn't pretty. She was dark and her cheeks were pitted like that bread. Pumpernickel. What the hell kind of name was that for a bread?

Sisia was a brick house, though. She liked to say it. A real mamma-jamma—36-24-36 back in the day. More like 36-30-36 now, but still Glorette heard men say, "Close your eyes, man, and open your hands, and you got something there, with that woman."

But it was the fingernails that Victor cried about. Long and squared-off and winking with gems or even a ring through the nail. Lynn Win had to bore a hole through the tip and hang the jeweled ring.

Claws. For animals.

But now only women were supposed to fight with them. You could scratch a man's face, but then he'd probably kill you. You could scratch his back—some men wanted you to dig nails into their backs, like you were out of control, and that made them lose it, their whole spines would arch and tremble. But some men, if you dug your nails experimentally into the wider part below their shoulder blades, the cobra hood of muscle, just frowned and elbowed your hands off. "Don't mark me up and shit," they'd say, and then Glorette knew they had a wife or woman at home.

But Glorette just used her regular nails. Her claws. The ones God gave her. The ones Victor said were designed different from apes and chimps, and different from cats and dogs. "I don't think we ever dug," he'd say. "Not like badgers or rabbits. And we didn't need the fingernails to hold onto food or anything. So it must be just for fighting, but we didn't have teeth like the cats or dogs to bite something on the neck and kill it.

"I think they're just leftover. From something else."

Sere had a vein on his temple, from his hairline toward his left eyebrow, like twine sewn under his skin. When he played his flute or drums, the vein rose up but didn't throb. It wasn't red or blue under his brown skin, not like the white baby Glorette had seen once at the store whose skin was so pale that blue veins moved along its head and temples like freeways.

But Victor's temples were smooth and straight, though he thought all the time, read and wrote and did math problems and studied for graduation tests and played music and didn't just listen but wrote down all these bands' names and dates and song titles. He asked her once, "This one, the one you like so much. 'Poinciana.' What is it?"

She thought for a long time. "A flower? I don't know."

One crystal of salt from a cracker on her tongue. The cracker exploding like hard-baked snowflakes and pieces of rock salt on her molars. Then a white sludge she could work at while they walked.

She had to have saltines when she was pregnant with Victor.

Sisia's aunt used to eat starch. White chunks of Argo. Only one she wanted. That box with the woman holding corn. Indian woman. Corn turned into knobs of snow that squeaked in the teeth. *Like new sneakers on a basketball court,* Chess used to say when they were young.

The corn husks were green skin when they peeled off. The kernels milky white when pierced by a fingernail. How did that turn to starch?

The leaves of the coca wherever those Indians grew it. And how the hell did it turn to little chunks of white? Baby powder cornstarch flakes of Wite-Out powdered sugar, not crystals, not cane sugar and molasses, like her mother would only use, like Louisiana. They cut the cane and crushed it in the mill, her mother said. Mules going round and round. Then the juice had to boil and boil and boil and finally sugar crystals formed. Diamonds of sweet. Diamonds of salt. On the tongue. But this chunk—which she picked up out the empty dryer drum while Jazen watched, her twenty in his pocket—she couldn't eat.

It had to turn to gray smoke inside her mouth, her throat, her lungs. Insubstantial. Inconvenience. The convenience store.

Controlled substance. Possession of a controlled substance, but if you smoke it or swallow it if they pull up, you ain't in possession. It's possessin you. Ha. Sisia laughing. Chess laughing. Come on. Let's go home.

He liked to pretend her couch was home.

Swear he would ask her to make grits. The tiny white sand of corn. Not crystals. Not chunks.

Call it cush-cush back home, her mother used to say.

Victor had eaten grits at his grandmére's house and loved to call it that. Cush-cush.

Victor was sleeping now. His math book open on his chest. Sere's brain. My brain? He had the third highest grades in the whole damn school. His ramen was in her hand. The plastic bag handles were rolled into pearls by now.

She walked down the alley behind the taqueria, more for the smell of the put-away beef than anything else. Ain't no charge for smelling. She paused beside a shopping cart parked against the chain-link fence. The slats of vinyl worked through the fence. Sideways world. She smoked her last rock in a pipe the man had given her. Pipe made of an old air-freshener tube blown larger with a torch.

The chunk was yellow and porous. Small as aquarium rocks. The fish in the pet store went in and out of the ceramic castle. Her head was pounding. Maybe he gave her some bad coca. A bad leaf.

Someone was behind her. Sisia. Sisia was ready to quit for the night. Glorette was tired now. She had Victor's ramen in her hand.

She heard a voice kept up all behind front teeth. "Old crack-head bitch," the voice said. "See if that hair real now. One a them fake falls. Drink yo damn soda? You ain't gon pop nobody now."

Not Sisia.

Fingers dug into her braid, at the base of her skull, and pulled hard enough to launch Glorette backwards, and then the silver handle of the shopping cart was beside her eyes, and the girl was tying her hair to the handle.

"Real enough," the girl said. "But this ain't the eighties. You ain't Beyoncé. You some old J.Lo and shit. You finished."

She was still behind Glorette. Her footsteps went backward. Was she gone?

Glorette couldn't untie her hair. Her hands shook. She was bent too far. Spine. So far backward that she could only look up at the streetlight just above. She felt pain sharp like a rat biting her heart. Teeth in her chest. A bad leaf? *I tasted salt*. A crystal. The teeth bit into her chest again. Just a muscle. Victor says just a muscle like your thigh. *Flex*. She closed her eyes but the streetlight was brighter than the moon. Yellow sulfur. The sun. Like staring into the sun until you were blind, until the thudding of your heart burst into your brain and someone slid chalk sideways into perforated stripes across your vision until you couldn't see anything.

Andrew Brown

JAMES BROWN is the author of several novels and a memoir, *The Los Angeles Diaries* (Morrow/HarperCollins).

the screenwriter
by james brown

The Las Palmas Behavioral Modification Center is located on the outskirts of Palm Desert, not far from its more famous counterpart, the Betty Ford Clinic, in the neighboring community of Rancho Mirage. Both cities are renowned for their spectacular eighteen-hole golf courses, plush landscapes, and million-dollar retirement homes. But water is not natural to this otherwise barren land, and without it everything but the indigenous snakes and lizards would shrivel up and die. In the summer months temperatures reach 110, often higher, and in the winter come the powerful winds that darken the sky with clouds of dust and debris. Life here stops where the water ends, and it's that borderline, on the cusp of survival and devastation, that strikes me as exactly the right place for the alcoholic and addict who spends his days constantly navigating between the two.

From Los Angeles, depending on traffic, it's a good two hours or more before you escape the congestion of the San Bernardino Freeway and turn onto the less traveled Highway 111. From here it's a narrow two-lane blacktop that cuts through Palm Springs and Rancho Mirage and takes you still deeper into the desert. The land is flat and dry and the distant mountains are steep and rocky. A few miles past the city of Palm Desert, you turn off the highway and onto another stretch of blacktop that twists and bends and leads you, finally, to the Las Palmas Behavioral Modification Center.

It's a sprawling, Santa Fe–style structure made of stucco and adobe and painted white. Outside the main doors is a rock garden with cacti and desert flowers and a small waterfall. At first glance it looks like it might be one of those trendy, out-of-the-way desert spas for people in the know, a quaint hideaway for L.A.'s hippest, but as you come closer, when you step through those front doors, you recognize it for what it is: a hospital for the mentally unstable and those wrestling with their own self-destruction by way of alcohol and drugs. The latter group comprise the majority of its patients, though many of us fit neatly into both categories. Directly after my release from St. Mary's Hospital in North Hollywood, where I was treated for second-degree burns on both arms and a host of contusions from head to toe, I take up residence at the Las Palmas BMC.

I arrive in the late morning, accompanied by my best friend, Tim O'Neill, who's taken it upon himself to drive me here. It is also at his urging that I choose this rehab over dozens of more local ones. According to Tim, it has a high success rate with its patients and an excellent reputation within the film community for its discreetness.

Unlike the Betty Ford Clinic, there are no photographers lurking behind the bushes, no *National Enquirer*, no news cameras. Even executive-level alcoholics and addicts can pass unnoticed through its doors and return clean and sober with no one the wiser for it. Why my friend thinks I need protecting, however, I have no idea. My place on the totem pole of movie making is just a notch above the caterer in the last of the rolling credits. And it's not like my drinking or using is or has been any secret for quite some time now.

"This is the best thing for you," he says, as we climb out of his car. He drives a Mercedes SUV, exactly like my ex-wife's, only a different color. "Like it or not," he adds, "this is your home for the next twenty-eight days. Don't get any bright ideas and try to bolt."

Given that it's in the middle of the desert, I assure him that I won't be going anywhere in the foreseeable future, particularly in my present condition. It's been nearly two days since my last drink, and I'm beginning to feel really sick. I'm beginning to sweat. "Clean up your act," he says, "and as soon as you're out of here, I know I can get you some work. A lot of people still believe in you."

I know what kind of work he means, the kind I used to turn down. TV dramas. Cop shows. Sitcoms. Of course now I'd be grateful to get it. As for Tim's mention of those who still believe in me, he's talking about my meteoric rise to the higher echelons of screenwriting, followed by my equally meteoric descent years later when the drugs and alcohol took ahold of me. Tim, on the other hand, is a screenwriter turned TV producer, and he's at the top of his form by any measure. He slaps me lightly on the back. I can see the concern on his face.

"Are you okay?" he asks. "You're not looking so good."

"I'm all right," I say.

"C'mon, let's get you inside."

As with any hospital, the amount of admitting paperwork is staggering, and the Las Palmas BMC is no exception. Had I been in better health, the process may not have seemed so overwhelming, but soon after Tim leaves I feel the shakes coming on. I'm a real trooper, however, and instead of asking the head counselor if we could postpone these admission procedures until I can at least hold a pen steady enough to sign my name, I push forward. I follow the man down a long, wide hallway to his office where I take a seat across from him at his desk. He's around my age with thick glasses and a bushy mustache, and while I sit there, sweating, I wonder what he thinks of me. I wonder if to him I'm just another casualty in that long procession of drunks and addicts who pass through his life, few probably ever staying sober for any real length of time. It has to be frustrating, and I wonder if he cares anymore. I wonder if it even matters. He glances down at my arms, which are both wrapped in white gauze from the burns I suffered in the accident.

"What happened?"

"I burned myself."

"How'd you do that?"

"It's a long story," I tell him.

Reaching into one of the drawers, he takes out some sort of form, or questionnaire, and lays it flat on his desk.

"I have to ask you some questions," he says, "and I need for you to be completely truthful. How long has it been since your last drink?"

"About two days."

"How much, on average, would you say you've been drinking?"

"About a quart a day."

"Of hard liquor?"

"Vodka usually. Sometimes bourbon."

The mere mention of liquor triggers my thirst. I want a drink, I want it now, and I want it badly. My hands are shaking, so I hide them in my lap.

"What about other drugs?"

"Like what?"

"Let's start with heroin. Do you use it? Have you ever used it?"

"I've done it a few times," I tell him. "But not in the last few years."

"Intravenously?"

Needle users always look the worst, and it's a bum rap because it's the most cost-efficient and expeditious way to get it into your system, offering the biggest bang for your buck. But I leave that part out, not wanting him to get the wrong impression.

"Sometimes. Yes."

"How old were you when you first started?"

"Heroin? I was fourteen. Drinking? I'd say ten or eleven."

"What about cocaine?"

"I've used lots of it. Too much."

"How much is that?"

"When I'm bingeing, I'd say three or four grams a day."

"And how often do you binge?"

I shrug.

"I don't really keep count," I say. "Maybe a couple times a month."

As we talk he is taking notes and checking off boxes on the form. He has on a sport coat and a red-and-white–striped tie that he likes to tug on now and again between questions. I'm starting to feel nauseated. I wipe sweat from my brow with the back of my hand.

"How long is this going to take?" I ask.

He smiles. "What's the hurry?"

But he knows damn well.

"I need something to steady my nerves."

"That'll be up to the doctor," he says. "Tell me, when was the last time you used cocaine?"

"On Christmas Eve."

"Any methamphetamines?"

"Only when I can't get coke."

"But you use them?"

"Yes."

At first, when he started asking these questions, he struck me as nonjudgmental. But as the process continues, and I admit to more abuse, he appears to grow irritated. He looks at me and takes a deep breath.

"Let's try another approach," he says, "and see if we can't save us both a little time. What drugs, Mr. Lewis, haven't you abused?"

I have to think about this for a while.

"Ecstasy," I say. "I've never tried that but I've pretty much done everything else, from Percodan, OxyContin, and quaaludes to LSD. Marijuana, I don't like, never have. To cut to the quick, my problems are with booze, coke, and speed. I've been using them all since I was a kid, but it didn't really get out of control until around my late thirties."

Again he smiles. That smug, knowing one. I'm quickly coming to dislike this guy.

"Or so you think," he says. "Alcoholics and addicts almost always cross the line into addiction years before they're ever aware of it. I'm betting you're no different." Then out of the blue he asks, "Do you have thoughts of suicide?"

I'm caught off guard.

"What?"

"Do you ever think about killing yourself?"

It's my firm belief that anyone of any intelligence has at some dark point in life seriously weighed the pros and cons of checking out early. But I also know that if I'm honest, I'll be treated as a threat to myself and they'll throw me into the lock-down psych unit. Which means I won't be going anywhere until the shrinks say I'm psychologically fit. That could be a whole lot longer than the typical twenty-eight days of rehab.

"No," I lie.

"Never?"

A wave of nausea passes over me.

"I think I'm going to be sick," I say. "Where's your bathroom?"

Inside of an hour I'm in the throes of full-fledged withdrawal and the formalities of the check-in procedures are temporarily placed on hold. I'm escorted directly to the staff doctor where it's determined that I'm in the first stages of delirium tremens. The nurse gives me a healthy dose of Valium, and because my blood pressure has rocketed off the charts, I'm also administered an additional shot of Clonidine, a powerful antihypertensive, to further reduce the possibility of stroke.

The combined effect of these drugs knock me out, and when I wake, when the drugs have worn off, I start to panic. My heart beats fast, and I'm still sweating. I'm still shaking and sick to my stomach. The room is dark, and for a minute or so I'm completely disoriented, not knowing where I am or what's happening to me. I sit up. I look around. The door is slightly ajar and a wedge of light falls across another bed in the room. Someone's in it, curled up in the fetal position, and I can hear his labored breathing. He's shivering under the sheet, like you do when you have a bad fever, and every now and then he moans. I lie back in bed and stare at the ceiling, knowing full well now where I am. I think of my daughter. I think of my ex-wife, and I ask myself, what's wrong with me? How come I can't straighten up? What have I done to my family? What have I done to myself?

I've hit a real bottom.

I've hit a brand-new record low.

It's around this time that a nurse slips into the room pushing a cart. She turns on the light on the nightstand between our two beds and gently places her hand on the shoulder of the curled-up figure.

"Eddie," she says, "how you doing?"

"Not so great."

"It's time for your medication," she says.

He has to sit up now, and when he does I see that he's just a kid, probably no older than my daughter, and he's drenched in sweat.

"What happened to you?" she asks me.

"I burned myself."

"How'd you do that?"

"It's a long story," I say.

I swallow the pills with the water and she takes the cups from me and leaves. Maybe fifteen, twenty minutes later, just before I go under, I hear Eddie in the next bed. "This is fucked up," he says under his breath. "I ain't never doing that shit again." Then it sweeps over me, whatever it is in the pills she gave me, and I'm down for the count again.

For both of us it goes on like this for the better part of two days, our sweating and shaking, passing in and out of consciousness. It's a rebellion of the body crying out for the drug it's been trained to need. The heart pounds. The head throbs. You can't hold down food, and every nerve ending is on fire. Except to use the toilet, neither of us has the strength to get out of bed, let alone leave the room. The detox process is exhausting, and when the tempest finally subsides, and I believe I can speak truthfully for Eddie as well, we're overcome with relief and gratitude.

After that we sleep.

And it's a wonderful, deep sleep.

When I finally wake up, I look over at Eddie in the next bed and find him staring at me. It's night, and the light on the stand between us is turned on. I feel immensely better, though the term *better*, in this case, is relative; even slight improvement, given where I started out, is a major breakthrough. I tell myself that this is it.

That I will change.

There will be no more drinking. No powders. No pills. No potions. From this day on I will make my first earnest, and hopefully last, attempt to put it all behind me, finally and forever.

Eddie asks the running question of the week. "What happened to your arms?"

"I burned them."

"How'd you do that?"

"It's a long story," I say.

"I got time," he says.

He's propped up on one elbow and I notice his arm, the left one. It's black and blue at the bend from sticking it with needles. Though I already know the answer, I turn Eddie's question back on him.

"What happened to your arm?"

"Heroin," he says, but he pronounces it "hair-ron," as they do in the ghetto. I also detect a trace of pride in his voice, one typical of the heroin addict, especially the younger ones. It's the mother of drugs, and in the hierarchy of addiction there's a certain romance, a certain prestige factor, in being strung out on smack. A few years ago his attitude wouldn't have bothered me, but now I see myself in this kid, on the fast track to destruction, and that mind-set troubles me.

He nods at me. "What're you kicking, man?"

"Booze and coke."

"I like coke, too."

Again he's a little too enthusiastic with volunteering this information.

"I'm starving," he says. "Want to get something to eat? The cafeteria's closed but the lounge stays open all night."

Until now I hadn't thought about it, but I'm famished, too. I rise slowly from the bed, still unsteady on my feet. I'm wearing a T-shirt and a pair of sweatpants. Eddie has on the same. In the closet I find my tennis shoes. I put them on and together we emerge from our dimly lit room and into the brightly lit lounge, a little broken maybe, a little shell-shocked for the experience, but nonetheless alive.

In the days to come Eddie and I will be subjected to a grueling schedule designed to get and keep us clean and sober. Breakfast is served at 7 a.m. followed by an hour-long group therapy meeting. After that it's a drug and alcohol–education class, which satisfies one of the state requirements for those who've lost driver's licenses on DUI charges, myself included. Then it's off to individual counseling. Then comes lunch. An hour later we have a study session with the *Big Book* of Alcoholics Anonymous, copies of which all patients receive on their first day. We break again for dinner and afterward we endure a lecture on the damaging physiological and psychological effects of alcohol and dope on our bodies and minds. And every other night, Sundays included, we attend either an A.A. or N.A. (Narcotics Anonymous) meeting held here at the hospital but open to the community. I switch off between the two, since I've earned lifelong memberships in both, though I feel more at home with your run-of-the-mill alcoholic. Eddie switches off, too, mainly just to hang with me.

Tonight, after dinner, we flip a coin: heads it's A.A., tails N.A., and it comes up heads. The meeting is held in the rec room at the far end of the hospital, and Eddie and I get there early to help set up the tables and chairs, make coffee, and put out the A.A. literature. The leader of the meeting is one of our head counselors. His name is Dale Weiss but he's better known among the staff and patients as Tradition Dale for his strict and unwavering allegiance to the principles of Alcoholics Anonymous. One glance at his face and you know he spent the better part of his fifty-odd years drinking hard and heavy before he ever sobered up. He has the telltale bulbous nose, and across it runs a thin spiderlike pattern of broken blood vessels. In his heyday, I'm sure the whites of his eyes were bloodshot and yellowed with jaundice, but now they're clear as ice, and that's how he looks at you. An intense stare, eye to eye, until you glance away.

"How many days you got, Lenny?" he asks.

"I think about twelve."

"You think or you know?"

"I know."

"You need an exact date," he says. "You need to keep an accurate count. I have 3,672 days, and God willing, tomorrow it'll be 3,673."

Tradition Dale is big on God, which has always been a stumbling block for me. Though I'm no atheist, I'm not exactly a churchgoer either, and I have a tough time embracing the religious aspects of A.A. The disciples say I need a Higher Power and that this Higher Power can be anything I want it to be, the options ranging from a doorknob to the group itself. "Fake it," they say, "till you make it." But I have trouble with that line of reasoning, too. It's like lying to yourself until you're convinced the lie is true.

People begin shuffling in five minutes before the meeting is supposed to start. It's a small group, maybe fifteen or so, about half of them patients at the BMC, the others visitors from the surrounding communities. Eddie and I've arranged the foldout chairs in a circle, and Tradition Dale takes a seat at the head of it. He passes around three laminated placards, one with the Twelve Traditions of A.A., another taken from Chapter Five in the *Big Book* called "How It Works," and a third with "The Promises," which is all about the important, life-affirming benefits of sobriety. The first two are read aloud as a kind of preamble before the sharing of stories begins. "The Promises" is saved for the end, so as to put a spin of optimism to even the darkest of meetings.

And they can get pretty dark.

One of the greatest realizations to come from A.A., at least for myself, is learning that there are plenty of others out there just as messed up and troubled as me. Some more so. It's no consolation but it does give me an odd sense of belonging in a world that by and large considers people like me weak-willed, moral degenerates. After the preambles are read, Tradition Dale calls on one of the group to share. In this case it's a young woman with a bony, angular forehead and sunken cheeks. A borderline anorexic. I'd say she's in her late twenties, and she looks scared. She looks emotionally fragile, as if any second she could burst into tears. I've seen her in other meetings, but she's not a patient here.

"I'm Gloria," she says, "and I'm a grateful alcoholic. I'm glad I've been asked to share because I'm going through hell right now. It's been a year since Charlie died, and I know they say it's supposed to get easier with time, but for me it only gets worse." She pauses. She looks around the group. "I don't think I'll ever be the same. He was always happy to see me when I came home, always there to cheer me up when I was feeling blue. You couldn't ask for a better companion. We went everywhere together. Did everything together. Now he's gone and I still can't believe it. Last night I woke up thinking he was in bed with me again, but when I reached over to touch him there was no one there. The sheets were cold." Again she pauses, this time to stare down at the floor. Her pain seems genuine, and I find myself feeling for her. "My friends," she says, "tell me to look on the bright side—that we had twelve wonderful years together. And no one can ever take that away from us. I've been thinking about getting another puppy, but it wouldn't be fair to Charlie. I mean, it's just not right, especially so soon."

Eddie is sitting next to me. He leans over and whispers in my ear. "Has she been talking about a dog?"

I shrug. "I guess so."

I don't like to think of myself as a cruel or insensitive man. Certainly you can deeply love a pet. At the same time, however, it strikes me that this woman has issues independent of alcohol and drugs and that maybe she'd be better off sharing her feelings with a good psychiatrist.

If addiction has one redeeming value it's that it does not discriminate, crossing all ethnic, economic, and social barriers. In this group of BMC patients, we have a doctor who used to prescribe his own morphine sulfate, a paramedic who couldn't keep his hands out of the med kit, a housewife strung out on wine and anti-anxiety pills, and a Beverly Hills building contractor hooked on OxyContin. Then there's my pal, Eddie Salinas, a sixteen-year-old heroin addict, and a thirty-something-year-old crackhead who hails from the friendly city of Compton, home to the notorious Crips and their beloved brethren, the Bloods. He has prison tats covering both arms, and on his neck, in fancy script, is the name *LaKesha*. Dale asks him to talk next.

"I'm Ronnie," he says, "and I'm a dope fiend and a drunk. My father was a dope fiend and a drunk. My mother was a dope fiend and a drunk. Both my brothers are dope fiends and drunks. Getting wasted is a way of life." This guy doesn't so much talk as shout, and he can't seem to sit still in his seat. I've heard him share before and I like his passion. I like that he's a little over the top, since the rest of us are usually more subdued. "Normal, for me, is being fucked up. Normal, for me, is getting sick on Thunderbird wine. Normal, for me, is spending every cent I make on rock. Can't pay the rent, no problem. Just do another rock. Electric company turns off the power, no problem. Just do another rock. And when the money's gone, and the dopeman don't answer the door to you, you do what you got to do. Pimp your wife. Pimp your daughter. Rob some punk, split open his motherfucking head. Ain't nothing stop me from getting the rock till the police send my sorry black ass back to prison where it belongs. Who all here would go that far?" He looks around the group, trying to register his effect on us. He wants to shock. He wants, I think, to show us that his addiction is somehow stronger and more real than ours because it comes from the streets. "That's the monkey," he says. "That's the jones. Let me tell you all something, and then I'll shut up. When I get out of here, first thing I'll do is fire up that crack pipe. And you know what? Listen now," he says, "because this is the kicker. It won't be because I want to. I mean, I know rock's bad. I know it takes me back to prison. Every time. But I'll do it anyway. I'll do it because of one thing. Because," he says, "it's who I am."

On that hopeful note, Tradition Dale calls on the doctor to speak, the morphine addict, who confesses to having intercourse with his female patients after he's knocked them out with a potent anesthetic. After that it's the building contractor from Beverly Hills whose foray into addiction started with a minor back injury and a generous prescription for OxyContin, a synthetic narcotic similar to heroin. Others in the group share, too, but these are the highlights of the meeting, and when the hour is up everyone rises from their seat. We form a big circle. We all hold hands and recite what's called the "Serenity Prayer": *God grant me the Serenity to accept the things I cannot change, the Courage to change the things I can, and the Wisdom to know the difference.* This is followed by individual outbursts of various A.A. clichés:

"Keep coming back."

"It works if you work it."

"And it won't, if you don't."

Communality has never come easily to me. By nature I'm a cynic, and in my book any public display of camaraderie is automatically suspect. I'll accept as truth man's darker nature far more readily than I will his goodheartedness, what little there is. Still I know I'm in exactly the right place. Still I know I belong here, that I'm no different or better than anyone in the group, and when I leave the meeting that evening I somehow feel uplifted. I feel, somehow, that I'm making progress.

On the way back to our room I stop at the pay phone across from the nurses' station and tell Eddie to go on, that I'll catch up. We're not supposed to use it after 8 p.m., and it's well past that, a few minutes before 10, but the nurses' station is closed for the night and the hallways are empty. I dig into the pocket of my sweatpants and come up with a handful of change. I haven't spoken with Alex and Nina for a couple of weeks now, and I want to hear my daughter's voice. I want to let them both know I'm making real headway. That I'm pulling it together this time. I deposit the coins. I dial the number.

Alex answers, and she sounds groggy.

"Did I wake you?" I say.

"No, I'm just lying here on the couch watching the news."

I want to ask if she's alone but I know better. It's none of my business anymore, and the last thing I want to do is get her started.

"How's Nina?"

"Fine," she says.

"Can I talk to her?"

"She's not here."

"Where is she?"

"Out with her friends."

"But it's a school night," I say. "It's almost 10 o'clock."

Alex laughs, a scoff. "This from her father in rehab. C'mon," she says, "give me a break. Since when did you start caring about your daughter?"

"I never stopped."

"Get off it, Lenny. I'm the only parent here. While you were off getting fucked up, who do you think raised that little girl?"

I have no answer for her, none that doesn't shame me, but it doesn't mean I ever stopped loving Nina. And for that matter, Alex, too.

"Anyway," she says, "let's change the subject before I lose my temper. My lawyer's been trying to get ahold of you but they have some stupid policy there about only friends and family and they won't put his calls through."

"What's he want now?"

"He wants to make an offer."

"You mean *he* wants to make an offer," I say, "or *you* want to make an offer? On what? What for? Just get to the point."

There's a long pause, and when she speaks again her voice is dead calm and businesslike. "I'll let him fill you in on the details," she says, "but basically we've agreed not to press charges if you'll sign over your half of the equity in the house. The way I see it, we're doing you a tremendous favor. Seriously, you're looking at attempted murder, or at the very least attempted manslaughter."

"For Christ's sake, it was an accident."

"That's your version."

"You know I'd never try to hurt you or Nina."

"Save it for the judge. I'm sure he'll agree that plowing your pickup truck through the house was just an innocent mistake."

At that she hangs up.

For a while I stand there in the empty hallway, listening to the hum of the receiver, wondering why it is that we can't ever talk civilly. Why it is that we always end up arguing? At what point did we surrender our marriage? At what point did I cross the line from recreational use and social drinking into addiction, where I needed a drink, a line, a pill, anything just to make it through another day? What began as fun, or escape, had somehow turned deadly serious through the years. And in the end it wasn't so much about getting high as numbing myself to the guilt and shame that accompanies a lifetime of abuse.

I return the receiver to its cradle and head back to my room. There I find Eddie lying belly down on his bed, writing in a notebook under the dim light of the table lamp.

He looks up at me as I come in. "Have you started your letter yet?"

"I will tomorrow," I say.

"It's due tomorrow," he says. "You'd better get on it. That counselor is a real bitch."

Eddie is referring to our group-therapy leader whose approach to sobriety involves belittling his patients, dismantling the self, or the ego, so that he can supposedly reconstruct it for us from scratch. His assignment calls for us to write a detailed letter of apology to the one person who we believe suffered the most from our drinking and drugging. We're asked to make a list of all the times we let that person down, how we hurt and humiliated them, and we're not allowed to make excuses for ourselves. No rationalizations. No justifications. We're to take full responsibility for our actions, and when we're done with the letter, instead of sending it, we're supposed to share it with the group and then destroy it.

For me, that one person would have to be my ex-wife, though Nina runs a close second. For Eddie, it's his deceased mother, the only person, he says, he ever truly loved. In my case, the wrongdoings go back further than I can possibly recall, but at the top of that list are the many nights I didn't call or come home. These are followed by the needless arguments and turbulent mood swings. Then come all the promises I made to quit and never kept, not to mention the thousands and thousands of wasted dollars I put up my nose or drank away at some bar. All this and more I put into that letter, writing deep into the night, long after Eddie's fallen asleep. It comes out to thirty-two handwritten pages—or that's where I stop anyway. Toward the early morning hours my eyes grow heavy and I drop off.

I don't put much stock into the importance of dreams. I don't believe much in symbols or hidden, subconscious meanings. In fact, I rarely ever remember my dreams. But this one is different. It's the kind that seems so real that when you wake up, for those first few seconds, you're absolutely certain it happened. That you were there. That you *are* there. In it I'm sitting at the edge of a dock looking out over the ocean, and beside me is a bottle of vodka. I know I'm not supposed to drink it. I know if I do I'll erase all the progress I've made. That it'll trigger the craving. And once the craving is on, I'll be off and running—next stop, the dopeman's house. But I pick up the bottle anyway. I uncap it. I raise it to my lips and drink, and I can taste it, I can feel it going down, the actual burning sensation in the back of my throat. This is where I wake up, flooded with guilt for having drank again, and then relieved, suddenly, when I realize it's only a dream.

Now the room is just beginning to grow light. Outside the sun is rising, and I roll out of bed. I go to the bathroom and douse my face with water. What happens next is totally out of character for me, but I get down on my knees in front of the sink. I place my hands together. I close my eyes.

Part of me feels silly.

Part of me wants to believe. In what, in whom, I have no idea. And the funny thing is, for me, it doesn't really matter. It is after all the act, not the message, that ultimately gives form to prayer.

Frank Delia

JERRY STAHL is the author of the narcotic memoir *Permanent Midnight*, made into a movie starring Ben Stiller and Owen Wilson, as well as the novels *Perv—A Love Story*, *Plainclothes Naked*, and *I, Fatty*.

twilight of the stooges
by jerry stahl

So it's 1980-something. I'm nowhere.

Suzy, this older white lady I buy cocaine from, tells me she'll give me a free gram if I help her do some.

I say, "Sure, why not?"

She says, "Exactly." Then, before my eyes, she gets on her hands and knees on the cat pee–marinated shag carpet. She raises the salmon nightie she lives in, exposing a pair of sixty-three-year-old, weirdly hot, baby-smooth ass cheeks, which she introduces as Heckel and Jeckel's albino cousins. Jiggling her cheeks the way body builders will jiggle their pecs, left-right-left, she makes them talk to each other.

"Heckel likes to get spanked. Bad little crow!"

"Jeckel, you're such a freak."

After fifteen minutes, or maybe a day, Suzy pretends to get annoyed with her chatty buttocks. She tells them to shut up. As I zone in and out, grinning like I haven't seen Miss Chatty Cheeks 5,000 times already, I am simultaneously wondering how long I can go without asking/begging/stealing another hit, and obsessing on the name of the guy who did Topo Gigio on *Ed Sullivan*.

By the time I write this, I am acutely aware of how old remembering The Ed Sullivan Show *makes me. Tennessee Williams routinely shaved a year off his age. When people caught him he'd explain that he didn't count the year he worked in a shoe store. I sometimes think the same could be done with drug years. They don't count. Though probably they count more. Like dog years. My liver, in point of fact, is well over a hundred. It sometimes forgets its own name and will doubtless be placed in a rest home by the time you read this.*

Suzy's TV is always on with the sound off. After a while you begin to think the rays soak into your head and over the blood brain barrier with the rest of the shit you're putting in there. Suzy resembles Miss Hathaway, Mr. Drysdale's horsy secretary on *The Beverly Hillbillies*—if Miss Hathaway had been locked in a dark room and force-fed Kents, cocaine, and gin for twenty-seven years, while bathed in color Sony light.

She reaches back and hands me a straw, a regular sweetheart. "Okay, soldier, pack some in there."

"In the straw?"

"In my *ass*. Jesus! How dumb are you? Put some powder in the straw, put the straw in my ass, and blow."

"I've done worse for less," I say with a shrug, trying to convey an emotion I do not even remotely feel. In fact, there is actual screaming in my head, a voice that sounds alarmingly like Jimmy Swaggart. (More TV-adjacent damage; I might as well be in the box, getting transmissions directly into my pineal gland.) I am never not awake Sunday morning at 4, when Jimmy comes on in my neck of the world.

Am I nervous or am I happy?
Why are you staring?
Fuck, HELICOPTERS!

Right before I angle toward the target, I start to feel chiggers under my skin, and I fight the urge to scratch myself bloody digging them out. This is when I hear Jimmy Swaggart start speaking directly to me: "Hey, loser! You're about to blow drugs into the anus of a woman old enough to be your mother. You know what Jesus says about that?"

Happily, I am so cocaine-depleted I instantly forget that I'm aurally hallucinating, and that I itch. You don't know you're having a white-out until you come out of it. I just kind of *blink to*. I remember that I'm trying to keep my thumb pressed on one end of the straw while I slip the other end in Suzy's pink O without spilling any coke. (Her sphincter, for reasons I can't fathom, makes me think of a dog toy.) I hold my breath, mouth poised by the business end of the tube, the length of a *TV Guide* away from the bull's eye. I have a weird pain in my spleen. Though I'm not sure where my spleen is. I just know it's unhealthy. And I should go to a dentist, too. I can only chew with the left rear corner of my mouth.

"When I say do it, *do* it!" Suzy says, and launches into some kind of Kundalini fire-breathing that expands and puckers her chosen coke portal. For one bad moment I am eyeball to eyeball with a jowly, Ray Harryhausen Cyclops, who won't stop leering at me. Then I avert my gaze and take in the pictures of Suzy's dead B-celebrity husband on the wall. The Teddy Shrine . . . *That's better*. Suzy met her late husband when she was a call girl. (Many of her clients were half-washed-up New York stage actors.) In a career lull, Teddy appeared in a number of *Three Stooges* vehicles. But not, as Suzy would interject when she repeated the story—which she did *no more than ten times a night*—"the good *Three Stooges* . . ." Teddy made his Stooge ascendance in the heyday of Joe DeRita, the Curly-replacement nobody liked. "Twilight of the Stooges," Suzy would sigh. "People even liked Shemp better than they liked DeRita."

Suzy worked a finite loop of peripheral celebrity anecdotes . . . Bennett Cerf liked to be dressed like a baby and have his diaper changed . . . Broderick Crawford liked to give girls pony rides. Goober from *Andy Griffith* was hung like a roll of silver dollars but had a dime-size hole burned in his septum. She also claimed that her apartment on Ivar, a cottage cheese–ceilinged studio a short stagger up from Franklin, used to belong to Nathanael West. I can still see her tearing up, missing a dear friend: "The midget from *Day of the Locust* died the same day John Lennon was shot."

I spent more time with Suzy than my own wife, which is a whole other story. After a certain point, junkies are rarely missed when they're not home. (If they happen to have a home—as opposed to a place they still have keys to, from which they can steal small appliances.)

A half-second before I think she is ready to blast off, Suzy abruptly turns around and chuckles. "I ever tell you how much Larry Fine loved his blow? The man was a hedonist . . . How do you think his hair got that way? He wanted to be the white Cab Calloway but it never worked out."

Luckily I don't spill anything. Did I mention the white-outs? I did, didn't I? Why am I telling this story? It's not even a story. It's just, like, a snippet from a loop. Like Suzy's bottom-feeding mono-logues. I don't have memories. I just have nerves that still hurt in my brain. Shooting coke does that. Even more than smoking it, when you fixed you could just wipe the inside of your skull clean as porcelain. Coke was about toilets and toilets were shiny white. Especially at 4 a.m. with the lights on and the bathroom door locked. Sometimes the blood in your head would crash over your eyeballs and you'd just go blind for a while, but you wouldn't notice till you could see again—when you came back and realized you were standing there, knuckles buckling, one hand propped on the wall, the other compulsively flushing and re-flushing the toilet, for the whoosh that could make you come.

I've done okay since getting off all of it—the dope and the cocaine— but I still think, much as the smack destroyed my liver, the coke shorted my synapses. All systems will be firing and then, next thing I know, I'll blink into vision again and realize I've gone blank. It's not so much as if the power's been diminished, it's as if the power just suddenly . . . goes out. Can we feel anything as sharply as the absence of a specific feeling?

What the fuck does that mean?

What was I just talking about?

Never mind. It's not coming back.

When I think about getting high, what I remember, viscerally, is not the dope rush—those faded years before I stopped the dope—I remember the coke hitting, that fork-in-the-heart jolt, like you dipped your toe in a puddle and tongue-kissed a toaster.

Before the needle was halfway down, you could see God's eyes roll back in His head.

So I twitch back and there's this gaping Eberhard Faber eraser-colored hole, two hummocky cheeks yanked open, scarlet chipped fingernails against baby skin.

"Hey, Whitey Ford, throw the dart through the hula hoop, dammit! What's the puzzle!?"

So (first time's always the hardest) with no further ado, I stick the straw into Suzy's ass, careful not to inhale, and blow the Pixy Stix's worth of flake into her alimentary canal, or whatever it is, and watch the teeny mouth shut tight around its deposit.

Suzy squirms. "Unggghh-uhhhh . . . Oh God . . . NNNNNNGGGGGG!"

Then she twists her head around, glassy-eyed. *"I'm a regular Venus flytrap!"*

That's when I realize I left the straw in her. I look everywhere but it's gone. Sucked right up with the blow. Should I tell her? Would she get mad when she found out? What if she cut me off? Or was there some kind of ass-acid that could eat a straw to pulp—so she'd never know?

Suzy mistakes my panic and paralysis for awe. "Impressive, right?" Smacking herself on the flank, she adds, "I used to smuggle guns for the Panthers in there. There's a man named Jackson who could tell you some stories, if he was in a position to tell anybody anything."

Then she giggles, doing a little wiggly thing with her bottom. "A lot of guys paid a lot of money to be where you are right now! Now blow some more, Daddy. Blow! Blow! Blow!"

I reload from a Musso & Franks ashtray full of powder and go in for Round Two. Her capacious anus quivers like some blind baby bird. And this time (with a fresh straw) I close my eyes, unload the blow, then quickly get up and weave into the bathroom to shake up a shot. I should put some dope in but can't find it—and can't wait—and before I have the needle out I'm on the floor, doing the floppy-fish. It takes everything I have to slap a chunk of tar on tin foil and take a puff to stop the convulsion. I make it back out to the living room. (Blinds always pulled, no day or night, like a one-woman keno lounge.) I never saw Suzy get off her couch to pee. I never saw her eat. I never saw her do anything but cocaine, generally up her nose—or, on special occasions, the odd ass-blow.

Suzy didn't geeze, she thought it was low class. She left the freebasing to her roommate, Sidney, a shut-in who could generally be found in his room, sniffing a pillow between hits. Sidney hadn't left his room, Suzy liked to say, since *The Rockford Files* was new. His claim to fame was playing drums behind Lenny Bruce at a Detroit strip club.

I didn't have any money, so I would keep Suzy company. I never had to be anywhere.

Suzy is still talking when I come back from the bathroom. She never stopped talking. It was not quite white noise. Suzy's clients were a talk show host, a couple of soap stars, a slew of jingle musicians, one name actor who required oz's mailed to him on the set, and my favorite, a TV evangelist famous for his high-rise hair and his multi-hour rants from a cowhide chair in Pasadena.

"I know what you're thinking."

Suzy's voice is jagged with pleasure. Her nose so permanently blown out she sounds like she's just unplugged her iron lung. "You're thinking, 'Suzy musta stole the ass-blow move from Stevie Nicks.' Well, you're wrong, baby. It's apocryphal. Stevie Nicks kept a guy on the payroll whose only job was to blow coke up her ass. Well, not his only job. His other job was to make sure she didn't stop for KFC on the way back from a concert. She'd put a broken nail file to her throat if the driver didn't stop for a half-dozen nine-piece boxes. She was a chicken hoover, if you know what I mean."

"I know what you mean."

"I know you know," Suzy says, lowering her nightie, squirming with pleasure as she eases her behind back on the couch.

"Did I ever tell you about the time Larry got Shemp drunk and they put a hooker's eye out in Canter's?"

Only 5,000 times.

"I never heard that one."

"Here, have some more."

Years go by.

Celeste Wesson

ROBERT WARD has written six novels, including *Red Baker*, winner of the 1985 Pen West Award for Best Novel. His novel *Cattle Annie and Little Britches* was made into a movie starring Burt Lancaster and Diane Lane. Ward has been a writer/producer on the hit TV shows *Hill Street Blues, Miami Vice, New York Undercover*, and *The Division*. His journalism and short fiction have appeared in *GQ, Rolling Stone, Antaeus*, and many other magazines. He lives in Los Angeles with his wife and son.

chemistry
by robert ward

This is the story of how I, hardheaded and some might say hard-hearted, Roger Deakens, actually learned something about the highly touted, but seldom seen, spiritual side of life and found my own true love.

My little tale begins in a bar, The Lion's Head, my favorite old haunt, the great hang for journalists, novelists, village politicos, and the occasional famous actor from the Theatre In The Round, which was just down the street, on the other side of Sheridan Square.

The dark, friendly dive where I met Nicole.

She was trim-hipped, with shining black shoulder-length hair, and she stood between the service station and the last seat at the bar, my usual spot.

I slid onto my stool and was immediately attracted by her perfume. Subtle, classy, a fog of desire. She had a long, sensitive, fine-boned face, and small pearl earrings. She wore a dark tweed business suit that accentuated her tight, athletic body. I ordered my usual, Scotch and soda, from Tommyboy, the 300-pound Yeats-quoting bartender, and tried to remember if I'd ever seen her in the Head before. I thought not, but there had been more than a few nights over the past six months when I couldn't remember much of anything at all. No, I figured, she must be a new girl, probably worked in one of the office buildings nearby, perhaps one of the restaurants that had been springing back up after a few rough seasons.

She sipped a glass of white wine, not looking at me at all, which was fine. I had plenty of time. That was my edge with women. I could wait them out. A lot of guys come on to every girl with the same kind of game-show-host jokes and fast riffs, but that's not me. I've learned through hard-won experience that when you're trolling for love, you've got to be "riff specific." Tailor each and every riff to the particular girl in question. That's how you get them to fall in love with you, which after all is the ultimate goal. Or at least it was my goal. I never felt that it was satisfying to merely get them to undress, to open their beautiful legs. No, I wanted them to want me, to need me, to love me. I'm talking about the hurting kind of love, where they'd beg to see me the next day and the next and the next. They wanted to be my girl.

But I didn't want a girl. Not that way. Love wasn't my thing, not back then. Not that I didn't care about them. I did, like another man might care about a vintage car. I was a young man, the field was ripe, and I had become a connoisseur of hearts. Okay, technically speaking, I broke their hearts. But, come on, they loved it. Well, at least some of them did. Or else why would they keep coming back?

In those happy days, I liked to think of myself as an artist, an artist of seduction. An overblown, self-regarding epithet, to be sure, but I did have a more than modest talent for love. What were my talents? Well, first off, I could size up any woman within the first two minutes. *Oh, what do we have here? Short, spiky hair, glasses, Levi's . . . must be the intellectual type.* The way to proceed here is to drop some little thing about a lady poet. I'm not talking about Sylvia Plath, for God's sake. Even a frigging football lineman can quote something from Plath. She's just another pop suicide now. No, with this kind of "sensitive rebel type" you have to mention a woman poet only women revere. Like, drop a nice line from, say, Mary Oliver. That's the kind of poet close to a bright woman's heart, the kind she's sure that no man would even know about. Oh yeah, you lay a little Mary Oliver on her and she starts thinking, *Wow, this guy isn't bad looking and he's so sensitive, as well. Maybe, just maybe, he's the man of my dreams.* Yeah, that's the thing. You want to be her dream lover, you have to pay consummate attention to the details.

But details aren't the only thing. Oh no . . . You have to appear to be a fun guy, as well. Sensitive plus fun. If you're too sensitive, after all, you might just as well be some kind of pushover. No, you have to show you're a little dangerous, but fun-dangerous, not deadly dangerous. And what better way to show this than to have your ready vial of pure white cocaine with you.

Ah, with the coke plus the riff-specific sensitivity, you were just too good to be true. (Which pretty much sums up what I was . . . way too good to be true, ever.)

Anyway, after a few laserlike riffs, which honed in on something the woman couldn't see coming, and a few spoonfuls of the requisite powders, well, she was pretty much all yours.

Man, I know it sounds cold but it wasn't . . . not really. It was fun, sharp, predator-and-victim fun. And what's more fun than that?

Not to mention the fact that I got something else out of it. I mean, besides the obvious things. Can you guess?

Nah, you're not smart enough.

Reverie. That's right, reverie. Of the two or three hundred girls I bedded with my artistic approach, I could remember about half of them in stunning detail. I mean, every lick of their tongues, the curve of their thighs, the way they looked in naked profile. I could see them down on all fours; I could see them on their backs, their legs open. I could see them up against the wall, their asses out, their long legs spread, begging for it again.

Yes, I could replay my conquests any time, night or day. At my little pad, there was no need for television. I had my own movie theater, Roger's Memory Lane, and in every frame I was the star. And some beautiful, fantastic creature I'd picked up was my costar.

And, I might add, I was very picky. I didn't exert all this energy or attention on just anyone. No, the girl had to have a certain quality, and she needed to present a specific technical problem for me. A challenge, if you will.

Now take this girl . . . the one in question, Nicole. There was something special about her, not just her great dark looks. At first I wasn't sure what it was . . . so I waited, watched.

Then I began to see. There was a sigh after she sipped her wine. The way she wearily shifted her weight from one great-looking leg to the other. She was beautiful, but above all, she was tired. Right away, I guessed she'd been through something tough. That told me how to tailor my opening gambit. What she needed was a little coke and sympathy. Well, reverse that. Sympathy first, then coke.

Fortunately I had a ready supply of both. Sympathy, in New York City, perhaps more than in any other place, is essential to seduction. For making women fall in love with you, sympathy is a basic ingredient . . . like, say, bread or water to a starving man. The city is so full of truly creepy guys that most women spend half their time frightened, wary, bummed out. If you don't have a fine reservoir of feigned sympathy, you really have no shot. And as for the chemical side of the equation, I'd just purchased a gram or so of coke from my local dealer, a guy named Wease, who stood at his post at the south end of the bar. The Wease, as his customers called him, sold decent, cheap blow. Granted, sometimes it might have a little crank in it—the kind that made you grit your teeth for about fourteen hours—but basically it was good, reliable stuff. And the nice thing is, if you got greedy and snorted all the shit up, all you had to do was hustle down to the other end of the bar, and there he was, ready with another handy little packet to enrich your emotional life.

Yeah, I thought, looking at the surreal sheen of her black hair, *this promises to be a very exciting night.*

"Roger Deakens," I said, smiling in my most understanding way.

"Nicole," she said, smiling in a sad way. "Nicole Draper."

A great name, a great-looking girl. Classy, with that touch of sadness. I felt my heart begin to beat.

"You okay?" I said, using my soft, caring voice and doing "concern" with my eyebrows.

"Is it that obvious?" she said.

"You just look a little down," I said. "Hard day?"

"Hard week," she said. "Our stock is down and my boss is going nuts. Not to mention that he's hitting on me every chance he gets."

"Oh man, I hate that," I said, trying out my PC chops. "And let me guess, you go over his head, complain, and you're gone."

She smiled and nodded her head. I saw her nostrils flare a little. God, she was a good-looking woman. And those lovely, small breasts, obviously all her own.

"You got it," she said. "But I don't want to bum you out."

"You're not," I said. I shook my head and sighed.

"What?" she said.

"Oh, it's just I wonder sometimes . . . when two people meet in a bar, why there's all this pressure to be witty and happy."

I could see a certain measure of relief spread across her lovely face.

"That's true," she said. "Which is why I never come to bars."

"So how come you're here tonight?" I said, doing my good-guy, smiley-face thing. (A cross between, say, rakish Mel Gibson in *Lethal Weapon* and country-boy innocent Ron Howard playing Opie.)

"Meeting my boss," she said.

"But I thought you just said . . ."

"I did. But he wants to get together with me to 'discuss certain problems in our mission statement.'"

"Oh," I said. "I get it. And while he's explaining these deep problems, he's playing footsies with you under the table."

"Exactly," she said. "Only it's more than footsies. He actually groped me during a presentation last week."

"Jesus," I said. "What an asshole."

"Yeah," Nicole said, smiling, "but he's the top asshole. Nothing I can do. Short of quit and bring in the lawyers, and you know where that gets you."

I sighed and took a sip of my drink. What a bummer. We'd established a real connection, I mean, even a kind of rapport, and now her jerkazoid boss was coming and she'd have to leave. I excused myself and went into the men's room, which was just opposite the bar.

Once I'd locked the battered old door, I put the toilet cover down, had a sit, took out my little vial of coke, and dipped in the spoon. The white flakes were big, chalky, and when I snorted them up, I was pleased to find they didn't burn the lining off the inside of my nostrils. Indeed, this stuff actually *was* coke and not some weird Wease combination of Mannitol and greaser speed. Within a few seconds I felt that ebullient lift in my head and the racing of my heart. Ah, that was good, truly good, and if I could just add the fair, elegant Nicole to the mix . . . Images of delight flashed through my head: Nicole lying in bed in front of me with her garter belt on, her legs open, on her knees, her lovely lips parted. Ah, but what of the boss? How could we rid ourselves of the boss?

I got up from the toilet, checked the mirror to see if I had any telltale white residue under my nose, and headed back to the bar.

She was still standing there, but she was no longer alone. Looming next to her was a hulking guy with a $200 haircut and a tan Burberry coat, the kind that would have cost me a month's pay. Obviously, the boss had arrived, and before I could walk the three or four feet to the bar, he'd edged even closer to her and put his arm on her back, moving it up and down in a familiar way.

Perhaps it was the drugs that made me do it, perhaps the challenge, but before I could think the thing through, I found myself opening my arms and stepping to Nicole's left.

"Nicole," I said. "I can't believe it."

She turned and looked at me. Stunned. The boss, a big, dark guy with thick eyebrows and a broad bear's nose, was shocked and, better yet, annoyed.

"I was just over at your office and they told me you might be here."

She hesitated for about a nanosecond, then went along with my performance.

"Terry," she said, winging it and throwing herself into my arms.

The combo of her fabulous little breasts pushing into my chest and my cocaine high filled me with a kind of soaring inspiration.

"It's so great to see you, baby," I said.

I kissed her on the cheek, and after beaming at her like Mister Sun himself, I looked up at the boss, who stood looming, glowering, totally usurped.

I pretended not to notice the scowl on his broad, thick-lipped face.

"Hi," I said. "Terry Andrews. I'm Nicole's fiancé. Just in for the night from Chicago."

"Fiancé?" he said, his head jerking like I'd backhanded him in the mouth. "Nicole, you never mentioned that you were engaged."

She smiled and looked at him with big, innocent eyes.

"You never asked, Ronnie," she said.

"But I assumed that . . ."

She ignored him, put her arm around me, and beamed into my face.

"Terry, this is my boss, Ron Baines."

"Hey, Ron," I said. "Great to meet you."

I flashed my hand, but he pulled away from me like I had a fungus on my fingers.

"Yeah, well, you're from Chicago, how come you're here?" he said, blurting out the words with a barely disguised hostility.

"I had a few days off between meetings, so I got the first plane out this afternoon. Man, I miss my baby. She's a real great girl, huh, Ron?"

"Right," Ron said, gritting his teeth and quickly tossing back his vodka. "One in a million. You staying long?"

"Not that long," I said. "Just long enough to get married."

There was a long silence after that. Finally, Nicole spoke up. "Oh, Terry, you're serious?"

"Why not?" I said. "That is, if Ron will give you the morning off. I bet he will, too. You're a married man, aren't you, Ron?"

"Well, yeah, technically," he said, biting his lower lip.

"Oh, separated?" I asked.

"Not yet. I mean, practically."

"Oh, you don't want to do that, Ron," Nicole said. "What about the kids?"

"Yeah, the kids," I said. "You have to consider them. How many do you have, Ron?"

"Three," Ron replied, sounding as though he'd announced that nuclear war had just commenced in New Jersey.

"That's great," I said. "Well, Ron, I hate to take this little girl away from you, but it's kind of a big night for us. I'm sure you understand."

"Yeah, well . . . yeah, right," was all he could come up with. He looked down at Nicole's finger. "How come you don't have a rock on your hand?"

"Tomorrow, Ronnie," I said. "We take care of all that tomorrow. Well, we have to run, pal. I just want to say what a pleasure it's been to meet you. Great to know my baby is in such good hands . . . professionally speaking, of course. Take care."

I looked up at Tommyboy, who gave me a smile from the side of his mouth, as I put my arm around Nicole and hurried her out of the Head. When I looked back, Ronnie-baby was hanging over the bar like a dead sentinel. It couldn't have been sweeter.

Out on cold, dark Christopher Street we laughed and hugged one another.

"That was wonderful," she said. "How the hell did you come up with that?"

"Inspiration, my dear," I said. "The source of which is your beautiful face, your stunning eyes, your raven-black hair."

She looked at me and actually blushed.

"You're wonderful," she said.

"We're both wonderful," I said.

Then we kissed, one of those long, passionate public kisses, the kind that makes love a spectacle. The kind that draws attention from everyone on the street, and the kind I always loved for exactly that reason.

And yet, this time, this time something happened. You know all that heart talk—I mean, how one kiss can make you lose your heart, your heart skipping beats, zing went the strings of my heart—all that kind of pop crap, the likes of which I had never felt before? Well, this time, God help me, something happened. Kissing those lips, feeling her breasts press into my chest, I not only wanted her sexually, I wanted, God help me, to take care of her, too. Oh God, what was happening to me? I wanted to cherish her. I was gone, wasted, down the blue drain of love.

I literally pulled myself away from her. This wasn't happening. Not to me, Roger Deakens, adopted son of Alfie.

It was the coke . . . had to be the coke . . . *Yeah*, that's what it was, the cocaine. What the hell had the Wease put in that shit? Maybe some kind of goddamned love potion? Yeah, that was it. That had to be it. He was jealous, very, very jealous of me and all my success with women. He'd even said so on more than one occasion. I remembered the night we'd both been hustling this blonde from Iowa, Susan something, a real looker, and he'd really wanted her, felt, he told me later, something really strong for her, and I'd just whisked her away doing my riff-specific Kansas corn-fed routine. Yeah, I'd aww-shucked her right into bed. And he was pissed because he knew that I didn't give a damn if I ever saw her again. That really pissed him off. He'd even said he'd get even with me someday, and this must have been that day. He'd put some kind of goddamned erotic love potion in the coke, but even as I entertained these thoughts, I knew it wasn't so. Nah, that was bullshit. That was crap I was telling myself so I wouldn't feel this horrible and yet so unbearably wonderful feeling of losing control, of slipping away . . .

Oh God, what had happened to me? As we walked toward Seventh Avenue I had my arm around her and I felt, really felt, that if I lost Nicole I was doomed, that I would do anything for her love, that if I didn't have her and keep her, my life would be nothing but the proverbial empty shell.

And then we were waiting for a cab, and she hugged me and said, "God, I want you inside me. I want your cock in me so bad."

And I heard myself groaning with lust, with a need that was worse than any lowly junkie's H-jones.

And she said, "My place. Let's go to my place. I'm just two blocks away on Barrow and Hudson."

"Right," I said. "Right. Let's go. I've got some coke with me."

"Fabulous," she said. "I love coke."

And then we were running across Seventh, stopping every two or three feet to kiss, to grope one another, and I knew that it was all over. Impossible as it sounded, I was finished, dead, totally whacked on love. By the end of this very night, I knew without a shadow of a doubt, I would ask this complete stranger to be my wife.

"Oh God, I can't stand it," she said, as I groped her in the elevator at 72 Barrow Street.

"Baby, baby, baby," I said, knowing it was a hopeless cliché but not caring anymore. Originality, it occurred to me, doesn't matter when you're in love. Neither does being riff specific.

We scrambled out of the elevator on the fifth floor. I put my hand up her dress and felt her unbelievably tight ass, as she opened the door, moaning.

Then we were inside. I can't describe the place . . . only her lips, her hair, her arms around me, my hands under her blouse, the incredible tautness of her nipples.

"Nicole, Nicole, Nicole," I repeated like an idiot.

"Roger, Roger, Roger," she refrained. I'd always hated my name but now it sounded like pure sex.

I kissed her hard, harder, my tongue found her throat. We staggered across the room as I pulled up her dress and put my hand into her throbbing, wet cunt. It was literally pulsating with pleasure and she screamed when I put my middle finger up her asshole.

She fell back against the wall, and I pressed my hard cock into her. A picture fell down. Crashed to the floor. I laughed wildly. This was real sex, not one of my carefully orchestrated little games. And I loved every second of it. And yet it was terrifying, for I felt wildly out of control.

I took off her suit top and started in on her blouse but she pulled away, panting.

"I need to see you naked first."

"Really?"

"Yes, believe me, it'll be worth it. I need to see your hard cock, baby."

I felt suddenly frightened. I was used to giving the orders. But now . . . God, I only wanted to please her.

I stood back, unbuttoned and slowly unzipped my pants. Smiling, I let my pants drop to the floor as I started kicking off my $300 shoes.

She smiled back as she saw my cock, and I knew she was mine. All mine, my lovely Nicole. Oh man, I loved her. I did . . . I wanted her. I needed her. I would fuck her until she screamed, begged for more, then screamed again, again, again . . . Or maybe, maybe this time it would be me doing the screaming and begging. I no longer cared.

"Do you like it?" I said, looking down at my hard member.

"Yes," she said. "Oh yes, I do."

"Me too," said a voice from behind me. "That's a real winner, for sure."

I turned, breathless, and to my horror saw the boss, Ron Baines, coming through the unlocked front door. There was a .38 in his right hand. "What the fuck are you doing here?" I yelled.

He didn't say a word, but ran right at me, raised the gun, and smashed the butt into my skull.

I felt a hot flash pass through me as I fell into a very undignified heap on the floor.

Blood rolled down my nose, over my lips. I was drowsy and my head pulsated with pain, but I was still conscious. I looked up at Nicole, my Nicole, for some kind of help, if only moral support.

But she didn't look like Nicole anymore. She was staring down at me as if I were a bug under a microscope.

"Get his hands," Baines said.

She reached down, and I weakly pushed her away. That was another mistake because Baines whacked me again with the gun butt, and this time I fell on my back, barely conscious. Blood ran down my neck and collar. They tied my hands behind me with some kind of cord that cut into my wrists, nearly cutting off my circulation.

Lying there in my own blood, I felt like an old dog whose body was covered in tumors.

"Now I could gag you, but we have to talk to you first. You scream at all, you get this." He reached in his pocket and pulled out an old-fashioned push-button knife. He hit the button and I was staring at a saw-toothed eight-inch blade.

"I won't scream," I said.

"Good. By the way, you were really excellent back there at the bar," Baines said. "The whole fiancé bit was a real good improv. You're fine, for an amateur."

"Look," I said, "I have a hundred bucks in my pocket. Just take it."

They looked at one another and laughed.

"He thinks we want money," Baines said.

Nicole reached down and held up my chin. "Look at this picture," she said.

I looked at the snapshot she thrust at me. A young blond woman with a nice face, a cheerleader's freshness, but with slightly big teeth. The photo looked to be several years old. The woman seemed vaguely familiar.

"I don't know her," I said.

"You fucking liar," Nicole replied. "She met you in that same bar two years ago. Her name was Gail. Gail Harden."

I tried but I couldn't quite recall her. Still, there was something—that overbite.

"You remember her, don't you?"

"No," I said. "There's some mistake. I never knew her."

She kicked me in the ribs with her high heels. I groaned, shook my head.

"You were all she could talk about. Roger, the ad genius. Roger, who made love to her for five weeks. Roger and she were going to get married."

"Married? No. No way I ever told her that."

"Then you do admit you knew her."

Now I remembered. Two years ago. I had just gotten back from the Hamptons and wasn't quite ready to give up my good times. She was sitting in the Head one evening, just before it got dark, dressed in this pretty little flower-print gown. She just looked so young and summery. The perfect way for me to launch back into work.

"Okay," I said. "We went out for a few weeks. Three, maybe four times, but that was it. And I never promised her anything . . ."

"Bullshit, you gave her coke, right?"

"Maybe."

Now it was Ronnie's turn to kick me in the ribs. I groaned and thought I could feel my organs leaking blood.

"Okay, I did. So what? Everybody does a little toot or two. C'mon. It wasn't like it was her first time."

"No, but it was the first time she'd fallen in love. Then you dumped her. She called you over and over, begged you just to call her back, to be her friend."

"That's not how it works," I said. "When it's over, it's over. I didn't want to lead her on. I never promised her anything. You bring her here and ask her in front of me. You'll see."

"That would be kind of hard," Nicole said. "My sister went home to Minnesota and hung herself. She left these poems all about you."

She dumped a book that looked like a journal in front of me. It fell open and I saw poems written in colored inks. The kind a junior high school girl might have written.

"No, that's a lie," I said.

She stuck another picture on the floor. A police photograph of Gail hanging from an attic beam. She had on that same summery floral dress. She had long, beautiful legs, like her sister's. Suddenly, I didn't know why, I began to pray, "Oh God, God, God . . . You can't blame that on me. She must have been unstable to begin with, right? She must have been crazy."

"She loved you. You turned her onto drugs, made her crazy for you, then you dumped her. You murdered her, as surely as if you'd kicked over the chair she stood on."

"Who are you, her brother?" I said, crying.

"No, I'm Nicole's husband, asshole. We planned this for a long time. We were going to invite you out to dinner with us . . . but you turned the tables on us. But it doesn't matter. You can just as well drink your dessert right here."

He pulled two small vials out of his big Burberry coat. One red, the other blue.

"See these?" he said. "One works like battery acid. The other will just make you violently ill, but you might survive. We're going to give you a chance. Drink either one, then wait five minutes. You'll know. They're both bad, but the poison makes you start to bleed from your ears, nose, and asshole. The other one will only destroy most of your intestines."

"Bullshit. You're nuts. I'm not drinking either one of them," I said.

"If you don't," Nicole said, "we'll knock you unconscious and pour the one with the poison down your throat."

Up until that point I'd been scared but somehow numbed by the whole thing. I mean, there was an air of unreality to the whole strange affair thanks to the coke, but it was rapidly wearing off.

"Which one will it be, Rog?" Baines said. "The red bottle or the blue?" He put them close to my lips; that's when I began to scream.

"Help me! Help, they're killing me!"

"Wrong answer," he said, slamming the gun butt down on my head.

I came awake in a white room, my stomach burning, my throat scorched by fire. I tried to talk but it felt as though someone had used a flamethrower on me. Then I tried to move my arms, to signal somebody for help, but I was strapped to a gurney, like a madman. That made sense because I *was* a madman, a madman burning alive from the inside out.

I thrashed my bashed-in head from side to side, looking for help, making dying-bird noises.

Suddenly, the white curtain flew back and there was a tall woman who looked like a doctor peering down at me through thick glasses. Behind her was . . . Wease. My coke dealer.

"Weease," I croaked.

"Keep calm, Mr. Deakens," the doctor said.

"Gonna . . . Gonnaa . . . die," I croaked. "Poisoned."

Wease moved forward.

"No," he said. "They pumped your stomach. You're gonna make it, Rog."

"Besides," the doctor said, "whatever you drank wasn't poison. It was a habanero-pepper drink. It only feels like it's going to kill you."

I fell back on the gurney and shut my eyes.

"What the fuck you drink that stuff for?" Wease said.

"Made me," I croaked.

"Who?"

"Don't know. People . . . met at the Head."

Every word felt like someone poking barbed wire into my throat.

"Oh, the chick at the end of the bar and the big guy in the coat?"

I nodded, a bilious stream of liquid fire coming up my throat and nose.

"The police are going to want to talk to you, Mr. Deakens," the doctor said. "And you too, sir."

She glanced at Wease, who furtively looked away from her into the hall.

"Hey, I was just in the 'hood and heard a scream," he said. "I don't need to talk to any cops."

Before she could say another word, Wease was out the door. Guess he wanted to get rid of his stash before the Village cops came.

I started to give a little laugh, but the pepper drink came up inside me again, and I fell back, gagging, choking, and generally sounding like a guy with throat cancer.

The doctor put a needle in my arm, and right before I fell asleep I thought of the damnedest thing. Not the way they'd tricked me, not the way they'd beaten and humiliated me, but instead I thought of Nicole's kiss. The softness of it, the perfection of her flesh. How I was sure, so sure, I loved her. How even now, after all this had happened, I wanted to kiss her again. Absurd as it was, it was almost a happy memory, and I'd have been content to go out with it, but right before I lost consciousness I saw the sister, Gail Harden, hanging from the rafters, and I wanted to die. *Just let me go to sleep, God, and never wake me up again.*

I was weak as a kitten when they let me out of St. Vincent's the next day. Two detectives, Barrett and Strong, came to see me, and I managed to whisper the whole damned story to them. About halfway through I broke down and said, "Maybe it would have been better if they had finished me off." Strong, a big guy, with a mobile, sympathetic face, put his big hand on my shoulder and shook his head.

"You can't think that way," he said. "Girl kills herself, could be a ton of factors."

"Yeah, but I was the main one," I said.

The two cops looked at each other.

"You got your house key?" Barrett said.

I fished into my pants. It was gone.

"Maybe we better take you on home," Strong said. "Let's call for the wheelchair."

We were a block away from my place at 77th and West End when I saw a lamp and clothes, my clothes, spread all over the street. Mostly underwear and mismatched socks, a few old paperbacks, a pile of CDs.

I followed the cops to my third-floor walk-up and saw the front door lying there, half torn off its hinges. Inside, it looked like a hurricane had swept through the place. My Eames chair was smashed, "Murderer" was written all over my paintings. The silverware was gone, the lava lamp I'd kept around for laughs, smashed. Books, records, CDs, all smashed into a thousand pieces.

In the bedroom, a strong box I kept far back in the closet was gone. Which meant so was $10,000. Somehow I didn't mind.

"They got you good," Strong said.

"We're gonna dust this place," Barrett said.

"Fine," I said. "That's great."

I picked up an overturned chair and sat down in the midst of all the debris. It was like I was the emperor of some Third World country that had suffered a coup d'état.

During the next few hours, more police came . . .

The cops made calls on their cell phones. Pleasant technicians came and did their work, just like on television. People were sympathetic in my building, but there were no witnesses.

I went to the precinct and ran through mug shots until my eyes were red, but found no one who looked like either of them.

In the coming days I felt strangely disassociated, out of my body. And then that phase ended and I began to feel a monster depression, as though I had a thousand pounds of fat hanging off my frame.

I dreamed constantly of Gail Harden. It was as though the photograph had come to life. I saw her doing a lot of coke, getting wired out of her mind, then stepping on a chair, putting the noose around her neck . . . and then swinging to and fro, while outside the snow fell silently over Minnesota.

Night after night the same images. And every time I saw her I fell deeper and deeper into the snow outside her house. I was caught in a snowdrift and my blood and bones turned to ice.

I tried to forget it, her, I tried to forget Nicole's kiss—the first kiss I'd ever been really struck by . . . Zing went the strings . . . of the murderer's heart.

But it was no use. I felt the kiss on my lips, and saw the vials of poison in front of me, one blue, one red.

I'd always thought I was strong, very strong. But I knew now I was weak, nobody could be weaker than me.

I made it down to the Head and spent 500 bucks on coke, thinking that it was the only thing that would pull me out of it.

Every day I snorted the shit just to get out of bed. Every afternoon, every evening, and every night.

But the images of Gail Harden wouldn't go away. If anything, the coke made them stronger.

I lay in bed at night, my nose running, my head pounding, listening to Billie Holiday on an old CD. That's when I started to hear it in the kitchen. A sound, like a chair being moved. I leapt from my bed, made it out there, but I was too late. She had hidden. In the closet, in the pantry, in my filthy little toilet. I couldn't see her, but that didn't matter, I knew she was there. Gail Harden was coming back.

How I wished it was Nicole.

At some point Barrett and Strong caught up to me. I was walking down West End, going nowhere, when they pulled up in their Cavalier and beckoned me to get in.

I did as they said. Nowadays, I did as anyone said.

"How you doing?" Barrett asked.

"I'm Mister Wonderful," I said.

They looked at one another and smiled.

"Well, maybe you'll be doing better when you look at this," Barrett said.

He handed me the photograph of Gail Harden. Hanging around. Still dead.

"Yeah, what of it?"

"It's a fake," Strong said. "Well done, but a fake. Been Photoshopped."

"Really?"

"Yeah, really. What's more, there's no record of any Gail Harden committing suicide in Minnesota during the past three years. The whole thing was a hoax."

"Take a close look at the photo."

I did.

"What do you see?"

"I still see Gail Harden hanging . . . very dead."

"No, you see Nicole Harden hanging there. Wearing a blond wig."

"No," I said. "I slept with Gail Harden and I'd know . . ."

"That's right," Barrett said. "You remember anything about her?"

"She had a very . . . shy kiss."

"She coulda faked that," Strong said. "What about her body? Any distinguishing marks?"

I thought for a second, then: "A cat. She had a cat face tattooed on the inside of her left thigh."

"Right, and what about Nicole? She have one, too?"

"I don't know 'cause she made me take my clothes off first."

The two detectives looked at one another and smiled.

"Of course she did. She didn't want you to see her naked. They couldn't have pulled the 'dead sister' act on you if you had seen the cat on her thigh."

I stared down at my feet. There was so much I wanted to tell them, but they wouldn't have listened.

Finally, I looked up.

"But why?" I said. "Why did they go to all that trouble?"

They looked at one another and shrugged.

"A game," Strong said. "Basically, the two of them are con artists, set up lonely guys, steal all their money. But these two, when they pick out a mark, they like to make it a little more dramatic. Like it's a movie. Or reality TV. It's no fun unless the vic really suffers. You know what I mean?"

"Yeah," I said. "I know, all right. I know just what you mean."

"Yeah," Barrett said. "You know the show they had on a few years back where the guy thinks he's an action hero in a movie but everybody else knows he's a schmuck? That kind of thing. No offense intended."

I laughed at that, and felt small, the incredible shrinking schmuck.

"We're getting more bizarre crimes than ever these days," Strong said. "It's not enough to rob and beat a guy, you gotta fuck with his mind, too. Everybody wants to direct."

"Oh," I said, realizing how lame it sounded.

"So make sure you change your locks and watch out for strange women wearing wigs," Barrett said.

"You bet," I replied. "Thanks for coming by."

"Bet that's a load off your mind," Strong said.

"Yeah, it sure is."

"You want a ride somewhere?" Strong asked.

"No thanks. I'll walk."

I climbed out of their car, gave a little wave goodbye, and headed down the block. They made a U-turn and cruised up West End.

I had only walked about two blocks when I started laughing. They were good guys, if a little rude. They'd probably seen the desperation on my face, noticed that in the past week I'd lost so much weight that my pants fell down on my hips, like I was some cholo wannabe. They could tell by the hollow look in my eyes. They knew how to read the signs. That was their job.

So they'd cooked up that story about how Gail Harden was really Nicole, how Ron and Nicole were just fucking with me because they were evil gamesmen. How it was all an offshoot of reality TV. But in the end, nobody was really hurt.

Hey, no harm, no foul, right?

But I knew better. They'd have to do a lot better than that.

Gail Harden was dead, all right. How did I know? Because she was living there in my apartment. Of course she was. Only it might not have been Gail. It might have been Nicole. Gail, Nicole . . . one or the other was hanging over the pipes.

I know. I know. You think I've gone nuts, that I'm unsettled by what happened to me, but I say you're wrong.

And how do I know?

Well, I found her that very same night, hanging from the pipes in my kitchen, turning north, south, east, and west, and all the time, whispering, *"When will you admit it, Rog? When will you finally admit you love me?"*

I cut her down, washed her face, cleaned her rotting flesh. But it was no good, she got up in the night and tied herself back up there. She was a real Johnny-one-note. The same lame riff over and over again. Whispered and all noose raspy.

"When will you admit it, Rog? When will you finally admit you love me?"

"When you can kiss like your sister," I said.

But she didn't laugh.

It took me three days to finally get it. She was right, dead right, if you will. I was living in denial. She was my own true love. My only true one. Gail or Nicole. Nicole or Gail. Didn't really matter how you named it.

Thursday, I cut her down for the last time and told her the words she died to hear.

"I love you, baby. How can I not love the woman that died for me?"

Now, when it gets dark, we sit there in my kitchen, drinking white wine, snorting Wease's good white powder until our noses bleed. I tell her not to worry, not to fret, because at last I've learned how love chooses you, not the other way around. You think you're in control, but oh baby, that's the greatest illusion of all. So I tell her I love her . . . Gail, that is. Or is it Nicole?

Sometimes her ghastly face changes and I just can't tell.

But whatever, whoever, these days I'm straight and true.

No more fucking around for this guy.

When I go to work now I speak only when spoken to. When I have my lunch, I eat alone. When the workday's done, I stop to see the Wease and come right home.

And trust me, I stay there until it's cutting time. Then my girl and I kiss, hug, drink our wine, and do a little blow.

You wouldn't believe the things she says, the worlds she knows.

And at last, when black night looms over the unreal city, we cling to one another just like all the other desperate, wired lovers, in my warm and blood-red bed.

part iii
the corruption

Guy Dill

KERRY WEST, a welder by trade, is a writing tutor for the University Writing Center at California State University, Los Angeles. West's only published works, other than "Shame" in this volume, are two short stories that appeared in Los Angeles City College's *Citadel*.

shame
by kerry e. west

Nicole!" Lorna shrieked at her twelve-year-old daughter. "Get in there and feed the babies." This was actually more about getting the kid out of the room than anything else. Nicole wordlessly tromped into the bedroom knowing quite well what we were up to.

Lorna whipped out the mirror and razor. Uncle Jeff pulled out the crank. I watched with impatient fervor. The three of us were like slobbering dogs, intent on a single-minded endeavor: a good, harsh toot up our sniffers. And any thoughts of what may have been wandering through the mind of the young girl in the other room were obliterated by this urgent social priority. Hey! Whadda-you-want? We were addicts. We just needed the kid *out* of the room so we could guiltlessly burn out our nasal canals—as if Lorna really gave a shit anyway.

"Where's the key, Mom?" came Nicole's raised voice from within the bedroom; it was a voice with nuances that often seemed matured years beyond what should have been normal for a twelve-year-old. The voice was unemotional and businesslike; she stolidly had the household routines down. It always impressed me how reserved Nicole remained around her mom, but then in her mom's absence she would instantly revert to her independent, playful, but far from naïve self.

"You don't need the key. Get them food *now*, and keep it quiet!" Lorna hollered back; she had a scowl on her face with tension lines wrinkling the corners of her eyes. Lorna, with the character natural to a screaming banshee, gave a daunting performance of stern parental control, and Nicole, and her two-year-old and three-year-old sisters, usually obeyed.

Lorna turned back to the main issue at hand and began to chop. She paused a second to brush back a long, light-reddish lock that had annoyingly fallen forward from behind her ear and into her face. She continued: *chopchopchopchopchopchopchop* . . . for a *long* time. Actually, it was only for about half a minute but, eager as I was, it seemed an eternity. She drew out some lines. I remember looking at her pale-skinned, freckled face, the matching flesh on her big-boned arms, and I remember thinking what a large girl she was. Oh . . . I don't mean corpulent; I mean hefty and muscular. She certainly had no beauty to speak of, and I possessed no sexual desire for her. She'd'uv probably kicked my ass if I'd tried anything anyway. Lorna proceeded to nostrilize the glittering powder and passed the mirror to Jeff.

Now, the family's Uncle Jeff was a precious find. He was a pleasant guy. He was cultivated. He was the most delightful druggie you could ever hope to know—should you wish or *need* to know one. His tamed soul made him an incessantly jolly man, content to live out life with a fresh blast every ten minutes. Very unselfish guy, too, and I don't mean this just because it was *his* stash we were doing up in the living room. He just liked sharing in good company; this, regardless of the enhancement to supply-and-demand that was bound to result. Jeff was a lofty six-foot-two, plump, and he supported a tarnished-silver, longhaired Genghis Khan moustache that flowed around and down the sides of his mouth. And his nose was large and red with a straw stuck up it.

He finished and passed the mirror to me. *Finally*. The line was smaller than I had hoped for.

"Say, Lorna? Did you get your check yet?" I asked conversationally as I bent over the mirror, inhaling, then releasing a sound wave apposite of relief, "Ahhh." I was hoping she'd be able to pay her part of the bills, or at least some of her part—I'd been having enough trouble with "unpredictable" utility disconnections. I had been renting my guesthouse to her. It was not really a large enough dwelling for her family, but they managed. Lorna slept on the living room couch, and the girls used the only other available room as a bedroom. What had become a real problem, though, was that Lorna never used any of her welfare check for rent or utilities. Never. She always got over on me somehow. It wasn't until years later that I was able to understand how she suckered me into accepting them as tenants in the first place.

She answered with an arrogant grin, "No. But I'll let you know when I do."

As usual, this predictable answer caused my anger to flare up for a second. I thus found it necessary to promptly establish some priorities and said to her, "Cool. Can I have another line?"

So there it was. It was a situation that was more costly for me than if I'd lived alone on the property, a situation superseded by the delicious incentive that their Uncle Jeff was a darn good connection, one I didn't want to lose.

Anyway, good . . . we did another round. When my turn came, I snorted *hard* so as to lay down a thick and speedy blanket over those vast reaches of my nasal canals that may have yet remained untainted—this time, *Wow*! Satisfaction guaranteed, let-me-tell-you. Graciously, I then excused myself to go out into the yard to give my van one of its meticulously scheduled oil changes.

Minutes later—lying out there under my van—the shit *really* kicked in. My teeth clenched and ground against themselves. My periphery narrowed; my concentration pinpointed heavily on the task at hand. And then my heightened ambition sensed all the cruddy grease clods encrusting the van's underside. Sidetracked now, I grabbed the first purposeful utensil within reach—a screwdriver—and began arduously scraping away all the caked-on deposits from the bottom of the engine. This single-minded contagion spread and I started on the frame. Next would be the transmission. So there I was an hour and a half later, still frenziedly preparing for an oil change, when Nicole and her baby sisters came barreling out through the side door of their bedroom. Uh-oh! They looked to be on a mission.

The girls, all blondes looking nothing alike, were pretty much a riotous bunch. Whenever those three erupted into the yard, the three-year-old, little curly haired Autumn, would break into a full and flashing smile the moment she'd see me, gleefully calling, "Kee-ee. Hi, Kee-ee." That seemed to be the extent of her vocabulary, to which I'd be required to reply, "Hi, Autumn." She'd return with, "Hi, Kee-ee." To which I'd again reply, and so on and so on, until I was the one to give in to this contest.

Then, in her usual waddling fashion, followed the youngest: scraggly haired Jessica. Jessica, always with a variety of purplish sores on her face and arms, never uttered a word. Two years old and she still wasn't able to talk at all. Well, she'd come stumbling out the door with her giant, wide-open eyes, taking in the whole yard, giggling frantically, and acting like a million Christmas gifts were now hers to ransack. She always seemed infatuated with the world, always tagging along behind Autumn, emulating her every move.

And finally, of course, there was the preordained babysitter, Nicole. Nicole could be a handful of monkey business if she wanted to be. But during "business" hours she had an absolute yet incredibly compassionate ability to keep her sisters in check. When Nicole spoke, the little ones would listen acutely, earnestly falling in before her like her own private little army, an integrated machine tuned to her every command. It always seemed to me that the two younger ones might have thought *she* was their mother, as well.

Now Nicole, despite all the responsibility that her mother would lay upon her, naturally needed her own diversions and wouldn't hesitate to seize any opportunity that allowed her to sway from everyday procedure. Such it is that she would offer to assist in *my* chores whether I needed help or not. I think this finagling may have been a perfect excuse for legitimately disobeying her mother: "But he needed help, Mom," she'd always plead, all the time knowing I was too soft to favor a contradiction.

Anyway, the three girls inevitably found my prone body hiding under the van. And Nicole leaned over to offer her assistance but I turned her down. I mean, after all, an oil change is a one-man job, isn't it? So Nicole let her sisters help instead. And *boy*, did they help. Autumn came over to one side to distract me, "Kee-ee. Hi, Kee-ee." Jessica stole a socket wrench from behind me and ran. Shoot! Now I had to get out from under and chase down the tool. Meanwhile, Autumn was left wide open to take off with the filter wrench. Here things got tricky. Since Autumn had a head start before I'd returned from tracking Jessica—and you can bet she went in the opposite direction—this gave Jessica all the time in the world to take her pick of the rest of my tools while I was off stalking Autumn. Apparently, all this was quite entertaining for Nicole, for she simply sat quietly on a bench giving me sweet, wide grins as I darted hither and thither.

You know? I'd almost swear under oath that since the two younger ones were so verbally limited, they all used telepathy to gang up on me. Can you not help but love such shenanigans? The ultimate joy of this world should be nothing larger than kids having a real ball.

Later that night there came an aggravated banging on my door. I answered in irritation, becoming delighted as soon as I saw whom it was. "Hi, Jeff! Come in. *Come in.*"

He entered looking more than a little concerned and told me straight out, "Lorna just got popped after she came over to cop some shit."

"Oh, man! What a hassle. How she gonna get out?"

Jeff, already motioning for a mirror, replied, "Not a problem, I bet. They're probably going to let her out on O.R. in the morning. Right now, man, I need to check on the kids." His mind spaced for a second, then he began crushing the small rock he'd pulled out and asked, "Know how to change a diaper?"

I looked at him dumbfounded. I didn't *even* want to touch that one. And I think neither did he, judging from his expression. So, with that startling revelation in mind, we both saw the highly fitting rationale in reinforcing the stamina of our polluted bloodstreams. We did so and dispatched the mirror.

As we walked over to the guesthouse, we consoled each other with the fact that we could always ask Nicole to do the diaper thing if need be. When we neared the door, Jeff called to Nicole to open it. She did; she had a cheery grin and let us in. An Olsen twins video was on the television.

Jeff spoke despondently to his niece: "Nikki . . . your mom's in jail."

"I know," she said brightly. "She called and told me." Nicole was definitely not upset. She almost seemed exuberant. Perhaps the evening was running more smoothly for her without her mother's interventions. Either that or Nicole had simply lit up to the fact that her Uncle Jeff had arrived. She utterly adored her Uncle Jeff. He was much like a father figure for her, yet she never gave him reason to reprimand her. He was stern but kindly, and perhaps devoted more time to Nicole than did anyone else. Lorna, on the other hand, couldn't, for she was a very busy woman; busy tweakin' around the clock just as most the rest of us were.

"Nikki, did you eat dinner? Did your sisters get fed yet?"

"Yes, Uncle Jeff."

"Where are they?"

"They're in their beds."

Then Jeff turned to me, an unsure gaze in his eyes, and said, "I'd better check on them," and I followed him while Nicole indifferently went back to sit in front of the television.

We passed through a doorway draped over with a heavy woolen blanket, and I realized I hadn't been in this room for quite some time. As we drew back the blanket, an appalling odor woofed out to slap us startlingly in the face. It was very dark in there, too dark to see. Jeff felt around for a light switch, found one, and snapped it on. The two of us, blinking vacantly as our eyes adjusted, froze for an instant, horrified as the sight before us materialized. We both quickly glanced to check each other's reaction, reactions that were meaningless in light of what we were looking at. We again peered back into a room neither of us had seen since the day Lorna moved the kids into it.

The room was a shambles of microbe-ridden rubbish heaps. Stuffed animals and rumpled clothes were strewn everywhere, with the majority of them heaped in a pile on the floor of the doorless closet. Under this bedlam lay a mishmash of kitchen knives, a hammer, a shower head, waterlogged toilet paper, paper clips, the closet door, you name it. The room's only decoration was another heavy, brown blanket nailed over the solitary window and feces-smeared walls. In one corner on the floor was a rancid pile of loaded diaper bundles. Out of the corner of my eye those bundles appeared to spasm when we first turned on the light, but it was just the cockroaches trying to take cover. There were only two pieces of furniture: a playpen and a small crib. I saw no bed for Nicole.

Autumn sat on her rump in the playpen, grinning and staring at us but saying not a word, not even a single "Kee-ee." With her were a couple of mangled toys, a pillow, and a dirtied dinner plate. Her hands, mouth, and blouse were mottled with food. There was no way for her to stand erect—covering the top of the playpen, secured in place with padlocked motorcycle chains, was a section of wrought-iron fence.

Jessica was asleep in the crib, which had a thick-corded fishnet draped over its top; it was pulled taut down the sides and tied off underneath. Movement was limited. For Jessica, sleep was likely a blessing. Her restriction didn't seem as severe as the playpen situation until Jeff pointed to the soiled colorings of the sheetless mattress; it seethed with soggy patches of some weird dark and moldlike growth. I only then began to relate the sores Jessica always bore to the meaning of "crib rot."

Suddenly, Jeff directed a blaring roar at the other room, which startled me and woke up Jessica: "*Nicole!*" He paused to swallow for control and then continued angrily, "What have you done here? Unlock this playpen *now*."

And I heard the meek reply from the other room, "I can't. Mom has the key."

We stood there a moment . . . bewildered, to say the least.

It was then that a large assortment of envelopes partially covered by a ragged jacket and several tiny socks strangely summoned my attention. I moved sulkily over to them and apathetically brushed aside the jacket with my foot. The items seemed vaguely familiar. I stooped down for a closer look. Behold! What did I find but . . . *my mail*? Here were the unopened phone and power bills that I had sworn to the utility companies—after several disconnections—I never received. And I began to see the logic: If I didn't get the bills, Lorna couldn't be held for what she owed. I cursed out loud, already raging beyond forethought for the younger presence in the room.

I looked to Jeff for support but he looked both nauseated and in a struggle to control his rage. The little ones thought we were there to play; they were thrilled. From the other room I heard Nicole stifle a sob.

How do you reckon a course of action when you are so caught up in your own concerns—and your own *habits*—that you are unable to perceive the full weight of a very serious problem? And open confrontation of this very problem could certainly threaten the frequent drug trafficking so conveniently wrought through my tenant's door. In that moment, it seemed there were only two available options: Avoid making waves with a charade of ignorance, or take all-out aggressive action despite the consequences.

I am ashamed to say I chose inaction.

After I had taken a bolt cutter to Autumn's chains, I retired to the main house and Jeff remained with the kids for the night. I really, really needed something to lift my spirits, yet there was to be no consolation in subsequent toots. Nor did I have the high and faithful expectations I usually did at the sight of Jeff, when, around midnight, he snuck over to use the phone. Strangely, he too did not feel reassured that supplemental blasts would fortify our moods.

Fortunately, he had his glass pipe handy so we could smoke some hits instead; smoking crank gives a completely different, more brain-deadening effect.

"The fuckin' phone's been turned off again," I complained in response to his request—in those days neither of us had cell phones.

"Listen. I *gotta* go make a call. Can you keep an ear out till I get back?" And he left, trailing a ribbon of bluish smoke behind him. At the time, I merely figured he had personal business to tend to. All the same, the chore was no big deal for me as long as it didn't entail reentering the guesthouse again. Even should one of the girls have awakened, I trusted that Nicole would be far more qualified than myself at handling any quandaries. Fortunately, all remained peaceful.

Jeff returned, bid me goodnight, and I passed out. And I never saw the girls again.

Late the next morning I awoke to deadening silence. Something seemed wrong, for silence is not natural where children do dwell. Kinda freaky! A sense of dread spread over me along with a terrible urge to run out there and see what was going on—I immediately broke into my own stash so I could load in a waker-upper. Ouch! . . . Nothing burns like *that* first thing in the morning.

As I stepped through my back door, I could already see the guesthouse door was slightly ajar. I advanced and rapped on it. There was no answer. "Hello . . . *hello!*" I called. No answer. I slowly pushed the door open the rest of the way and was not surprised to find no one there. Circumstances being what they were, I did not think it tactless to proceed. The girls' door to the yard was also fully open. It felt strange; it *was* strange. All seemed the same as I last saw it except that the bathroom lacked amenities. No toothpaste, no hairbrushes, no girls, no Jeff, no note. Silence.

I tried phoning Jeff several times that day, got tired of running out to phone booths, and finally drove by his house, only to harvest the same result. Damn! I realized I should have stocked up while he was around. It meant I'd just have to go over to Pacoima and settle for some lower-grade shit.

Four days later there came a banging at my door. I answered in a downcast temperament, becoming delighted as soon as I saw whom it was. "Hi, Jeff! Come in. *Come in*." Needless to say, we went through our traditional formality before commencing with the idle chatter.

That done, I chattered, "What happened?"

Turns out that the phone call Jeff had gone to make was directed to some cousins of the girls' father—Daddy himself being in prison—who'd leapt into action, swooping down from the mountains where they lived to scoop up the girls and spirit them away. As their uncle explained, they'd secretly had this in the works a long time. They'd already pulled the legal papers and were just waiting for their chance. It had all been expected. Meanwhile, it was *not* Lorna's first drug offense, which hung her up a week before they rescinded the bail and let her out on O.R. The courts, though, quickly made provisions that, until she proved herself under a year of random drug testing, Lorna was banned from all communication with her kids and from the welfare benefits connected to them. Matter of fact, the only person *not* banned from visiting the girls was Uncle Jeff.

"They live on a ten-acre ranch with horses and miniature goats and pigs. Both cousins have jobs and are financially supplemented by their church, and the church has already filled the girls' closets with new clothes." Jeff continued, "By the way, I want to trade some shit for that old gas-driven lawnmower of yours. We're gonna build Nicole a minibike so she can ride it around the ranch."

I was *ecstatic* and demanded exclusive rights to the oil change.

One evening three months later, I went over to Jeff's to party. He'd already been smoking heavily and I was making a commendable effort to catch up. He piped in, "Hey! I have something for you," and nonchalantly leaned back in his chair to reach for a small photograph on the shelf behind him. He handed it to me. It showed a helmeted Nicole racing madly down a dirt road on her minibike, chased by a rip-roaring golden retriever that was in turn being pursued by a screaming little lunatic named Autumn. Aside and closer in the foreground was Jessica. She had a tiny piglet cradled gently in her arms whence upon she gazed protectively.

I beamed approvingly at the photo. Looking up, but not really caring, I asked in afterthought, "So what's Lorna been up to?"

Jeff screwed up his lips and looked me straight and stonily in the eyes. "She's pregnant again."

Anne Fishbein

DEBORAH VANKIN is the Books Editor and Food Editor of the *LA Weekly*. Her writing has also appeared in the *New York Times*, on NPR, and in several national magazines. Deborah has taught novel-into-film at L.A. City College and has authored chapters in the forthcoming books, *Taschen's Los Angeles* and *Based on a True Story (But with More Car Crashes)*, a collection of essays on film. She has lived in England, Israel, and Tokyo, Japan, and now resides in the Silverlake area of Los Angeles.

viki, flash, and the pied-piper of shoebies
by deborah vankin

I lost my virginity three times—each occasion marked by the presence of coke. The first time, a medical procedure, came at the hands of Viki, our family doctor and my mom's best friend. They'd met the night my mother, brother, and I moved into a low-rent high-rise on a downtown Pittsburgh side street. My mom was out of cigarettes that night and Viki, who lived in the neighboring apartment, bought Kool Menthol Lights by the carton. It was the early eighties; single mothers bonded over things like that back then.

Viki was a former teen beauty queen, now in her early forties, who wasn't submitting gracefully to the aging process. "Huh? Huh? Does this look cute or *what?!*" she'd say, fingering her jaw-length, silky blond bob in our hallway entrance mirror when she arrived for weeknight happy hours. A gimlet, straight up. Viki was five-foot-nine and disproportionately leggy in tight Sassoon jeans—the dark blue kind, with script across the back pocket—and for emphasis, she'd jerk her bony hips to the right, then swivel a half step to the left, before slowly, cautiously, backing away from the mirror as if she were having separation anxiety parting with her reflection. "Nice, huh? Fifty bucks it cost me to go blond." Then she'd break into this unnerving, too-wide smile.

This was our family doctor. And when I turned thirteen—"a woman now, *officially*," my mom bragged to whomever at the supermarket would listen—I was not only bat mitzvahed in a tailored lavender pants suit that matched the one in my mom's closet, but I was sent off to Viki for my first "Women's Wellness Exam."

I walked. Living in East Liberty, a busy commercial district, we hardly ever used the crappy silver Pinto except, from time to time, to lug groceries. And Viki's office was just a few blocks away. Aside from a cluster of elaborately framed degrees and academic awards hovering above the reception desk, Viki's practice was sparse, disturbingly devoid of activity. She'd converted the basement of a small-frame Victorian into a medical office and had just one employee, an obese Latvian woman named Odessa, who had a lisp and the most pronounced dimples I'd ever seen—as if someone had gone into her fleshy cheeks with a needle and thread and stitched a tight little notch into each one. Odessa had no medical training nor a valid work visa; but she was a friend of a friend and she needed the cash. Plus, Viki looked thinner and cuter by comparison—the real reason, I suspected, that she kept Odessa around.

While the cramped examining rooms in the back were strictly medical-looking, with lots of chrome, crinkly white paper, and cold tile flooring, the waiting area had clearly once been a child's bedroom—and still could be, if you ignored the assorted cholesterol and AIDS-awareness brochures on the window sill. There were giant rainbow-colored butterflies sponge-painted across the upper crown molding and the nubby blue carpet featured a hopscotch pattern. "Fun, huh?" Viki had boasted when she opened for business. But really, she'd simply exhausted her divorce settlement and had no money left to replace it with beige plush.

As I waited for my appointment, it occurred to me that I'd never run into any other people at Viki's. Who *were* her other patients? If you didn't know exactly how much it had cost Viki to go blond, or that she habitually put crushed ice in white wine to keep it cold, or that she sometimes did coke ("just to stay awake, like for finals during med school"), would you take her seriously, like a real doctor? Would you depend on her to keep you well?

Thirty minutes I'd been sitting there when, finally, Odessa whirled herself around in the deluxe office chair that she'd insisted upon from the catalogue, and marched back to nudge Viki. There was some indiscernible quarreling, then stomping around, followed by the clank and clatter of steel instruments dropping. Then: "Damn, where *is* it?" Clank. "Fuck." To which the response was a sort of sharp, singsongy outburst that, even in Russian, had the ring of condemnation. Odessa was laying into Viki for *something*. Then: quiet. A somewhat unsettling stillness took hold of the place, followed by a soft chopping, as if Viki were back there mincing herbs.

When Viki emerged, striding into the room confidently as if her white lab coat were a brand-new designer jacket she'd just scored on sale, her eyes were wide and her pupils dilated. I suppose on some level I knew she wasn't amped up on caffeine. Lots of my mom's friends did coke; it was always around at parties, along with crackers and a fragrant hunk of cheese.

"I'll be with you in just a . . ." Viki ducked below the reception desk, then popped back up with a stack of mail, distracted, flipping through a book of coupons. "You know, it's just been crazy-busy today."

I nodded empathetically, as if I weren't the only patient there.

"Odessa" she said, "has someone been calling and hanging up? It happened to me twice this morning. Twice. Like it was deliberate." She tossed the mail aside and thumbed through her messages. "Okay, let's get a look at you. Why don't you get undressed."

As I slipped into the green paper gown, I could hear Viki outside the door, still going at it: "But are we still getting that *static* on the line, like someone's listening?"

Viki checked my weight. "One-twenty, nice," she smirked. "Bet you look cute in a bathing suit." From her tone, I could tell this wasn't a straight-up compliment; it almost sounded like a challenge. Then my height: "Tall for your age. I'm tall, it's sexy, you'll see." Another one of those sassy, crooked smiles. "And *I* still got it, right?" Again, the tone was clear: This wasn't a question. Viki laughed, then sniffed brusquely, as if warding off a cold. "Allergies."

"You know, when I was your age I had lots of boyfriends. My mom had to keep a schedule on the fridge just to keep track." She checked my nascent breasts for lumps. "So, do you have a boyfriend?"

"No, not really."

"But you've obviously fooled around, right?"

"Um . . ."

"Come on, I'm not that out of touch. Do you think you might, you know . . . soon? *You know* . . ."

She slipped on a pair of plastic gloves. Then the womanly part of the exam.

"All looks good. Do you want me to go ahead and clip your hymen?"

"What?"

"You know, so when it comes time, it won't be complicated. Really, it's no big deal."

"Um . . ."

"It'll be easier, believe me. That's what I did when I was your age."

I couldn't think of any excuse not to. It seemed to make sense. I mean, I trusted Viki; she lived next door. So I shut my eyes and, for some reason, I thought of butterflies.

Afterwards, as I was dressing, Viki locked herself away in the bathroom for quite some time. Again, the mincing of herbs followed by another allergy attack. Viki did this occasionally, and I knew better than to wait around for a proper goodbye.

On the way home, aside from the swatch of cotton gauze in my underpants, I didn't feel any different—just lighter, as if I'd lost or left something behind. I thought about the day Viki had alluded to, that moment in the future when I'd appreciate this practical maneuvering and reap the benefits for real. And I wondered if it was true what the girls at school said about the girls who, *you know*: Did I walk differently now?

◌

The second time I lost my virginity, I was on a college road trip along the Susquehanna River with a frat boy named Flash. Sophomore year. Flash was short and stocky and regardless of how hot and muggy the Pennsylvania weather, he'd always wear those itchy wool camping socks—gray with red trim—scrunched way down around his ankles. From his just-blossoming beer belly, one could imagine Flash, twenty years forward, kicking back in a cream pleather armchair from Sam's Club while taking in the last quarter of a pivotal football game. But Flash had a great smile—hence, the nickname—and he always had coke.

Perhaps now, years later, Flash is a grizzled newspaper man writing obituaries or ad copy in a dusty corner cubicle (he wasn't dumb), because Flash liked words. He had an affinity for rattling off synonyms, especially for the names of drugs—proof, he no doubt believed, that he was "in the know." Flash was the "goodies buyer," he bragged, for a fraternity we'd dubbed the House of Skull. Flash was "suburban street" long before hip-hop had become popular.

"Blow, snow, flake, toot, marching powder," he rattled off as we flew over the potholes of the bumpy, gravel-coated driveway. "Rock and roll!" he wailed. Then he leapt out of his 1987 red Jeep Wrangler Laredo, proudly, protectively tapped the side pocket of his khaki shorts, and shot me an expectant, conspiratorial grin. It was almost charming. His parents' cabin had been empty for months and when I emerged from the master bathroom a few minutes later—which was fusty and moldy-smelling, with a little pile of polished river rocks resting in a dish on the sink—Flash was already cutting lines with a razor from his Dopp Kit. The one I'd planned on shaving my legs with on the off chance we went water-skiing.

Our backpacks were still lying in the hallway, but the stereo was already blasting: Billy Idol. Priorities. I noted the plethora of frosted pink in the decor, collapsed beside Flash on the living room couch, and set my feet on the edge of the glass coffee table. "Don't rock the boat," Flash whined, and he pushed my legs aside. "You'll spill." He was fully absorbed in divvying our supply and didn't even look up when I leaned forward in a stringy bikini top. I ran my finger across the glass surface, collected a trace of powder, and sucked it off, smearing it over my gums with my tongue. Numb. I appreciated numb in all its varying forms—even if that meant spiritually.

"Dance for me," Flash said, finally breaking his concentration.

He knew it was a long shot. I never danced. I avoided parties because I had trouble saying no when some seemingly well-meaning boy walked up to me and asked, guilelessly, "Care to dance?" Like it was a 1940s USO event and we'd be doing the jitterbug. Or the opposite: an unthinking and drunken tug of the wrist to get me up from my bar stool. There were exceptions: nights at crowded frat parties when the wood dance floor, warped from years of spilled beer, filled to mosh pit capacity, and I could fall into the throng of people, letting it rough and tumble me until I was adequately flushed, covered with sweat, and no longer cared. But for the most part I preferred private parties, like this one.

"No. *You* dance. For *me*," I teased Flash.

"Come on, babe. I'm not kidding. I'm doin' all the work here."

I leaned back and let my head drop off the back of the couch, contemplating the sparkly cottage-cheese ceiling. Flash (all proud and regal looking, presenting me with his supine palm) passed me his World Philosophy textbook, which had six meaty lines carefully arranged on the cover, as if he were the butler serving a tray of champagne.

I eyed them appreciatively. "I'm still not gonna dance," I said.

Flash rolled his eyes and we took turns sucking up the good stuff until the coke was long gone and my sinuses started to burn. For the rest of the evening, we subsisted on scraps of leftover snack food from the trip up—beef jerky, cheese curls, and warm

Mountain Dew—and since we could no longer sit still, we resorted to a somewhat frenetic and disjointed version of charades. We alternated positions in the front of the room, performing wildly animated renditions of song titles and TV shows, while the viewer basically ignored the game from the couch, eventually looking up and saying something like: "I give up."

"Lucille Ball, stupid. *I Love Lucy*. Duh!"

To mellow us out, we did chilled Jell-O shots off one another's bellies until the sky lightened up and I came to realize that Flash's parents' cabin was a riverfront property.

"Come have almost-sex with me," Flash pleaded, slapping the empty spot next to him on the oriental rug. There was a big difference back then, it's worth pointing out, between "sex" and "almost-sex." A girl could have engaged in "everything but," been promiscuous enough to make even Madonna proud, but still, no matter how skilled she was at giving head, crossing that last frontier was a big deal. It was "reserved" for someone special.

I settled in next to Flash and he kissed the side of my neck with his parched, sun-cracked lips before gnawing gently on my ear. "Bump, charlie, nose candy," he whispered. "She, her, lady flake . . ."

That's pretty much the last thing I remember from that night—Flash's warm breath on my earlobe, the litany of coke nicknames, and his itchy socks against my ankles as the ceiling fan whipped around, creating dark, elongated triangles that cut, repeatedly, across our strung-out faces.

The next morning, I woke up naked but for a wide-brimmed sombrero adorned, all the way around, with little bells—the kind you typically find on cats' collars. I've no idea where the straw hat came from or why I'd woken up wearing it; but it jingled with ear-splitting clarity as I made my way down the hall to the bathroom, the lumpy comforter draped around my bare shoulders and dragging behind me. When I flipped up the toilet seat, there, in the bowl, was Flash's limp and waterlogged social security card float-

ing around and around and around in the now blueish water. His
runny, blurred signature was still legible: *Ronald P. Anson.*

Ronald. His real name was Ronald.

Roughly a year after my rendezvous with Flash, my family moved
from Pittsburgh to Philly so that my mom could take a "real job,
with benefits" at Temple University. She was a clerk in the admis-
sions office but hell-bent on the idea that if she held the job long
enough, she'd somehow get smarter by osmosis. During this time
we vacationed in Brigantine, a sleepy South Jersey island nearly as
populated with dive bars and drug dealers as it was with washed-up
sand crabs and tall, grassy weeds. There was never enough money
for designer-brand clothes or frivolous food items or the slicker-
looking school supplies, but somehow my mom had managed the
mortgage on a small beach bungalow. She went in on it with Viki,
and they alternated weekends.

Situated just across the bay from Atlantic City, Brigantine was
a bedroom community for casino workers. Each evening, card
dealers and cocktail waitresses, hotel maids, bartenders, and
lounge singers made the trek over the bridge onto the glittering
Vegas "mini-me" strip. Here, barely out of earshot of gagging slot
machines spitting up coins, is where I lost my virginity for the third
time, the one I count as "official." I was nineteen, not yet aware of
what had really happened with Flash, and still holding out for "that
special someone." It's what goes on record in the annals of "important girl moments" in my mind because a) it involved another person, and b) I remembered it.

I was on coke quite literally that night—a makeshift bed of flattened cola boxes laid out discretely by a bank of sand dunes on the
beach. The little nook, sandwiched between a spindly wood fence
and a ten-foot-high mound of sand flecked with bits of jagged
shell, was a landmark of sorts—couples tramped there after dark for

some privacy—but it never received a deserved nickname, like "makeout point."

Sean was a bartender at the Big Brown Bar, or "B-cubed" as we called it, a local dive with a jukebox that leaned toward reggae and soul, and a shabby back porch that emptied onto the beach. We'd met in a darts tournament. As I stared down the bull's-eye, nibbling the inside of my cheek to harness my concentration, I caught Sean ogling. I reminded him of an old girlfriend, he told me later. I had the same pouty mouth.

What I came to notice about Sean, once he sparked my interest and I'd gone back, repeatedly, to B-cubed, was his erratic temperament. One night he'd be charged up and tending bar as if it were an extreme sport, all but tossing bottles in the air like Tom Cruise in *Cocktail*. The next, he'd be sulky and sullen, quickly irritated. But like so many of the girls who padded behind him, I sat there night after night—ingesting ridiculous amounts of greasy fried mushrooms and teaching myself to blow smoke rings from bummed Camel Lights—until he remembered my name. His mood swings would come to make sense. Sean made an okay living mixing drinks, but his rent came from coke.

B-cubed sported a somewhat uninspired nautical theme, with lots of dark wood and hanging, knotted rope. From the porthole above the toilet in the bathroom, one could see Atlantic City in the distance, a toy, snow-globe skyline glittering against the sooty sky, its fuzzy reflection calling attention to itself in the murky water below. Brigantine was to A.C. what Brooklyn had been to Manhattan in the 1970s: a place you aspire to leave. But Sean never got Saturday Night Fever. Sean took pride in hardly ever leaving the island. The last time he embarked from the fourteen-mile stretch of gravel and sand had been nine months earlier, to have a tooth pulled. Sean detested Atlantic City. "It's a playground for shoebies," he'd say.

"Shoebies," that's what they called the summering crowd. Because shoebies wore their weathered, strappy leather sandals, flip-flops from the five-and-dime, beat-up Converse All Stars onto the beach; then, after the methodical ritual of spreading out over-size towels, setting down coolers, and muttering some form of "ah, smell that fresh air," the flock of shoebies would enter into a flurry of buckle- and shoe-strap-releasing and the subsequent, near-choreographed wriggling of newly emancipated toes. The locals, they didn't mind hot sand on their feet. The locals went barefoot.

We were shoebies of the worst variety. We actually owned a house on the island. And B-cubed was situated, a little too conveniently, on the corner of our street, so that you had to walk past its rowdy entrance—which reeked of sweat, salt water, and coconut-scented tanning lotion—after every stint on the beach. The bar was popular not because it was any good, but because the owners were generous to underage drinkers and it was, simply, the nearest toilet around if you weren't the type to pee in the ocean.

Sean was in an especially spry mood the night we hooked up, full of jerky, happy movements and short bursts of laughter, all white teeth and lanky, toned limbs, lips so fleshy and red it was as if he'd just soaked them in a Dixie cup of Kool-Aid. I was sitting at the bar with several other shoebie girls from the city who had equally weighty crushes on Sean, facing the open door, when a yellow Camaro with a wheezy muffler pulled up and Sean slipped out. I recognized the driver from Island Pizza. He was still in uniform. Through the doorframe I could make out a slice of activity: Sean leaning a little too deeply into the driver's window, laughing nervously and glancing periodically over his shoulder. There was the quick, surreptitious exchange of cash accompanied by another cautionary glance in either direction, then a handshake and "See ya later, man. Yep."

Back inside, Sean was leaning against a pinball machine thumbing through a wad of bills, when the Camaro screeched to a halt and did a 360. He stuffed the cash in his pocket and headed back out, a nothing-to-hide lilt in his step, walking straight into the car's headlights—too overtly confident to be anything but scared shitless. The Island Pizza guys were rankled over something and, illogically, as their voices rose they bumped up the volume on their tinny car stereo.

Finally: "Can you turn that goddamned thing off?" Sean said. "Fer Christ's sake."

I couldn't make out what, exactly, the Island Pizza guys were accusing him of. But Sean's voice was fairly audible.

"No way, man, I work here. Weigh it out in the back of the car."

More protesting from within the Camaro.

"Nuh-uh, there's nowhere private here, I've got customers, I'm on the clock."

Perhaps I craved adventure, and this was my late-teen, melodramatic way of claiming it; or maybe it was the beer, which was finally kicking in; or possibly the confidence induced from finally having perfected the smoke rings. Who knows? But I strode outside and rammed up against Sean, as if I'd known him since we were kids. "You need a place to go?" I said. "Because my house is right there, the little yellow one on the corner."

That was the pinnacle of the drama, however. The Island Pizza guys, Sean's "clients," as he referred to them, had been mistaken about his cheating them. And to smooth over the discrepancy, they offered us each a line before finally cranking their car radio back up and rumbling off down the street. Sean and I walked back to the bar, but when we got there, he led me past B-cubed and onto the beach. "It's late, they don't need me anymore tonight," he said. "Come on."

As we reclined on the sand, I mistook the gnawing in my stomach, the butterflies, for some premature version of love. "You're so cool, you know that?" Sean said. "Thanks for doing that. Really, really cool. Yeah." He stretched out the "yeah," a Jersey thing. "Yeehhh." Then he held my face and stared into my eyes as if they weren't mine, in a way that was far too familiar, too loaded with intimacy, for the short time we'd known one another. "Yeah, you're all right." And then we did it; simple as that.

Later, as we lay in each other's arms, the cardboard cola boxes under our bare backs, Sean turned onto his side and kissed my eyelids gently. He traced the bow of my upper lip with his index finger—over and over again—and, just before nodding off to sleep, he silently mouthed what appeared to be *"Trina."* Which, even under the muted rumble and crash of ocean waves, isn't remotely close to my name.

I spent the next morning tanning with a school friend, Amy, who'd driven up to spend labor day weekend "with you!" she'd said. But she was a casual classmate, the type of friend who rotates in and out of your life according to the semester schedule; and I suspected she was really after a good browning of the neck and shoulders before classes started up the next week. I didn't particularly enjoy sunbathing; but the night out with Sean had been significant enough that only a grossly girlish activity—gossiping while baking baby-oil-slicked bodies on those silver foils, say—would do.

As I filled her in on the night before, our tangerine wine coolers nearly the exact shade of our toenails, Amy went from puzzled to agitated to flat out rude: "I don't get it. Why would you lie to me?"

"What do you mean?"

"You know I don't care how many people you've slept with. So why say Sean was your first?"

"I have no idea what you're talking about."

"I know about Flash. We have Mid East History together. He told me all about your road trip."

"But we didn't sleep together. I mean, we *slept*, but that was pretty much it."

"That's not how he tells it."

We went back and forth like this for a while, then Amy peeled the now warm and wilted cucumber slices from her eyelids and tossed them into the sand. She stood up and dusted off her roasted shins and calves. "Whatever," she said.

I sat on the beach alone for quite some time after that, wringing my brain for details about that night along the Susquehanna River; but all I remembered with any clarity was the careening coke binge and my last moments with Flash before, apparently, passing out.

Flash could have been lying, of course. *Amy* could have been lying, though I don't see why. She'd only recently taken a liking to Sean and she wasn't even a shoebie, not officially. But there was no way to know for sure after what had happened in Viki's office so many years earlier. No proof, in other words. So I wrote off the first time as unfortunate, the second time as a sloppy mistake, and I trudged back to join Amy inside the Big Brown Bar. It was Friday and still warm outside and, well, *the first time*—that was worth a round of shots.

After I returned to college for my senior year, Sean did a stint at the Jersey State Penitentiary for dealing. And when Viki was carted off to rehab that fall by her newly appointed fiancé—a "sea captain," he called himself, but really he just operated one of those boats that carried tourists across the bay—we sold the beach house because my mom couldn't keep up the payments. Flash, who knows what happened to him; but he was well-equipped with a large vocabulary, at least. And except for a few lines off the back of a navy three-ring binder on the way to a concert that year, I didn't bother much with coke anymore. I preferred beer and pot and mineral water with a spritz of lime. But one thing was certain: I walked differently now. I held my head up high and walked like a lady.

I had to. You know, consider the alternative.

Leslie Barton

NINA REVOYR was born in Japan and raised in Tokyo, Wisconsin, and Los Angeles. She is the author of *The Necessary Hunger* and *Southland*, which was a Book Sense 76 pick, won the Ferro-Grumley Award and a Lambda Literary Award, and was named one of the "Best Books of 2003" by the *Los Angeles Times*.

golden pacific
by nina revoyr

It all got harder when my mother left, three weeks ago now. That's when Chester started saying he needed somebody to drive around with, and there's no one left to go with but me. He's got a big car, would *have* to be to fit him in it; his belly's like a sack of potatoes stuffed under his shirt. When we came out to L.A. ten weeks ago, my mother looked at him once and said, "Don't ever go near him." My mother understood about men.

He grabbed me one day with a grubby hand, slid his fingers down my shoulder, said I looked older than I am, thirteen. Close up, he smelled like old tobacco and sweat. I pulled loose and stayed away, but now my mother is gone. I sit next to him while he puffs his cigarettes and watch the smoke curl toward the ceiling, looks almost pretty till the car fills up. He laughs when he sees my eyes tear from the smoke, me bent over to cradle my cough.

Every day at lunchtime we drive down to the school. All the kids come outside at 12:15, and we go so he can watch the little girls. Chester parks the car on the street right next to the schoolyard, under a row of big trees with leafy fingers hanging down. He's like an old animal washed up on the beach, brown and wheezing. The little kids don't see the fat man and the girl watching from the car in the shade. They're only five or six years old, same age my sister was. They look so shiny and pretty, chasing each other and laughing, in shorts and white T-shirts or bright blouses. Sometimes they fall and start crying and then the older girl runs over and scoops them up. She's got almond eyes and gold-brown skin, royal-looking, a Mexican girl. Chester doesn't notice her, though. He keeps his eyes on the small ones. His breath changes when they squat on the sizzling pavement, bony bottoms pressing tight against their shorts.

We left D.C. in June, right after school got out. My mother said too much was happening and she had to get away. She said the weather was bad for thinking. D.C. summers so sticky and hot they sweat the soul right out of you. It didn't matter that we left because she had no steady job, worked off and on, a lot of places wouldn't hire her because of her crumpled hand. Then a man she knew said he was driving out west to California, so we packed two bags and went with him. She had a friend in L.A. who said we could stay with her, but when we got here and called, the friend was gone. So we were stuck in L.A. with twenty-six dollars, the man who drove us on his way to San Francisco. All the clothes except the ones on our backs stolen out of the car in Oklahoma. Most of the money gone after two plates of greasy chicken and a night at the Golden Pacific Motel. We were right downtown, you could see City Hall. This place was supposed to be a motel, but it looked more like a bunch of boards standing up with some paint slapped on to hold them together. So old the whole building shook when they ran the washing machine downstairs. My mother's eyes sad the whole time she talked to the shriveled old man at the counter, said she'd never take me into a place like this except she couldn't do any better just now. Piss stains on the outside wall and dirty air that pressed like fog against the window. Inside our room there was a Bible under a chair leg where the end got broken off, grooves in the wall behind the headboard so deep I could lay two fingers in them. There was a freeway outside the window, and it was loud in the room, like the sound came in and got trapped there, bounced and bounced off all the walls.

It was the next morning we met Chester. We walked into the coffee shop down the street for breakfast, and he looked up from the counter, said he knew the Lord was looking out for him when He sent two such beautiful ladies his way. He was wide awake and cheerful, as if he thought he was somewhere else. My mother smiled like something hurt her, quick-shuffled me into a booth. Chester got up, stretched wide, sleeves slipping down his arms, and slid into the booth right next to her. He said he had no particular plans that day and wouldn't we like to go for a ride. L.A. was dangerous, he said, could eat people alive, especially those who didn't know their way around. I don't know how he figured out we were new. There were big rips in the fake red leather seats and I poked my fingers in them as he talked. My mother looked away from him, held her bad hand in her good one; it was dried up, shrunken, a bit darker than the rest of her. She kept saying we were busy, but anybody could see she was just putting him off, and Chester smiled at her the way she smiled at me when she knew I was lying. Chester's fingers are like splotchy brown sausages, and he has big liquid eyes. His forehead and upper lip are always wet, too, and when he walked ahead of us toward the door that day, I saw the sweat spread like disease across his back.

He paid for our room that night, twenty dollars. My mother didn't like the neighborhood—men hovered in doorways, caked in their own dirt, talking to themselves in low, lurching voices. Boys slid down the sidewalk, watery-eyed and wary, stopping to palm money for packets pulled from their big pockets, or to follow nervous men into cars or motels. We walked around the block once and saw shells of buildings with boards for windows, covered with graffiti, food, a few speckles of blood, the sticky yellow-brown patterns of piss. My mother hated the motel, but Chester had paid for it, and there was nowhere else to sleep except the beach. I would've gone—I like palm trees and water, the salty smell of the ocean— but my mother wouldn't have it, said no child of hers was going to sleep outside like a beggar. So every day for a week Chester drove us around the city, and every night he paid for our room. He took us to Hollywood, Venice Beach, the San Fernando Valley, and told us stories about what he'd seen there. He bought us burgers and burritos, poured beer into an empty Coke can so he could drink as we drove. He didn't tell us about himself—he had no job that I could see, and I didn't know where he got his money. My mother wouldn't talk much on these drives, not unless he asked her something, but Chester didn't seem to notice or care.

When we were alone in the room at night, my mother shut the window against the noise of the freeway and made plans. She said she was going to start looking for a job, something easy where she didn't have to use her hand much. She said she was going to get us an apartment, and me into school, and enough money together to buy us both some new clothes and pay Chester back. We prayed every night, and sat and looked at the picture of my sister Tammy she'd set up on the dresser. Tammy was always happy. Mother said that when she was born and the doctor slapped her, she opened her eyes and laughed. When she was older, she chattered and cuddled, took her Raggedy Ann doll everywhere; even strangers had to smile when they saw her. She was skinny; I could feel her bones poke my legs when she sat on my lap. Those nights in our room, my mother didn't want to talk about Tammy. I guess she had enough to think about with me, and I could tell she was worried. I stayed thin no matter what I ate, which wasn't much, because I couldn't eat in front of other people without feeling my stomach shove the food back up my throat. I had to scoot around a corner to eat the burgers Chester bought, and chase my mother out of the room to eat my dinner.

It was all right, though, until one night I went downstairs after eating a chicken sandwich to tell my mother she could come back inside. She was sitting in Chester's big tan car, and it was facing the other way, and the windows were rolled all the way down. It was sunset, the sky was hazy and brown, and I heard Chester talking in that big ripe voice of his, still cheerful but something else now too, and he was telling my mother that he wasn't the social services department, that he expected something in return for all his kindness. He said she'd better reconsider what she was saying because if he stopped paying for that room, she and I would be out on the street. But if she was smart and did like he told her, then he'd give her something special, something to take her troubles away and make her feel better. And as I stood there I heard an unfamiliar sound, and it took me awhile to realize it was the sound of my mother crying. I didn't recognize it because I'd never heard it before, not when we'd left D.C., not even when Tammy died. I stood there a second, but then my mother saw me in the rearview mirror, and she straightened up in her seat and stopped crying so quick I wasn't even sure I'd really heard it. Then she said something to Chester and opened the door, calling me over. She told me to wait in the car with the door locked until she came back out and got me, and then she hugged me, hard, the heel of her crumpled hand pressed tight against my ear. Then she and Chester went into our room and shut the door.

There's not more than fifty kids at the school Chester drives us to, which is a few miles away from the motel, in Culver City. I thought there were so few because it was summer, and the only kids who go to summer school in D.C. are the ones who have to. These kids get twenty minutes to eat their lunch, at picnic tables where the green paint is chipping so bad there's white spots big as quarters. Then another half hour to play before they go back inside. I wish my mother was here to see them, but it's probably better that she's not. Every time she saw a little kid on our drive across the country, she pressed her lips together and all the lines in her face got deeper. The kids in the schoolyard make me feel better, though—they all seem so young to me, only babies, still happy. But it's the older girl I keep my eyes on. Every once in a while she looks down for a second when she thinks that no one's watching, and I think how alone she seems, even with all those kids. Then she looks up again, and smiles at whoever's near her. Sometimes after they eat she takes the kids to the park right next to the school, lets them play on the slide and the swings. She pushes them gently, their small, sneakered feet tracing the arc of their swing; she laughs when they come squealing down the slide. After a while a bunch of boys show up, Mexican boys, thin nets over their hair, bright white T-shirts under plaid work shirts with the sleeves rolled up, and baggy tan pants buckled high. They look about the girl's age, or a little younger. Sometimes, when they scratch their arms and their shirts flap open, you can catch a glimpse of black metal. The girl's hands flash left and right as she touches the kids, gathers them in, takes them back to the school in a hurry. The boys are real respectful, though. They nod to the girl as she passes and don't start talking until the kids are all gone. Then they sit on the swings and rusting merry-go-round, laughter lifting from their circle like smoke.

One day the girl walks the kids past the car. She leans toward the window and asks if I have the time. I'm so surprised it takes me awhile to answer. Then she tells me her name, Yvonne, and asks mine. Right before she turns away she smiles, and that white smile flashing out of her gold-brown face is like a birthday gift, a burst of bright flowers. Her hair is clean and shiny, reflecting the sun; it twists and flows like smooth black water.

After that I start getting out of the car. As soon as the kids come pouring from the building for lunch, I get out, shut the door, and walk over to the metal fence. Chester doesn't seem to mind—he's maybe fifteen feet behind me, can hear everything that goes on, anyway. Yvonne comes to meet me, half an eye still on the kids. "I'm going to college soon."

"When?" I ask.

"Next month." She's real excited, as if she were getting married or something. It's a quiet kind of excitement, though, more in her eyes than in her voice, like she doesn't quite believe that it's true. She says the college is about five miles away, but the bus trip takes an hour—she'll take the commuter line that goes down Venice Boulevard.

"I just graduated in June," she says. "I'm the first one in my family to go to college." I can tell she's real proud. I am, too, although I don't know why. A gust of wind comes along and shakes the fence, makes a sound like twenty people rattling chains all at once. The fence is maybe eight feet high, diagonal squares set spinning on their corners, three strands of barbed wire across the top. I glance up at the barbed wire and then back to Yvonne, who's smiling.

"So what are you doing here?" she asks. I tell her my mother and I just came out from the east a few weeks ago, and I'm not doing much of anything because school hasn't started yet. "My mother went away for a while, but she'll be back soon," I say.

"Don't you get bored?"

"No, I'm kinda busy."

"Who's that man?" she asks quietly, gesturing toward Chester. I pause. "Just a man."

Then a little girl comes running over and hugs Yvonne around her legs. Yvonne leans forward to face her, and I think of how bright her red blouse looks against the gray concrete, the dead grass, the dry summer.

"Hi," I say to the little girl, but she says nothing, and those big round eyes fix on me from out of that chocolate-brown face.

"You look pretty today, Carla," says Yvonne, but the girl doesn't answer her either; she makes a strange, low noise, almost like she's in pain, although I can see she's smiling. Then she scrambles toward something chalked onto the pavement. It's on a slope, facing away, and it looks like a curving bell shape, with a half-circle on one side and two straight, branchlike parts on the other.

"What's that?" I ask.

"It's a Mary," Yvonne says. "Mother of God."

I stand on my tiptoes, peer down the slope, see the vague shape of a person, the thin legs and covered head. "Who drew it?"

"I did. I draw one every day. There's a whole bunch more on the other side of the schoolyard, and one by the park, and one over there on the sidewalk."

I look where she's pointing, to the right of me, and sure enough there's one on the sidewalk, right next to the car. "Why do you draw Marys?" I ask.

"I don't know," she says. "I've always drawn them."

The little girl squatting next to the Mary sticks her finger in her mouth and then rubs it against the chalk, smearing part of the outline. I don't tell Yvonne that her Mary reminds me of the police drawings I'd seen sometimes on the streets of D.C. I think of Chester in the car behind me and don't want to go back; when I do he'll be sitting there with his pants shoved down around his thighs. Yvonne turns toward the little girl, who stands up and runs back over to the other kids. She keeps looking at the drawing, even after the girl has left. We both stand there staring at the Mary, not saying anything, as if it might peel off the ground and fly away.

At first the only man my mother took into the room was Chester. Then there were others, until I had to wait for hours at a time in Chester's car, or in the coffee shop with the torn red vinyl seats. The owner of the coffee shop, Pedro, gave me hot dogs and grilled cheese sandwiches. I'd go around back to eat them, watch the cars speed by on the freeway forty or fifty yards away, and wonder where all those people were going. My mother still drove around with Chester and me in the morning, but she got quieter and quieter, and hardly said a word to either of us.

Then one day in the coffee shop, when she wouldn't even look up at Pedro when he brought her scrambled eggs, Chester leaned over the table and said real low, "I keep telling you, woman. I got something that'll make you feel better." My mother sighed and looked past him and said, "Okay." They sent me upstairs and went someplace else; I just waited and watched an hour pass by on the clock. When my mother came back to our room, her eyes were red and she was jumpy like a nervous animal. She moved from the bed to the chair to the bed again; she couldn't seem to keep herself still. She kept saying that she was thirsty, but when I gave her some water, her hand shook so bad she couldn't hold the glass.

After that it seemed like she was always off with Chester somewhere, asking him for something. Even when she was with me she didn't seem like herself; her hair was stringy and dull, and she was starting to lose weight. She didn't seem to sleep much, but she never got tired; I'd wake up and find her mumbling to herself. Then one day when I was changing the sheets, which I did every afternoon, I found a little plastic sandwich bag like the kind I used to take for lunch, with some clear, jagged pebbles inside. My mother grabbed it from my hands and started yelling at me, eyes wild. I was scared, but then she stopped, came and put her arms around me. "I'm so sorry, baby," she kept saying, and I could hear the tears in her voice. "I'm so sorry. I never meant for this to happen." She pulled away and put her head down, bad hand laying in her lap like a dead bird, and for a second she looked like she did the day we heard about Tammy. Then she got herself together and left. I don't know where she went, maybe to tell Chester to leave us alone, maybe off someplace by herself. When she came back, though, her eye was swollen and there was dried blood around her mouth. She went straight to the bathroom and shut the door. She wouldn't let me help her. That night one of the men who'd been coming around picked her up and didn't bring her back till the next morning. She'd never spent the night outside the motel before, but after that she did it three more times. Two weeks later she drove off with a man about 7 o'clock, his car blending in with all the traffic on the freeway. That was the last I saw of her.

I waited a couple of days, thinking the man just wanted her for longer than usual. Chester was pissed, said the man had cheated him, left with his woman and his best shit, too. He raged around, kicking his car tires and yelling at me like I'd stolen her. But he paid for my room and kept buying me food. The third night, though, he grabbed my elbow and shoved me into the room, said that debts left by the parent had to be collected from the child. He threw me down on the bed, pressed one fat arm across my chest, and yanked my shorts down with the other, popped the buttons. What I remember is his lips against mine, his tongue a slimy fish in my mouth, his skin so moist and rancid it was like I was drowning in his sweat. Pain so sharp between my legs I thought he'd stuck a knife inside me. The sound of the bed banging against the wall and the bunched-up sheet like white flowers in his fist. It was like he was hammering me down into something, making me disappear. His eyes were half-closed and he made high crying sounds like an animal having the life squeezed out of it.

After that there were others, some the same ones who had come for my mother. Chester told me I had to earn my room and board, kept my pockets stuffed with condoms, held clean cloths against me after as I bled and bled. He bought me new clothes, tight things it embarrassed me to wear. He sits in the parking lot or the coffee shop now and waits, talks to the men and gets their money when they're through. They don't leave, though, he won't let them leave, until I tell him they didn't hit me, and that they put on the condom I offered. They're all different, those men—some never say a word to me, some use language my mother would have covered my ears against, some talk to me awhile, before and after. Some bring a flask or bottle into the room, some the little plastic bags that Chester sells them. Most of them drive nice cars and dress in suits, sneaking over from their downtown offices on their lunch breaks. Two of them are lawyers, one works in a bank, another does something in movies. Sometimes they're young, no bristle of beard against my cheek, but most of them are older than Chester.

When I'm with them I try to listen to the sounds of the free-way, or to count, and not think about my mother, or what she would do if she knew what was happening. I look away when they take out their mirrors or their little glass pipes, and as soon as they leave, I run to the shower and scrub myself all over until it hurts. It doesn't matter, though. The dirt's under my skin, and I can't seem

NINA REVOYR // 163

to get it off me. The bed smells like the men, and me, and I don't want to sleep there; I curl up at night on the floor. Chester started buying me more food to fatten me up—spaghetti and bread and milkshakes—but it doesn't work, I can't keep it down anymore, even when I eat alone. I think of running away, but if my mother comes back she wouldn't be able to find me. So I stay.

Once a week Chester takes me somewhere nice, the movies or the mall or the beach. He buys me things—a radio, a small stuffed pig to sleep with. One time he even took out a pipe and asked if I wanted something to make me feel better. But I just shook my head no, because I saw what that did; I knew what it could do to me. Chester tries to get me to talk, but I don't say much, and I never laugh at his stupid jokes. Sometimes when we're driving around, I look out the window and start to cry, and he looks over at me between sips of his Coke-can beer. "Why you so sad?" he asks. "I take good care of you, don't I? Shit, at least you ain't out on the streets."

At 12:10 we pull up beside the schoolyard. I get out of the car to wait the five minutes till the kids come out, hoping Yvonne will be with them. She doesn't disappoint me. She steps out the door and smiles so wide I can see her teeth all the way across the schoolyard. As she comes toward me, I notice for the first time how she always walks a little awkwardly, faltering now and then, like her body's a borrowed car she isn't sure how to handle.

"Hi," she says, "I missed you yesterday."

"I was sick," I say. That isn't true. I was in the motel room with the banker.

"Are you feeling better?"

"Yeah."

"Want a candy bar?" She takes a Mars bar out of her pocket and sticks it through the fence. I take it. There are no Marys on the concrete today, but two on the side of the building. They're bigger than Yvonne, but nothing's in them, they're just outlines—cold, white, untouchable. "Aren't those clothes a little old for you?" she asks. She looks at me kind of sideways, then she glances toward the car.

"They're all I got," I say, and I start to tell her that Chester picked them out for me, but don't.

She looks over at the car again. "Listen," she says softly, "do you need some food? Some clothes? Cos I've got a whole bunch of stuff at home I could—"

"No thanks," I say, and I look quickly behind me. Chester's watching us now, his forehead wrinkled, his hands wrapped tight around the wheel.

Yvonne looks like she's about to say something else but then three little boys run up to her. They're cute, smiling and huffing, and they only come up to her waist. One of them makes a high, weird, wavering noise, and another answers him the same way; they sound like whales talking underwater. The first one holds his arms out toward Yvonne, asking to be picked up.

"Hey, handsome," Yvonne says, and then, "You're a little old for this, Miguel," but she picks him up anyway. She turns to me again, and the two boys on either side of her tug at the legs of her shorts.

"Hi, guys," I say. They all keep staring at Yvonne and don't say anything. I look at her. "Hey, how come the kids never answer when I talk to them?" I ask.

Yvonne looks at me like she's surprised at the question. "Don't you know?" she says, smiling. "They're deaf."

It's the mornings I think most about my sister. The picture my mother brought is still in the room, and when the men come in, I turn it face down on the dresser. Early mornings I have time, though, and I sit and look at it awhile. It was taken two years ago, when Tammy was three. She's laughing in it and looking off at something above the camera, and I remember the day it was taken, a Saturday, and that we all went out for ice cream after. When the picture was made and framed, we showed it to Tammy. She'd never seen a picture of herself before and she didn't believe it was her.

What happened was that Tammy came down with something, maybe pneumonia, no one ever knew for sure. She got a real high fever and my mother pressed ice bags to her head, put her in a tub full of cold water, but nothing brought her temperature down. My mother had no insurance, and we couldn't afford a doctor. Three days after she took sick, Tammy died. My mother went a little crazy after that, shaking Tammy like she could shake her alive, my sister's head flopping forward like that Raggedy Ann's. It was a few days later that we up and left for L.A.

One Friday we get to the school a little late. The kids have eaten already, and a bunch of them are climbing on the jungle gym. Yvonne stands next to them, laughing out loud and talking although she knows they can't hear. I look at the way the sun shines off her hair, the way she stands so straight and proud, and I think of how lucky she is, how she has everything, or at least she can someday. I get out of the car and go to the fence, and when she sees me, she starts to walk over.

"I brought you a candy bar," I say, and I have, a Milky Way that one of the lawyers gave me. But when I reach into my pocket, I pull a condom out, too, and the blue square of foil flutters down my leg and lands in front of my feet.

Yvonne sees it and her eyes get wide. "Is that yours?" she asks.

I keep my head down, not able to look at her, and I want to say I'm sorry. I can't seem to hold my face together, and I feel the tears begin to come. "Not exactly. I mean . . ." I move my shoulders a

166 // THE COCAINE CHRONICLES

bit, half-nod in the direction of Chester. She doesn't say anything, and I finally bring myself to glance at her. She looks like she can't believe it, but like she *has* to believe it, and then she steps up close to the fence.

"Why don't you come in here?" she says. "Let me call someone. Go around to the front of the building and come in."

Just then I hear the car door slam, and Chester yells, "Hey!"

I turn and look at him; he saw the condom fall, or maybe he heard Yvonne. He starts to walk over, glaring at me, hands open like he's ready to catch something.

"Come on, come in the school," Yvonne urges quietly, but I can't move, I feel stuck, and Chester's getting closer. When he's right behind me, I stick my fingers through the squares of the fence.

"Hey, girl, let's go!" Chester says, but I tighten my grip, and then I feel him grab the back of my shirt, pull so hard it starts to tear.

"Stop it, leave her alone!" Yvonne says, but Chester just ignores her, and starts pounding my fingers, hard metal cutting into my flesh.

Yvonne reaches out with both her hands and touches my fingers, hooked down to the second knuckle through the squares; it's the warmest touch I've felt in weeks, and I want to close my eyes and fall into it. But Chester's yanking at my shoulders now and I think, *I hate this man, I hate him*, and I think, *Please let me squeeze through these squares so I can be safe with Yvonne*. And I think how nice it would be to play in the schoolyard with the kids, who are finally looking over at us now, but my fingers are getting tired and the metal starts to hurt and he's pulling even harder and I let go.

Chester falls backward with the weight of me, but then he gets his balance again. He goes up to the fence and punches out at Yvonne, slams his fist against the metal so hard I see the blood on his hand when he pulls away. He drags me to the car, and I look back at Yvonne, her foot on the head of a Mary and her fingers looped through the fence where my hands just were. Chester throws me into the front seat and then shoves himself in after me, screeches away from the curb. He raises his hand, and I expect to feel it any second, but although his fist is clenched, he doesn't hit me. "*Goddamnit*, girl," he says, "we're never going back there."

And as he puts his hand back on the wheel and cuts hard around a corner, I look at him and say, "Where's my mother?"

"I don't *know!*" he yells, swerving into the middle lane, and then, again, softer, "I don't know."

I turn from him and look out the window, toward downtown, toward D.C., and I know that she's not coming back. Chester keeps driving, breathing heavy, and I don't say anything. But when we stop at a red light, I open the door and jump out of the car.

"Hey!" Chester yells, but I'm running already, toward the sidewalk, where I'll turn right, go down the block. I hear him get out and start after me, hear the honks of the people stuck behind his car. I'm on the sidewalk now, on Venice, heading west toward the school and Yvonne. Chester's not far behind; he's faster than I thought. We pass a taco place, a liquor store, a place that sells car radios. Chester's breathing hard, and every second or two I hear another scrap of his shouts: "Get . . . back here . . . girl! You . . . can't . . . get away!" And maybe he's right—my lungs hurt and I'm tired; maybe he'll catch up with me and take me back to the motel and it'll all start over again. But right now, this second, the wind is cool and the sky is clear; right now, I've left him behind me and I'm free.

Florence Hernandez-Ramos

MANUEL RAMOS has published several crime-fiction novels including the Edgar Award finalist *The Ballad of Rocky Ruiz* and a noir-tinged private-eye saga, *Moony's Road to Hell*. He lives in Denver, Colorado, where he is an attorney with the state's legal-aid program. His current writing project is a collection of short stories.

sentimental value
by manuel ramos

1988

The Sunday insert, tucked in among the comics and grocery coupons, had a three-page, color baseball article. *Latin American Ball Players. Latin Stars of the National Pastime. The Latin American Connection.* Latin?

Plenty of hype about the current crop of players. Sure, they were good. Who wouldn't want Canseco, or Valenzuela? And some of them born in the States. But they couldn't even be bat boys for Cepeda, Aparicio, Marichal, or Zorro-Zoilo Versalles, MVP that year it all changed for Ray. He had read about these players when he was growing up, had kept their cardboard images in a box with his glove. They were the men who inspired the skinny, quiet Raymond López.

He had been fast. Fifty stolen bases his senior year, good hands, a better bat. Ah, but his arm. ¡A toda madre! A cannon that made him famous, a starter for four years at North High, and a City League All-Star right fielder. That arm generated a couple of calls from bald short guys in plaid sport coats who said they were scouts. Talk about characters! Smoking their smelly cigars, going on about the big leagues like Ray was the next bonus baby and it was right around the corner.

"Just sign this contract and we'll hook you up in the Instructional League, buy your momma a house one of these days, boy. A little extra in it (*and for you, too, Mr. Scout, as long as you got my name on a piece of paper that locks me in forever, but if, just if, mind you, if I don't cut it, phfft! So long, boy!*). We'll even cover your bus ticket to spring training."

Mamá wanted Ray to continue with school, a community college, and that was fine with the scouts, but they couldn't provide any help.

"Let's see how you do against stiffer competition, boy, then we can talk about financial assistance."

And the scouts shook their heads, flicked the ashes off their cigars, and walked away, muttering about the waste of time, late for the next Latin or black or farm kid with the strong arm, fast legs, quick bat.

Clemente. Had to be included. Roberto Clemente. Nice picture, good-looking guy, for a P.R. First Latin in the Hall of Fame. Exactly 3,000 hits. Lifetime .317. Played in fourteen World Series games and hit in every one. The long throw to Sanguillén at home, right on the money, and *you're out!* Yeah, yeah, everyone knew about the New Year's Eve mercy mission, the horrible plane crash, and the special election to the Hall of Fame. So what? Ray knew what was really important about Clemente.

No mention, this time, of how they all hated him. Even Ray understood that and he was just a kid during that 1960 season when the writers bypassed "Bob" for MVP and gave it to Groat. Clemente had to wait six years, and by then Ray had forgotten about a baseball career.

The usual quote not included.

"The Latin player doesn't get the recognition he deserves. Neither does the Negro unless he does something really spectacular."

Not that kind of feature.

Ray trimmed the pages of the article, carefully applied glue to the edges, and gently centered them in a scrapbook. He waited for the glue to dry, took one last look at Clemente, then returned the scrapbook to the makeshift shelf where it sat with a dozen other scrapbooks. He threw the rest of the paper in the trash. It was time for Christina and he had to get ready. He pushed himself into the bathroom and began the ordeal of cleaning his body.

The hot towel felt good on his arms and chest. Of course, he couldn't feel it on his legs, what was left of them. Only three weeks since her last visit and he was horny as a teenage kid. Business had been good, thank God. Pumping his sax for the tourists down in LoDo might not sound like a real gig, but he made enough to pay the rent on his dump, eat a couple times a day, and every once in a while buy a bottle of Old Crow, or something close.

He anticipated her touch, her mouth, the feel of her breasts in his hands, the sounds she made when he worked his Chicano magic on her. God, he was hot already. Think of something else, man, don't get too worked up or Christina won't have anything to do.

Lefty Gomez, half-Spanish, half-Irish. Ray couldn't believe it when he read about Lefty in the *Baseball Almanac*. He assumed that the great Yankee pitcher, winner of the first All-Star Game, was a Chicano from California (he wouldn't have been Chicano, of course—what would they have called him back then?), but there it was, half-Spanish, half-Irish. A cover? Apparently not. "El Gomez," "Goofy." Colorful nicknames for a colorful personality, everyone said. One of the greatest, but Ray still felt disappointment because Lefty wasn't raza.

Ray had a way with baseball. He knew from the day he picked up a bat and hit his father's first toss back at the old man and knocked him on his butt. Ray, Sr. shouted, "Wise ass," and threw him some smoke. Ray swung and missed, but he stood his ground and the old man got this gleam in his eyes and a smile about a mile wide, and then he tried a curve and damn if little Ray didn't drill it in the direction of first base. Ray, Sr. couldn't spend a lot of time with little Ray, working at night, on the weekends, or on the road, doing anything to hustle a buck, but when he had a few hours they gathered the mitts and balls and bats he had scrounged from second-hand stores and junk dealers, and father and son played ball.

Ray slipped on his cleanest shirt. Christina liked him to be fresh and neat, she demanded it, and at fifty bucks a shot he thought he should try to maintain some standards. She was his last luxury, his only extravagance.

Why would the old man, a wetback orphan with a wife and three of his own kids before he was twenty years old, on the edge of big-city desperation, pick up on American baseball? It could be something as simple as playing the game in an overgrown field somewhere on the outskirts of Durango, Mexico. Sneaking in to watch winter ball. Sal Maglie and those other gabacho players who told the Major Leagues to get screwed, for a couple of years anyway, and then crossed the border to keep in shape, make their fortunes, until they realized where their bread really was buttered. Or it could be—he never let on—that the old man understood the more complex things in life, like the fact that his kids were definitely not Mexicans, and although they carried tags like Chicano or cholo or pachuco, they were American, even if he wasn't, just not quite as American as the snot-nosed, blond-haired children who wanted to play with little Ray, and what could be more American than baseball?

Nah. The old man just liked to play ball.

He rushed to the door when he heard the knock. Christina waited for him, smiling.

"Ray, how've you been? We got to get together more often, baby. I kind of missed you."

Christina earned her money. She bent over and planted a kiss on Ray's lips that almost raised him out of the chair, a crane lifting steel girders. She tongued him, rubbed his back, brought him back to life—miracle worker, Christina!—then eased up.

"How about a drink, Ray? I got some time."

Ray poured the last two shots from his bottle, then pulled two beers from the fridge and twisted off the tops with an easy flick. His meaty arms and thick wrists looked as if they could swing a forty-ounce bat with the precision of Ernie Banks.

"How's your boy, Christina? Haven't seen little Julián for months. Must be big, eh?"

"Jules, Ray. His name's Jules. He ain't no Spanish kid. He's a terror. Can't keep up with him. He's got all this energy, the terrible twos."

She swallowed the shot in one gulp and sipped the beer.

Ray could see the tiredness around her eyes, but he didn't check her out too closely. She was sensitive about her looks. Ray thought she was fine. She liked to show her legs. She wore tight skirts with slits up the side, or skirts so short that Ray knew before they had a date that she had a rose tattooed on her thigh. Ray told her often that she would be surprised how good she would look and feel if she laid off the coke. She needed it, she would answer with a grunt. Her line of work required something to get over, something to take off the edge.

In any event, she was getting old, she said, especially for what she did, and the extra dose of "fire in the blood" kept her on her feet—and her back.

But damn, Ray was already in his forties, what the hell can you do about getting old? Did Ray, Sr. get old, was he even alive, did he ever think about playing catch with little Ray?

"Bring him by, Christina. I'll show him my scrapbooks, teach him how to play ball."

"Oh, Ray. He's too little. He'll tear up your books. Maybe when he's older. You guys can play catch or something. Or teach him how to play some music."

Sure, Christina, whatever.

She stretched a line of powder on his wobbly table and snorted it quicker than Ray could get it together to object.

"*Oh yeah,*" she whispered.

Her eyes glazed and a faint reddish tint crept up her jaw line. She breathed deeply for a few minutes, then she shook her head and gave Ray one of the smiles that filled his dreams. She walked around the room, stepping out of pieces of clothing, and Ray watched in silence. He loved it when she stripped for him. Lacy black things with hooks and straps hung on her skin, jiggling when she moved slowly toward him. The rose sat like a bruise on her leg, warm and swollen, ready for his caress. She stood at the edge of his desk, turned away from him so that he could watch her wiggle her ass.

"Ray, you never showed me this. Wha's it?"

She held a baseball in her hands.

"Uh, Christina, be careful. My old man got me that. Here, give it to me."

And although he didn't want to ruin the mood, he rolled to her with a little too much speed, a little too much urgency in his response, and snatched the ball from her hand.

"Is jus' a ball, ain't it?" Her words slipped out half-formed. She wasn't wiggling anymore.

Ray relented. He handed it back to Christina.

"All right. But be careful. See, there it is, Roberto Clemente's autograph. The old man got it for me one time when he worked in L.A. Clemente signed it before a game with the Dodgers. He's dead, you know."

"Your old man?"

"Clemente. Plane crash. The ball's worth a lot of money. But it's about the only thing I got from my old man, so it's kind of special to me."

Christina returned the ball to its space on Ray's desk.

"You kept it all these years? How old's it?"

"Early sixties. I was a kid. Actually, I lost it, didn't know what the hell happened to it. But when my mother died, I came back from 'Nam for the funeral, and there it was in a box with her rosaries, pictures, and mantillas. She didn't have much. For some reason she kept this old ball."

Christina watched him drift away. His scarred face saddened, his body slumped in the wheelchair. She took his head in her hands and held him against her, smoothed the strands of wispy hair, and helped Ray in the only way she knew.

Clyde tried to stay calm. But handling his habit was not an experience that lent itself to calmness. And making the money by breaking into houses, apartments, and an occasional second-hand store, the kind that should not have alarms, only added to the tension. No wonder he always felt tired—except when he was riding the blow, of course. Then he could do anything, anytime, anywhere. Make love to the most beautiful woman. Pull off the most outrageous heist in thief history. Kick ass. Be the man.

Ripping off old Ray's sax didn't exactly fall into the historical category. Stealing the cripple's instrument, Ray's source of income, probably ranked as outrageous, pitiful but outrageous.

He tried to explain to Linda but she didn't get it.

"I can get twenty, thirty bucks for the sax. Ray keeps it in good shape. Take me five minutes to get it, maybe. His lock's gotta be a joke. And what can Ray do about it if I get in his crib and yank the sax? Not a damn thing. Nothin'."

Linda arched her eyebrows.

"But crap, Clyde. It's Ray. He don't harm no one. He's a little weird, but who around here ain't? And you know him, man. He knows you, too. What if he sees you? What if he turns you in to the cops? You ready for that?"

Clyde knew there was one thing he definitely was not ready for, and that was another lockup. He refused to consider the possibility.

"No way there's any risk. Ray drinks himself to sleep every night. Calls the juice his Oblivion Express. I heard him talkin' about it one day when he was on the corner playing for handouts, explainin' to that Jesus Saves preacher why he can't get up early for the coffee and doughnuts and sermon at the center. Goes out like a match in the wind. And in his chair, you think he's goin' to pull any hero stuff? Come on, it's a setup. Made for Clyde the Glide, smoothest second-story pro on the West Side."

Linda shook her head but she knew it was hopeless. And maybe Clyde could scrape enough together for a line or two, if he did an all-nighter and hit at least a half-dozen places. Ray's sax by itself wouldn't pay for a taste, much less a good time. It was stupid but it was Clyde's lifestyle, so to speak. To each his own.

Ray slept curled in a ball in his chair, clutching the saxophone he dreamed was his rifle. The street below his room shook with the noise from buses and taxis, ambulances screaming their warnings to the dealers, pimps, and winos prowling Ray's neighborhood. He slept through it all. He prowled, too, but the thick jungle that surrounded him held more terror than the actors in the midnight street scene could conjure up in their wildest drug-induced fantasies. He moaned and twisted his blanket into a sweaty, crumpled rag, but he slept.

The door creaked and Ray's eyes jerked open. For a horrible, ridiculous second, slant-eyed killers hovered around him, poked at him with their weapons, and Ray whimpered. The door eased shut and a shadow moved around the room. Streetlights bounced off the gleam of a knife blade.

"Get the hell out of here!"

Before the guy could react, Ray wheeled into the back of the intruder and knocked him over.

"What the . . . !"

The knife flew across the room. Clyde crawled on the floor, looking for the weapon, trying to regain the advantage. Ray ran over groping hands. A feeble scream mixed with the loud crunch of fractured bone. The thief struggled to his feet, turned around in circles, lost in the darkness, defenseless against the crip he thought would be easy. Ray moved smoothly, effortlessly. His strong, solid fingers grabbed the first thing they touched and flung it at the man. Dazed, Clyde stumbled out the door and collapsed at the top of the stairs.

Ray's neighbors flicked on their lights, threw open their doors, some with guns in their hands, and kicked the intruder sniveling on the stained, muddy carpet.

Ray wheeled to the hallway and picked up his baseball. The ink had been smeared by the impact on the burglar's greasy skin.

He held the ball with his viselike grip and carefully, slowly, used a Sharpie to fill in the words *Roberto Clemente* over the smudge.

Someone nudged his shoulder.

"Better get that door fixed, Ray. I walked right in. You okay?"

"Yeah, Art. Guess I still got my throwing arm. I think I know that guy. You recognize him?"

"No way. Dirty creeps around here. About time one of them got it. You really clobbered him. What the hell you hit him with?"

"This ball. Check it out. My old man gave it to me, about the only thing I got from him. It's worth some money, but it means more to me, it's kind of special. Sentimental value and all that."

Rich Alderete

DETRICE JONES was born and raised in San Francisco and is currently an African-American Studies major at the University of California, Los Angeles. This story is her first published work, and is based on her own life experiences.

just surviving another day
by detrice jones

There was a knock at my door. Then a jingle and he was in. Cheap-ass lock. I looked at the clock and it was 3:36 a.m. He turned on the light and began his search. I watched him, hoping he wouldn't find it.

"Let me get that money and I'll pay you back in the morning," he said.

"No. I need it for lunch."

"I'll give it back to you in the morning."

Yeah right. How was he going to do that? If he didn't have any money now, he wouldn't have any in the morning. He came over and searched near me and around the bed. It wasn't next to me. I learned quickly that it was one of the first places they looked. They had just given me the money no longer than six hours ago. I guess they had smoked up the little cash they already had. Which meant if he found the money, I wouldn't have any for tomorrow or the next couple of weeks when somebody got paid again. He found it in the little chest on my dresser.

"I'll give it back to you in the morning," he said as he left the room and turned off my light, as if I would be going to sleep anytime soon. I lay there and worried about food and eating for tomorrow. I had to get hunger off my mind. When I finally fell asleep, it seemed like it had been two minutes before the alarm clock went off. I hit the snooze and went back to sleep. This repeated five times. I finally woke up an hour later. I knew even if I missed first period, I would have to make it to my next class because we had a quiz that I couldn't make up.

After I got dressed, I looked for my dad. Like always he was nowhere to be found. My mom was in the kitchen. She pressed her blackened fingers on the stove looking for crumbs, little rocks or anything that was round and white. I made some toast so I wouldn't starve for the whole day. I didn't say a word as I tried my best to maneuver around her.

"Where Ronnie at? I gotta go to school."

"He'll be back soon."

Denial. I knew better. I took my time to eat and looked for some loose money around the house. I found fifty cents in the big couch. Beatrice saw that and had a slightly jealous look in her eyes. What the hell could she smoke with fifty cents? I went outside to see if I could find my dad, Ronnie. He was in the driver's seat of our van. At that moment I wished I wouldn't have talked so much in drivers ed, stopped procrastinating, and got my license sooner.

"You gotta get to school?" he asked in a mumbled, half-sleep voice, without turning his head at all.

"Yeah, I'm late, but I gotta go to second period, at least."

"I'ma have to give you that money this afternoon," he said, still looking straight ahead like he was unable to move his neck in either direction.

He drove like I was Miss Daisy. It took at least thirty minutes to get there when it should only take fifteen. I went to the attendance lady to get a tardy note. She knew my name, homeroom number, and grade by heart. Sometimes she would already have my note ready for me when I got there. I was there in time for the quiz I didn't study for. Nobody could convince me that I got anything less than an A, though.

During our nutrition break, I bought a Snickers from the student store. I was . . . kinda hungry.

"How was Mr. Springsted's quiz?" my friend Jessica asked.

"Pretty easy. Make sure you know about the Great Depression. Dates, how it affected minorities, shit like that."

"You think you did good?"

"I don't know, maybe a B. Hopefully. I didn't study."

"You said the same thing last time and got an A."

"I was lucky. Hey, you got some money I could borrow?" She looked at me and hesitated. She was going to say no. I could see it in her eyes. She must have been thinking about the money I already owed her.

"I'll give it back, I promise. I left my money at home today. I'll pay you back with all the other money I owe you."

"I only got a dollar to spare," she said while handing me the money.

"That's cool. Thanks. I'll pay you back tomorrow," I said, knowing she would forget. She always did until I asked her for some more. The bell rang. "I gotta go to class, you know how Mr. Gordon is about people being late."

"Yeah."

"I'll see you at lunch."

"All right."

"Good luck on that quiz," I had to yell at her down the hall.

"Thanks."

Mr. Gordon was known for not letting people in the class if they were tardy. You would have to wait in the hallway with all the other late people and not make too much noise. He would be madder if we made noise in the hallway when he was ready to let us in. He would ask us why we were late, then give us a lecture on why we shouldn't be late. Then, of course, there was the embarrassing walk back into class with the whole room watching. Later in the year I would learn to stay by the room during break. For now I had to damn near run to the class all the way on the other side of the tiny elementary school that they turned into a high school and packed us in like sardines.

Lunch took too long to get here. I always got hungrier when I thought that I might not be able to eat for the rest of the day, and a dollar wasn't gonna cut it. When I got through the crowded hallways to the place where my friends usually ate, they were almost done.

"How the fuck ya'll get ya'll food so early in that long-ass lunch line?"

They all laughed. They were something like little girls when I cursed. Coming from families with more money than mine, they were sensitive about that stuff. So cussing was always the fastest and easiest way to make them laugh.

"Why you always cuss so much?" April said.

"'Cause I can."

"Does your mom know you curse like that?" Erin asked, wiping cream cheese off her fingers.

"I cuss in front of her."

"She does," Keyona said.

"You bad," Erin said.

"Ya'll didn't answer my question. How did ya'll get ya'll food so early?"

"We got out of art class early," Erin said.

"One of ya'll got some money I can borrow?"

"You ain't got no money?" Keyona asked.

Obviously, I almost said with attitude. Why would I ask them for money if I had some? "I left my money at home." They were silent. "If each one of ya'll give me a dollar, I will be able to eat." Still, nothing. "I'll pay ya'll back tomorrow."

April gave me a wrinkled dollar out of her tight jeans.

Erin gave me four of the six shiny new quarters she had.

Keyona, reluctant to give me anything, asked, "Are you going to pay me back tomorrow?"

"I will."

She turned to her purse so no one else could see and pulled out a crisp dollar bill.

"Thanks, you guys. I'll give it back," I said, not knowing if I could live up to that promise. I would definitely have to repay Keyona tomorrow. I went to the lunch line and saw Jasmine and Jessica—the Big Ballers, even though they wouldn't admit it. They had the best cars in school. I would trade shoes with them any day.

I had already asked Jessica for some money earlier. I had to figure out a way to ask Jasmine for some money without Jessica getting mad.

"Jasmine, can I borrow some money?"

"I just gave you some money earlier."

"A dollar? I can't eat with a dollar."

Jasmine pulled out five dollars and handed them to me.

"Thanks, I'll pay—"

"Don't worry about it. You don't have to."

"You sure?"

"Yeah. It's all good."

Good. I could pay back cheap-ass Keyona and eat tomorrow, and my parents wouldn't know that I had some money.

After school I went to basketball practice. If I didn't eat lunch today, I probably would have passed out.

"Point guards lead from the front." My coach yelled at me because I was the last to finish the suicides. I hated being a point guard because I was lazy. My coach was right, though. I was the leader and shouldn't be last. We had to do three sets of suicides today because two people were late and one person on the team couldn't come. We ran most of the time during practice. It was more like a track team than anything because our coach was not a basketball coach. So we ran, rarely ran plays out of his store-bought playbook, and almost never scrimmaged.

Basketball was my form of meditation. I got a chance to clear my mind and focus strictly on the game. I didn't have the energy or time to think about the bad things that were going on in my life. I didn't think about school, stupid high school boys, or my home life. I didn't have to think about being scared to get a drink of water in the middle of the night because my dad might be in his paranoid state and try to stab me, his own daughter, because he thought I was trying to get him. I didn't have to think about my mom taking back the lunch money she gave me because they spent the rest of hers. I didn't have to think about my little brothers and sister who might not be safe.

After practice Erin got picked up, while April, Keyona, and I caught the bus. I knew I didn't want to go home this early.

"April, can I go to your house?"

"I don't care," she replied.

At April's house I would be able to eat real home-cooked food instead of Top Ramen. When I got there, I had to wait for her to eat before I did. I couldn't just raid the fridge like I wanted to. We ate baked chicken, fried okra, and rice. I always waited until the last possible moment to go home, sometimes missing the last bus and spending the night over there. I didn't want to go home, not tonight.

"April, your friend can't spend the night again," I heard her mother whisper to her through the paper-thin walls. I made sure I made the bus that night. I guess I wore out my welcome. Instead of saying *Welcome*, it says *Well . . .* I guess you can *come*.

It was piercing cold high in the mountains where April lived. The always gloomy and foggy city didn't help either. April, fortunately for her, was immune to the cold. The bus was fifteen minutes late, and I didn't get home until 1:30 a.m.

My mom seemed like she hadn't moved since morning. Still trying to pick up rocks. My dad, on the other hand, was in motion. Slow motion. He had his favorite knife in his hand, creeping around the house like a scared zombie. There was no use in talking to either of them. I had a little money so I would be able to survive another day. I took a shower and tried to hide the money somewhere no one would look. I had to find a good hiding place through trial and error. This time I simply kept it in my pocket and buried my pants deep in my dirty clothes bin. I went to sleep without even thinking about homework. I had more important things to worry about. It was 2:15 a.m. and I went to sleep as soon as my body touched the bed.

There was a knock at the door. Then a jingle and she was in. I gotta fix that door! I looked at the clock and it was 4:58. She turned on the light and began searching. Why did my mom have to come in tonight? I knew she wouldn't be afraid of a teenage girl's dirty clothes bin.

"You got some money?" she asked while searching me, the bed, and the mattress.

"NO! Ronnie took my lunch money yesterday."

"He did?"

"I didn't even get to eat," I whined, trying to make her feel bad. After ten minutes of searching, she gave up, only glancing at my dirty clothes. With her brain in this state, she wouldn't be able to remember what I had on today. She turned off the light, as if I would be going to sleep anytime soon, and closed the door.

I would survive another day.

part iv
gangsters & monsters

Bob Buck

EMORY HOLMES II is a Los Angeles–
based writer who has published works
as a novelist, playwright, poet, children's story writer, and journalist. His
news stories have appeared in many
publications, including the *San
Francisco Chronicle,* the *Chicago
Tribune,* the *Los Angeles Times,* the
New York Times Wire Service, *Los
Angeles Magazine,* and *Essence.*

a.k.a., moises rockafella
by emory holmes II

Y ou said I could have water. I want some water," Fat Tommy
said again.

"You can have water, Moises, after you tell us how it went
down. That's our deal," Vargas reminded him.

Fat Tommy didn't understand. He wanted some water. Why
these other questions? Why this Moises shit? He wasn't goddamn Moises anymore. That shit was dead; done. Why didn't
these pigs believe him? He felt so sorry for himself. None of it was
his fault. It was the Colombians and that goddamn Pemberton.
He was the bad guy. If they want their devil, there he is. But don't
expect Fat Tommy to commit suicide and snitch. That shit was
dead.

Fat Tommy was having a really bad day. His big shoulders
slumped. His money was gone. His business was gone. His high
was gone. He laid his arms tenderly across his knees. He narrowed
his eyes in the harsh light and squinted down at his arms. Still, he
had to admit . . . he certainly was well dressed.

"Don't give those white folks no excuses, Tommy," his wife
Bea had advised. "We ain't gonna get kilt over this asshole."

Bea had borrowed her mother's credit card and bought him
two brand-new, white, long-sleeve business shirts from Sears for
his interrogations and, regrettably, for the trial. That was such a
sweet thing for Bea to do. Buy him new shirts that the cops would
like. He loved his Queen Bea—she had been his sweetheart since
grade school, way back when he was skinny and pretty. Bea was
sexy, street-smart, and loyal to him. After he'd knocked her up,

twice, he had started to hang with her, help her with his sons, and had grown to love her.

Gradually, she had encouraged him to develop his unique sartorial style: his dazzling jheri curl (forty bucks a pop at Hellacious Cuts on Crenshaw); his multiple ropes of gold, bedecked with dangling golden razors, crucifixes, naked chicks, powerfists, and coke spoons; his rainbow collection of jogging suits and fourteen pairs of top-of-the-line Air Jordans (and a pair of vintage Connies for layin' around the pad). He had restricted himself to only five or six affairs after they got married. The affairs were mostly "strawberries"— amateur ho's who turned tricks for dope.

Getting your johnson swabbed by a 'hood rat for a couple of crumbs of low-grade rock—not even a nickel's worth—wasn't like being unfaithful, he figured. It was medicinal; therapeutic; a salutary necessity—more like a business expense. Like buying aspirin or getting a massage on a high-stress job. But that was all past—the whores, the dealing, the violence, the stress. He had resolutely turned his back on "thug life" six months ago, when he realized that a brother, even an old-time G like him, was vulnerable to jail time or a hit—after he had experienced the deadly grotesqueries in which Pemberton was capable of entangling him.

So, hours after that goddamn murder, months before he knew the cops were on to him, he'd flushed the bulk of his street stash down the toilet—1,800 bindles—and thrown away most of his thug-life paraphernalia, even his jack-off books, *Players* and *Hustlers* mostly, and his cherished *Big Black Titty* magazines, and faithfully (except when the Lakers were on TV, or *Fear Factor*, or *The Sopranos*) got down on his knees and read the Bible with Bea and promised to her on his daddy's life, and on his *granddaddy's* soul even, he wasn't going to disappoint her anymore. No more druggin', no more whores, no more hangin' out. No more street. Swear to Jesus . . .

"White folks like white stuff," Bea had explained that morning before he surrendered himself. They were in the bedroom of their new Woodland Hills bungalow, and Bea was standing behind him on her tiptoes and pressing her breasts against his back as they faced the dresser mirror. "They like white houses, white picket fences, white bread, and white shirts," she added grimly, peeking over his shoulder to admire her husband and herself in the mirror.

They both looked so sad, so pitiful and wronged, Bea thought. And all because of that shit-for-brains Pemberton. Fat Tommy thought so, too. Recalling those poignant scenes on that morning, he remembered that they'd both cried a little bit, standing there perusing their innocent, sad, sexy selves in the mirror. Little Bea had slipped from view for a moment as she helped Tommy struggle out of his nightshirt and unfastened for the final time the nine golden ropes of braid that festooned his massive neck, and then his diamond earring. Bea tearfully placed them in a shopping bag of things they would have to hock. She slid the voluminous dress-shirtsleeves over his backswept arms. Then her beautiful, manicured hands appeared, fluttering along his shoulders, smoothing out the wrinkles in his new shirt.

When Bea was satisfied with her effort, she slipped around in front of him and unloosed his lucky nose ring, letting him view her voluptuous little self in the lace teddy he'd bought her for Mother's Day, but which she had seldom worn. Then, while he was ogling her melons, she seized his right pinky finger, whose stylish claw he had allowed to flourish there as a scoop for sampling virgin powder on the fly and which he had rakishly polished jet black, and before he could stop her, she deftly clipped it off. Fat Tommy shrieked like a waif.

"It's better this way, Tommy," Bea assured him. She carefully placed the shorn talon in a plastic baggie. It resembled a shiny black roach; but for Fat Tommy, it was like witnessing the burial of a child.

"I'm keeping this for good luck," she told him, and stowed it in the change purse of her Gucci bag. She patted his lumpy belly, which protruded out of the break in the shirt like a fifty-pound sack of muffins. Then Bea buttoned the shirt and put on the new hand-painted tie with Martin Luther King, Jr.'s image on it that she'd had a Cuban chick make specially for him, the girl she'd met in rehab. She cupped his big pumpkin head in her hands. She had paid her little sister Karesha fifteen bucks to touch up his jheri curl. The handsome thick mane of oily black locks cascaded sensuously, if greasily, down his forehead and neck.

"Try to stay where it's cool, so the jheri curl juice don't drip on your brand-new shirt, baby," Bea said in a sweetly admonishing tone.

"This new ProSoft Sport Curl Gel don't drip like that cheap shit, baby," Fat Tommy explained. "It's deluxe. I gave your sister two more dollars so she would use the top-drawer shit. I want to make a good impression."

"I know you do, baby. But you're gonna have a hard time keeping it up in the joint . . . I don't think you—"

Her husband had stopped listening and Bea stared once more into Fat Tommy's eyes. He was such a big baby. Standing there he reminded her of a favorite holy card she'd cherished those two years she went to St. Sebastian's Catholic school before she met him. St. Sebastian, sad and pitiful, mortally wounded, innocent and wronged, pierced with arrows. She kissed him lightly on his shirt front and pushed him backward onto the edge of the bed.

"Pull yourself together, Tommy. I've got to go drop off the kids," she said.

Fat Tommy was still crying, sitting dejectedly on the side of the bed, long after she had dressed and gone out to drop their boys at her sister's new hide-out in Topanga Canyon. The boys woke up during the forty-minute drive to Karesha's as Bea vainly scanned the radio for news of Pemberton's arrest. She couldn't stop looking at her boys, couldn't stop cursing Pemberton under her breath and sadly reflecting on how that asshole had put them all up to their eyeballs in shit.

Bea's mother was looking out the window of her sister's place when she drove up. Her mother would drive the boys up to Santa Barbara and they would take a cross-country bus to Texas that night. The three women and the two infant boys cried until Bea's mother drove off in Karesha's pink Lexus, with Little Tommy and baby Kobe waving bye-bye from their car seats.

After their mother and the boys were safely away, Bea's little sister, Karesha, a cold, deadly customer in most circumstances, confided to her that she was a little nervous about the possibility of her own capture or the jailing and execution of her notorious former squeeze, Cut Pemberton, and what it all could mean for her Hollywood plans, and for her high-toned, social-climbing crew.

"You heard from him?" Bea asked, as she backed out the dirt driveway of Karesha's rented, brush-covered hideaway.

"I hear the Colombians got him. The cops don't know much about him yet. I'm sure he wants to keep it that way. Anyway, I trashed the cell phone," Karesha said quietly. "But if that sick motherfucker come 'round here I'm gonna send him to Jesus." She lifted her T-shirt and showed Bea the pearl-handled .22 Pemberton had bought her as an engagement gift.

When Bea arrived back home, the neighbors were out, watering their lawns, pretending they didn't know Fat Tommy was a prime suspect in a vicious murder.

"How do, Miss O'Rourke?" Pearl Stenis, the boldest of her nosy neighbors greeted her.

"I'm blessed, Mrs. Stenis," Bea said flatly.

She pulled into the garage and closed the door. She gathered herself a moment before she got out. She turned on all the lights in the garage and found a flashlight, and took a good twenty minutes making sure the Mercedes was clean of diapers and weapons and works and blow and any incriminating evidence.

When she was done, she poked her head into the house and called, "We're late, Tommy. I'll be in the car. Come on, baby. We got to be on time this time." She waited in the car and honked the horn a half-dozen times but had to come back inside. She found Fat Tommy back in bed, fully dressed, sobbing, with the covers pulled over his head.

"Where the hell were you, baby?" Fat Tommy complained. "I thought Cut got you."

"That niggah better be layin' low," Bea said. "These Hollywood cops would love to catch a fuck-up like that and Rodney-King his ass to death for the savage shit he done."

"I was there too, baby. Remember, I was there, too," Fat Tommy murmured.

"Don't say that, Tommy! Don't say that no more," Bea demanded. "Put that craziness out your mind. You wasn't there. You don't know nothing. You don't know nobody."

"It just ain't fair," Fat Tommy complained.

"Listen here, Tommy," Bea said sternly. "You don't deserve this beef. You don't know nothin'. You didn't see nothin'. You got a wife and family to protect. It was that goddamn Cut that fount Simpson. You didn't even know he was a cop. It was all Cut's idea. We wouldn't be mixed up in none of this if Cut hadn't . . ."

Fat Tommy began sobbing again. After a few minutes, he confessed that he had raided the emergency stash in the bathroom and had done a couple of lines to calm his nerves. He suggested that they do what was left. There was only a half-bindle anyway. He never did crack, the high felt like a suicide jump. Crack was for kids; toxic, cheap-ass shit meant to sell, not do. Fat Tommy was old school—White Girl all the way. Powder, he believed, was classier, mellower than rock cocaine.

Bea retrieved the emergency bindle out of the bottom of a box of sanitary napkins. There was only a portion of an eight ball left from the half-pound Fat Tommy liked to keep around the pad for Laker games and birthdays and other special occasions. Bea used her mother's Sears card to line out six hefty tracks of the white powder on the dresser top. Rolling their last hundred-dollar bill into a straw, the couple snorted quickly, sucking the lines of blow into their flared nostrils like shotgun blasts fired straight to the back of their brains.

"Damn, that's good shit," Fat Tommy said, feeling the cold drip of the snow, liquefied and suffused with snot, glazing the commodious interiors of his head and throat.

Quickly, the drug began to take effect: it eased its frigid tendrils down the back lanes of their breathing passages, deadening the superior nasal concha, the frontal and sepenoidal sinuses, creeping along their soft palates like a snotty glacier before it slid down the interiors of their throats, chilling the lingual nerves and flowing over the rough, bitter fields of papilla at the back of their tongues and ascending like a stream of arctic ghosts up through their pituitary glands, their spinal walls and veins, and into the uppermost regions of their brains. The pupils of their dark brown eyes became dilated and sparkling.

Fat Tommy shut his eyes tight. The darkness inside his mind began to fill with amorphous, floating colors. His big body seemed to be shapeless and floating, too. He looked down at the drifts of sugary dust remaining on the dresser. Almost 400 bucks worth of Girl—gone in six vigorous snorts. As Fat Tommy admired the smeared patterns of residue on the dresser top, Bea leaned down and broadly licked the last thin traces of powder. Normally he prided himself in always managing to lick up the leftovers before Bea got to them. But he was immobilized with grief; and he was frozen from his nose to his toes. Bea was frozen numb, too. The coke was ninety percent pure. Chilean. It'd only been stepped on once. Cream of the Andes. Bea blinked hard and looked up at her husband.

"I'm straight now," Bea said, noting a half moon of white powder showing around the deep alar grooves of Fat Tommy's right nostril. "Your slip is showin', baby," she added, pointing to his reflection in the mirror. Fat Tommy pinched his nostrils closed, shut his eyes, and took a sharp snort. The lumps of powder shot past his nasal vestibules and septum in white-hot pellets of snot.

His heart began to race. Neither of them said a word for a few minutes. They closed their eyes and surrendered to the high. When Fat Tommy finally opened his eyes, Bea was staring at him with a beatific look on her face.

"You look nice," Bea said. "Innocent . . . Don't let 'em punk you, Tommy. Just wear the shit outta this shirt and tie. Dr. King'll bring you through. All business. You know how to talk to white folks. Don't go in there like no G . . . talking all bad and shit, like you was that goddamn Cut. That's what they want. Give them your A game and you'll be all right. Remember. You wasn't there. You didn't see nothing. You don't know nobody. *We ain't gonna get kilt over some asshole.*"

Fat Tommy got in the car, gripping his Bible, sobbing and praying and assuring Bea and the Lord he loved them. Between his sobs he promised her he would savor her instructions and repeat them like a mantra: Don't say nothing that's gonna get us kilt *over some asshole*. She reminded him that his stupid-ass Uncle Bunny had done a nickel at Folsom on a break-in after Bunny talked too much. So—don't talk too much. Don't do nothing that will make you look guilty. They got nothing. That was the bottom line, Bea reminded Fat Tommy. They agreed if he was cool and smooth he had a chance to ease his way out of the beef with short time.

The cops were nice to him at first; they said he was a stand-up guy for turning himself in and helping out with the investigation. They had interviewed him all day. Fat Tommy said he didn't "need no lawyer." He wasn't guilty. The cops didn't seem to be concerned about his coke business so much as they wanted to know what he knew about the recent murder of the undercover cop—Simpson— right in the middle of the projects on Fat Tommy's home turf, La Caja. Fat Tommy assured him he "didn't have any 'turf' anymore, not in La Caja, not nowhere." Moreover, he certainly didn't know anything about a cop killing.

"We know you ain't no killer, Moises," Vargas told him a few minutes into the interrogation. "But you grew up in La Caja, where this murder went down. We figure you might know something. Point us to the bad guys. We know you're in bed with the Colombians. They're all over La Caja these days. One of them called you by name, Moises. He's quite fond of you. Says you're a big shot. You're looking at some serious time if you don't play ball. Play along and help us catch this killer . . . you'll be all right . . ."

Vargas offered him a jumbo cup of lemonade and four jelly doughnuts. His high had long ago been blown and he couldn't believe how hungry and thirsty he'd gotten. Vargas said that the pretty cop who had processed him that morning had asked to make the lemonade especially for him.

Fat Tommy said, "That was sure nice of her."

"Yeah. Officer Ospina is a sweetie. Drink up. That's the last of it . . . We need to get started," Vargas said, and smiled at him.

Braddock took the empty cup, crushed it, and banked it into the wastebasket in the back of the interrogation room.

"Great shot," Fat Tommy said. "Three-pointer."

Braddock and Vargas said nothing. Braddock walked to a chair somewhere behind him and Vargas turned on a tape recorder and intoned: "This is Detective Manny Vargas of the Homicide Detail, Criminal Investigation Division of the Van Nuys Police Department. I am joined with Detective Will Dockery and DEA special agent Roland Braddock. This is a tape-recorded interview of Thomas Martin O'Rourke, a.k.a., "Fat Tommy" O'Rourke, a.k.a., Tommy Martin, a.k.a., Pretty Tommy Banes, a.k.a., Sugar-T Banes, a.k.a., Slo Jerry-T, a.k.a., Big Jerry Jay, a.k.a., T-Moose, a.k.a., Moises Rockafella . . ."

"Uh, my name ain't Moises," Fat Tommy protested, interrupting as politely as he could. "Some bad people started calling me that. But I don't let nobody call me that no more." He tried his sexiest grin.

Vargas looked at him blankly and continued: "This a homicide investigation under police report number A-55503. Today's date is March 28, 2005, and the time is now 1349 hours." Then Vargas looked at Fat Tommy and said, "Could you state your name once more for the record?"

"I'm Thomas Martin O'Rourke."

"Address?"

Tommy gave them his parents' address. That's where he got his mail now.

"How old are you?"

"Thirty-four, officer," Fat Tommy said.

"Employed?"

"I was assistant manager at the Swing Shop . . ."

"Was?"

"I got laid off."

"When was that?"

"1992."

Dockery and Braddock rolled their eyes, then Vargas said, "What were you doing after you got . . . laid off?"

Fat Tommy fingered his Martin Luther King, Jr. tie. "Odd jobs, here and there . . ."

"What kind of odd jobs?"

"Church stuff."

"Church stuff?"

Fat Tommy sat up straight in his chair. "I'm a Christian, sir. And I try to help in the Lord's work whenever—"

"You get that fancy Mercedes doing this church work?"

"Naw." Fat Tommy laughed out loud.

"The street tells us you're a big-time coke man—that true, Moises? You a big-time coke dealer, Moises?"

"Oh no, sir. Not no more. All that shit is dead . . . I mean, all that stuff is dead . . . I don't do no drugs no more. I don't sling coke no more. I got a wife and family . . ."

"You high now?"

"What was that?"

"You under the influence of drugs or alcohol at this time?"

"No. Oh Jesus, no." Fat Tommy wished to Christ he was. He

couldn't make the cops believe him. They wouldn't give him any more lemonade, even though the girl cop said she made it specially for him. They wouldn't give him any more doughnuts—they said they were all out. Cops out of doughnuts! Now they wouldn't even give him water—and he was dry as shit. That Chilean coke had sucked all the good spit out of his mouth. The cops kept hammering away at his story. He shut his eyes. He was only pretending to listen, nodding yes, yes, goddamnit, yes, or gazing up at them with a mournful, wounded look in his eyes.

Their sharp questions droned on unintelligibly like the buzzing of wasps attacking just above his head. Then . . . the cops seemed to go quiet for a moment. Bea's admonitions echoed in his head and gradually, without realizing it, Fat Tommy allowed a wan smile to creep across the corners of his mouth. Still smiling, he opened his eyes into a narrow slit and gazed down at his handsome shirtsleeves, admiring the shiny contours, like little snow-covered mountains really, that the polyester fabric traced along his thick, short arms as they lay across his knees.

Christ, he loved this shirt!

"Somethin' I said funny, Fatboy? Somethin' funny?" Braddock yelled, momentarily breaking through his reverie.

Fat Tommy jumped a little, snapped his eyes tight a moment, then slowly opened the slits again and looked back down at his arms. Braddock continued mocking him. Fat Tommy burrowed himself deeper into his thoughts. He looked at his arms and knees. They were such good arms—good, kind arms; and great knees—great, great knees. He looked down at his hands and knees lovingly as the cops droned on. He decided, with a hot, white tear leaking out of a crack in his right eye, finally, that he loved his knees as much as he loved his dick or his ass—better, probably, now that he had found the Lord again. His regard for his ass and dick now seemed so misguided, so . . . heathen. And these knees were so much more representative of him—innocent, God-fearing, above reproach.

They had taken him all over—all over L.A., the Valley, even to Oak Town once on a church picnic. There was plenty of water there, beer and red pop and lemonade and swine barbeque, too. He was thin then, and pretty. Just a baby boy—so innocent, such a good young brother. The picnic was on the Oakland Bay, and they'd all rode the bus up there, singing gospel songs the whole way. There must have been a hundred buses, the whole California Youth Baptist Convention, someone said. And it was his knees that helped him get through it, basketball, softball, the three-legged race with pretty Althea Jackson. They were nine years old. Those were some of the best times in his life. And he was such a good guy, a regular brother, everyone said so, and now this lunatic murder and this fucked-up Pemberton, that devil, poking his bloody self like a shitty nightmare in the midst of all his plans.

Fat Tommy ached at beholding all these tender scenes—Bea, the picnic, the tears—all the images like flashing detritus in a river streaming across his upturned hands, it was just too much. He closed his eyes, but the river of images burst inside them, flooding the darkness in his head even more vividly than before: his first day at Teddy Roosevelt Junior High; the time he and Bea won third place at the La Caja Boys & Girls Club Teen Dance-Off; and his best pal . . . not that goddamn Pemberton . . . but Trey-Boy, Trey-Boy Middleton (*rest his soul*). That was his best friend. It was cool Trey-Boy who befriended him when everyone treated him like a jerk, and it was Trey-Boy who'd taken pity on him and helped him pimp up his lifestyle.

It was Trey-Boy. Not a murderer. A hip brother. True blue. Trey-Boy showed him how to affect a gangster's scowl, and helped him adopt a slow, hulking walk that could frighten just about anyone he encountered on the street. He'd showed him how to smoke a cigarette, load a gat, roll a blunt, cop pussy, weed, and blow. He had even showed him how to shoot up once. And Trey-Boy never got mad, even when that faggot Stick Jenkins bumped him on purpose and made him spill a good portion of the spoon of heroin he

had carefully prepared. Trey-Boy had pimp-slapped the faggot—
he called him "my sissy," and Stick had just smiled like a bitch and
turned red as a yella niggah could get—and everyone laughed.

He remembered how Trey-Boy had cooked up what was left of
the little amber drops of Boy they could scrape from the toilet seat
and floor and showed him how to tie-off and find the vein and
shoot the junk, even if he only got a little wacked—it was wacked
enough to know he wouldn't do that anymore. It wasn't fun at all.
He couldn't stop puking. It felt like now—in this hot room with no
water, under this white light. But he wasn't no goddamn junkie.
None of that puking and nodding and drooling shit was for him.
He was strictly weed and blow, strictly weed and blow. He wasn't
no goddamn junkie. Let them try to pin that on him. They'd come
up zero. Just like this murder. He wasn't there; he didn't do it. He
didn't see nobody; he didn't know nobody.

Trey-Boy had given him his favorite street moniker—Fat
Tommy. When Trey-Boy said it, it didn't feel like a put-down. It
was a term of war and affection. Fat Tommy was a lumpy 370
pounds but he didn't feel fat when Trey-Boy called him Fat
Tommy—he felt big, as in big man, big trouble, big fun—there's a
difference, really, when you think about it. A street handle like Fat
Tommy made him feel like one of the hoods in *The Sopranos*—his
favorite story. He'd made a small fortune with that name—not like
he made with Cut Pemberton, when the margins and risks got
scary and huge, and the fuckin' Colombians got involved, and people feared him and only knew him by the name Pemberton hung on
him, Moises—Moises Rockafella, the King of Rock Cocaine. He
didn't make big cake like that with Trey-Boy—but at least he didn't
have to worry about a murder beef, and the living was decent.

Such a wave of woe swept over Fat Tommy as he contemplated
all this that, softly, he began to weep. His whole bright life was
passing before his sad eyes: there were pinwheels of light; a whole
series of birthdays; his stint as a fabulous dancer; his wife, Bea,
again; his kids—Little Tommy and infant Kobe—cuties! cuties!

He didn't deserve this. And there was his old job as assistant manager at the Swing Shop —twelve years ago now—all those great records: Tupac, NWA, Biggie, KRS-ONE, Salt 'N' Pepa, shit, even Marvin Gaye. He knew them like the lines in these hands that now stared up at him, glazed and dotted with sweat. All the bright scenes of his life seemed to be fading, all of them diminishing like faces in a fog. Even the fabulous good shit that was coming, close on the horizon, that seemed to be diminishing, too. If only he could get a glass of water, or maybe some lemonade.

"I'm dryin' out inside," Fat Tommy pleaded, lifting his head slightly. He could not see Vargas, but could hear his footfalls pacing back and forth somewhere behind him.

"Steady, sweetheart. Steady. Just a few more questions and you're home free," Vargas said.

Tommy waited for the next question with the same despairing apprehension with which he had endured all the last. An hour earlier Vargas had the lights on so bright that when Fat Tommy looked up the next moment, he beheld not a pea-green interrogation room with a trio of sad-sack cops trying to sweat him for a cop murder he didn't commit—the whole room seemed to him as a single white spotlight, a moon's eyeball inspecting him on a disc of light. At many points during the long, arduous interrogation, the men drew in so close on the hulking gangster that the tips of all four men's shoes seemed to be touching. Now when Fat Tommy squinted into the light, it didn't even seem like light anymore but a kind of shiny darkness. And he felt as though he were falling through the brightness like a brother pitched off a 100-story building. Vargas switched the lights back to a single hot light again. The trembling darkness in the distance beyond the spotlight seemed like measureless liquid midnight.

"I need some lemonade!" Fat Tommy screamed. The voice startled him. It did not seem like his own, but rather like the voice of a child or woman screaming from the bottom of a well.

Dockery and Braddock pushed their chairs back from the cone

of white light that made Fat Tommy look like a Vegas lounge fly sobbing under a microscope. The scraping of their chairs was like an utterance of disgust, and they meant it to be that. It sent shivers up their own backs, and sent a great hot thunderbolt of fear down the spine of Fat Tommy O'Rourke. Vargas cut a rebuking glance at Dockery and Braddock.

"It's late," Vargas said, looking around for a clock. They had started this session just before 2 p.m.

Braddock pulled out his watch bob. To view the dial, he swept his hand through the cone of light that seemed to enclose Fat Tommy in a brilliant Tinker Bell glow, and the watch flashed like a little arc of buttery neon framed in white.

"Almost 6 a.m. Sixteen goddamn hours and not a peep from this shithead," Braddock said. He smacked the back of Fat Tommy's chair. Tommy shivered briefly and settled deeper into his sob.

Dockery felt around in his pant leg for his pack of butts and stood up. "Just a little longer, sport, and you can get back to beatin' off in yer cell," Dockery said.

"Yeah, beatin' off in yer cell . . ." Braddock repeated.

"I need a piss break," Fat Tommy said as politely as he could, then added with a smile, "and a big glass of lemonade."

"Good idea, asshole. Think I'll go drain the lizard," Dockery said, and looked at Vargas. Vargas nodded and Braddock and Dockery went out.

Fat Tommy sobbed on. He was still crying when Braddock and Dockery came back in laughing. They both held huge cups of lemonade and they were eating fresh Krispy Kreme doughnuts. Braddock tossed a half-eaten doughnut in the trash.

"I'm starvin', officer. I'm sleepy. I don't know about no murder," Fat Tommy tried again. He shut his eyes tight.

"Pale-ass pussy," Braddock muttered. "Yer gonna fry for this. Why don't ya quit yer lying?"

"I don't deserve this beef. I don't know nothin'. I didn't see nothin'. I got a wife and family. I ain't no liar," Fat Tommy complained. "Cut was the one who fount Simpson . . . He told us he was a snitch. Not no cop. It was all his idea. We wouldn't be mixed up in none of this if Cut hadn't . . ."

The room went dead quiet. Fat Tommy strained to hear the shuffling of the cops' shoes behind him, but could only hear his own heart beating, *thu-thump, thu-thump*.

Then Dockery said, "Cut? You never mentioned any Cut."

Fat Tommy could feel the life draining from his chest. He slowly opened his eyes. He began to hyperventilate and for the first time he could feel the jheri curl gel-deluxe begin to drip against his collar.

"You said I could have water. I need some water," Fat Tommy pleaded.

"You can have water, Moises, after you tell us how it went down," DEA agent Braddock growled from somewhere behind him.

"Tell us about this Cut," Vargas continued, piling on. "He got a last name?"

"Cut . . . um . . . Cut Pemberton . . . I think."

"And?"

"I didn't know him that good."

"Go on," Vargas said.

"Gots a cut cross his ear, go straight cross his lip, like he was wearing a veil on one side of his face."

"Yes . . . ?"

"Said he got it in a fight with a cracker when he was in the Marines. But I heard he got it in prison."

"Okay . . . go on."

"He can talk Spanish."

"Go on," Dockery said. "Cut . . ."

"Well, Cut was the onliest one that did it."

"Go on."

"Cut was one of them red, freckly niggahs from Georgia. Spotted like a African cat. I didn't even know him good . . ."

"Um-hum."

"Wore plaits standing all over his head."

"Plaits? Really?"

Tears were streaming down his eyes, but Fat Tommy grinned. "My Bea used to call him BuckBeet, 'cause he looked like a red pickaninny. That used to piss him off, 'cause of Buckwheat, you know?"

"Yes . . . Cut . . ."

"Yeah, Cut. First I knew of him . . . two years ago . . . when I was staying on Glen Oaks off Paxton . . . him and Karesha—my wife's sister—and my Uncle Bunny banged on my duplex at 'bout 2 in the morning looking for some crack."

"You mean Bunny Hobart—the second-story man?" Dockery broke in again. The detectives had two tape recorders going now, but Dockery never trusted electronic equipment and was transcribing everything Fat Tommy said on a yellow legal pad.

"Yeah, that be him," Fat Tommy said. He slumped back in the hard metal chair, trembling as he recalled the scene. "He knew Cut from the joint. Cut had just got out and was chillin' with Karesha. Cut was already dressin' like a Crip, all blue, talkin' shit. I could tell he was trouble. He used to strong-arm young Gs and take their stuff."

"And Bunny told him you were the big-time coke man," Braddock said. It was not a question.

"I was gettin' out of the business. I was gettin' out," Fat Tommy explained. "It was Cut that fucked up all my plans. He wanted to impress the big-time talent . . . I was only stayin' in till he could get on his feets."

"What big-time talent?"

"Colombians, La Caja Crips . . . it was them goddamn Colombians that told Cut about Simpson. They said he was a snitch—not no cop! Cut came up with the idea of settin' the guy up. I tried to talk him out of it; I tried to reason with him . . ."

"A regular Dr. Phil," Braddock said.

"Yes, sir," Fat Tommy said quietly. His heart was sputtering like an old Volkswagen.

"Catch your breath, son," Vargas said. "Get our boy King Moises some lemonade, will ya, Dockery?"

Fat Tommy flopped his big grease-spangled head down into his hands. From the top of his jheri curl to the soles of his size-18 Air Jordans, everything about him was huge, extroverted, and showy. Now, he sat hulking in the metal chair, trying in vain to make himself smaller, hoping that the willful diminishment of his great size would in turn minimize in the minds of the cops the appalling grandeur of his recent crimes. He sat there in his bright white tent of a shirt with his Martin Luther King, Jr. tie strung tight round his bulging neck like a painted garrote.

Far above the dull cacophony of the cops grinding away at his statement, Fat Tommy O'Rourke—a.k.a., Moises Rockafella, La Caja's King of Rock Cocaine—could hear a plaintive, high-pitched wail, a shrill, sad voice, strangely resembling his own. He prayed to Christ it was someone else.

Teresa Moody

BILL MOODY is the author of the
Evan Horne mystery series. The lat-
est release is *Looking for Chet Baker*.
Moody is a jazz musician, a DJ at
KSVY in Sonoma, California, and
teaches creative writing at Sonoma
State University.

camaro blue
by bill moody

Hello? Yes, I want to report a stolen car. Robert Ware. Oh, for Christ's sake. Okay, okay. I don't know when. Last night sometime, I guess."

Bobby Ware tried to calm down. He gave his address and license number and continued to answer questions. "It's a blue 1989 Chevy Camaro Sport." He listened to the other questions and lit a cigarette.

"It was in front of my house. Oh yeah, there was a horn too. What? No, not the car horn. A tenor saxophone in a gig bag. What? Oh, a soft leather case. Yeah, that's right. Okay, thanks."

Bobby hung up the phone and sat for a minute, smoking, thinking. "Fuck," he said out loud. "Fuck, fuck, fuck!" Finally got his dream car and some asshole stole it. *Man, I gotta move*, he thought. *Too much shit in this neighborhood.*

He got up, paced around. Barefoot, cut-off jeans, sandals, and a Charlie Parker T-shirt, his daytime uniform, trying to think who he could borrow a horn from for the gig tonight.

He was working in a quartet at a club on Ventura, backing a singer who was trying to convince everybody she was the next Billie Holiday, but she wasn't fooling anyone. But hey, a gig was a gig. Three nights a week for three months now, so he couldn't really complain.

He replayed last night in his mind. He'd come home, tired and anxious to get in the house, and totally spaced, leaving his tenor in the car. That wasn't like him or any horn player, but too late now. He sat down and turned on the TV, hoping he wasn't going to see his Camaro in one of those car chases the city had become famous for.

When Lisa got home, he was still sitting in front of the TV, watching the news, but there were no stolen car reports and no news from the police.

"Hi, baby," Lisa said. She was carrying a bag from the Lotus Blossom Chinese takeout. "You hungry?" She set the bag down on the kitchen table and walked over to Bobby.

She was in her Century City law-office outfit—skirt, blouse, half heels, her hair pulled back in a ponytail. She sat on the arm of Bobby's chair and kissed him lightly on the lips, then let herself slip over the arm onto his lap.

"What's the matter?"

"Somebody stole my car."

"Oh, baby, and you just had it serviced and waxed."

"Tell me. But it gets worse."

"What?"

"My horn was in the car."

"Oh no, did you report it?"

Bobby pushed her off him. "Of course I fucking reported it."

Lisa held up her hands. "Okay, okay."

Bobby sighed. "I'm sorry, babe, but you know what the chances are of getting back a stolen car in L.A.?" Especially that car. Bobby had read somewhere that Camaros, even older ones, were popular among car thieves. By now it was probably stripped clean at a chop shop, and somebody was trying to figure out how to put the saxophone together.

For as long as he could remember—at least since high school—Bobby had wanted a Camaro. He could never afford a new one, and good used ones were hard to come by. Then one afternoon, driving back from the store, he'd found this one parked on a side street with a "For Sale" sign in the window. A blue Camaro Sport. One owner, all the service records, and the car looked like it had hardly been driven more than to the store. Now it was gone.

* * *

He took Lisa's Toyota to the gig, after dredging up a tenor from a former student who wasn't sure he wanted to pursue jazz anymore. Bobby had helped him pick out the horn so it was a good one, but it wasn't Bobby's old Zoot Sims model he'd bought from a guy on the street in New York.

After the second set, he was standing in the parking lot behind Gino's with the bass player, a tall thin guy who played good and didn't care anything about singers. They watched a tan Ford Taurus pull in, and two guys in rumpled suits got out and came over.

The bass player cupped the joint in his hand and started walking toward the club. "Cops, man."

"Are you Robert Ware?" the older of the two asked Bobby. The younger one watched the bass player walk away.

"Yeah. Is this about my car?" Bobby was wary. They didn't usually send detectives out for stolen cars.

"I'm afraid so," the older cop said, casually showing Bobby his ID. He looked at Bobby for what seemed like a long time. "We found traces of cocaine in your car, Mr. Ware."

"No, that's not mine," Bobby said. "I'm not into coke."

The younger cop nodded, smiling knowingly at Bobby.

"No, seriously, man. Coke is not my thing." He held up his cigarette. "This is it for me."

The older cop took out a small notebook and flipped through some pages. "Do you know a Raymond Morales? Hispanic male, twenty-nine years old."

"No."

"You didn't let him borrow your car?"

"Borrow my car . . . What are you talking about? I don't loan my car to anyone. Ask my girlfriend."

"We did. She told us where to find you."

They all turned and looked as the side door opened and the bass player peeked out. "Hey, man, we're on."

"Listen," Bobby said, "can you guys wait a bit? We have the last set to do and then we can talk."

The two cops looked at each other and shrugged. The older one said, pointing across the street, "We'll be at Denny's."

"Cool," Bobby said. "You did find the car, right?"

The younger cop looked at him and smiled again. "Oh yeah."

Bobby found them in a back booth drinking coffee and eating pie. He sat his horn on the floor, slid in next to the younger cop, and ordered coffee.

"So? What's the deal on my car? When can I get it back? Was there much damage?"

The two cops glanced at each other. "There was some damage," the younger one said.

"Oh fuck," Bobby said, loudly enough that a couple in the next booth turned and looked. "I knew it. Totaled, stripped, or what?"

"Bullet holes," the younger cop said.

"What?"

"Mr. Ware," the older cop began, "your car was involved in a high-speed chase early this morning. Raymond Morales was driving. He apparently ran out of gas. He emerged from your car with a weapon and fired on the pursuing officers. They returned fire and Mr. Morales was shot at the scene."

"Jesus," Bobby said. He sat stunned, not knowing what to say.

"The driver's side door has holes, the window was shattered, and there were several bullets lodged in the seat."

"Is he . . . ?"

Both cops nodded.

"I'm sorry," Bobby said, wondering about Raymond Morales.

"It happens," the younger cop said.

"Your girlfriend said you reported there was a saxophone in the car?"

"Yeah, that's right."

"We didn't find it."

Bobby looked at both of them. "What do you mean, you didn't find it?"

"Wasn't in the car," the younger one said.

They talked some more without giving up much information about the incident or when he could get his car back. The older cop gave Bobby his card and said they'd be in touch. They left Bobby to finish his coffee and think about Raymond Morales.

Two days later Bobby got a call from the older cop. Lloyd Foster, Bobby remembered from the business card. "We're done," Foster said. "You can pick up your car tomorrow morning."

"Anything new?" Bobby asked.

"Like what?" When Bobby couldn't think of what to ask, Foster said, "See you in the morning."

Bobby was prepared for the worst when he arrived at the impound garage. Foster and the younger cop were waiting for him. Bobby was surprised to see the car mostly intact. The entire driver's side window was gone. The techs had cleaned it out, Foster told him. When he opened the door, he saw the small round holes in the seats where the bullets had lodged.

There were dark spots on the seat—blood stains that hadn't been entirely erased—and there was a strange smell Bobby couldn't place. He looked at the two cops.

Foster shrugged. "Techs use all kinds of compounds, liquids to secure evidence. It'll go away eventually."

Bobby walked around the car. On the passenger door there were some minor dents and paint scrapings from when Morales had sideswiped a car or a telephone pole or something else in his attempt to get away.

"Why didn't he just, you know, give up, instead of trying to shoot it out?"

The two cops exchanged glances and shrugged.

They handed him some papers to sign to release the car and gave him copies. Then they watched him get in the car and adjust

214 // THE COCAINE CHRONICLES

the seat. Morales must have been short—the seat was closer to the wheel than Bobby kept it. He nodded at them, backed the car out of the garage, and drove off. In the rearview mirror, he caught them watching him till he turned the corner.

He pulled into the first gas station and filled up. He used the Yellow Pages to find a glass repair shop and jotted down the address of two not far away. Ed's Auto Glass was the first.

"We can do it while you wait," the man at the desk said. "What happened? Somebody try to break into your car?"

"Something like that," Bobby said. "It was stolen."

"Wow, and you got it back. Lucky," he said, sliding a clipboard across the counter so Bobby could initial the estimate form. "Give me an hour."

Bobby went for a walk, bought a Coke at a convenience store, and smoked, thinking about Raymond Morales dying in his car. He pictured the car, out of gas, skidding to a stop, Morales throwing the door open, hiding behind it, firing at the cops, the glass shattering, bullets embedding in the seat, and then falling backwards as a bullet struck him in the chest. He couldn't get the vision out of his mind. All for some cocaine. How much? What was it worth? His life?

He got home before Lisa and examined the car's interior inch by inch, not knowing what he was looking for but unable to let it go. He felt under both seats, up in the springs, in the channel the seat slid back and forth on. He even lay under it with a flashlight, knowing the cops had already done this but not trusting their thoroughness.

He opened the hatch, raised the flap where the spare tire was kept, took the tire out and felt around the compartment, shined the flash everywhere, but it was no go. The car was clean.

The only evidence of the incident were the holes in the seat and the dark stain. Raymond Morales's blood.

"Hey, you got it back," Lisa said, getting out of her car. Bobby hadn't even heard her drive up.

"Yeah." He shut the hatch and locked it, as Lisa walked all around the car.

"Looks okay," she said.

He nodded and shrugged at her look. "No horn." He opened the driver's side door and showed her the bullet holes in the seat, the dark stain.

She just stared. "Jesus, kind of spooky, isn't it?"

Bobby got on Lisa's computer and went to the *Los Angeles Times* website to check on obituaries. He skimmed through starting with the date after his car was stolen and found it five days after:

Raymond Morales, 1974–2004. Beloved son of Angela Morales. Survivors include his sister Gabriela. A memorial service will be held Wednesday, May 15 at . . .

Bobby jotted down the date and time and glared at the photo of Raymond Morales, obviously taken a few years before his death. It was almost like a high school yearbook photo. Just a nice look-ing kid, three years younger than Bobby. He told himself he was only going out of curiosity, maybe to see if someone had any infor-mation about the horn, but he knew it was more than that.

He drove into Inglewood Park Cemetery and found the site easily. There were at least thirty or more tricked-out lowrider cars and a single limo parked along the curb. A plain tan sedan Bobby recognized as Foster's car was also there.

Bobby parked as close as he could and got out. A ways in on the lawn, among the hundreds of tombstones, he saw the small crowd gathered around the grave site. Foster and the younger cop were standing behind the fringe of mourners. Foster turned as Bobby walked up.

"Interesting," he said to Bobby. His younger partner turned and smiled.

"What are you guys doing here?" Bobby asked.

"Routine," Foster said. "We know Morales ran with some of these dudes. We're just compiling some information." Foster looked at him. "What about you? Car spooking you?" This made the other cop smile again.

Several of the young guys turned and glared at Bobby and the two cops. They were all slicked-back hair, ponytails, sunglasses, sharply creased chinos, and black shirts. A couple started moving toward them but were held back by others. Bobby moved away to stand alone.

At the center of the gathering, two women sat by the casket as the priest finished. Bobby guessed they were the mother and sister. The younger woman raised her eyes briefly and looked at Bobby, then touched her mother's hand.

Bobby turned to look back at the cops as they walked toward their car. He took a deep breath and wondered if this was such a good idea. As the service ended and started to break up, the young guys walked past, stared at him curiously with hate in their eyes, and went to their cars. Soon the loud sound of souped-up engines and glass-pack mufflers filled the air.

Bobby stood still, hands clasped in front of him, not sure what to do next, when Raymond Morales's mother and sister walked by. The sister looked at Bobby strangely as her mother stopped and also looked at Bobby.

"You were a friend of my son's?" she asked, studying his face.

"Well, no, not really," Bobby said, surprised that she spoke to him. "I, ah . . ."

"High school," the sister said. "Taft High School. I know you. Bobby Ware."

"Yes," Bobby said, taken aback.

"I'm Gabriela." She smiled briefly. "You played a saxophone solo at the school assembly. I was a freshman when you were a senior."

Bobby let his mind travel back ten years. He'd been in the marching band and the jazz ensemble, and he had played at the senior assembly. "Well, yes. I didn't think anybody remembered that."

"Come, Gabby," Raymond's mother said, starting toward the car, already losing interest in Bobby.

Gabriela followed her mother, then stopped and turned. "That was your saxophone, your car, wasn't it?"

Bobby stood mute, realizing she knew everything, watching her dig in her purse for a pen and a slip of paper. She scribbled quickly and pressed the paper in his hand. "Call me," she said. Then was gone.

Bobby waited for the mourners to clear out. He saw one group of three guys pause at his car and stare, then look over at him, before they got in a black Chevrolet and drove off.

The next morning Bobby dialed the number. "Barnes and Noble," a voice said. "How can I help you?"

Bobby thought it had been a home number she'd given him but quickly realized she wouldn't have done that.

"Can I speak to Gabriela Morales, please?"

"Let me see if she's in," the voice said.

Bobby was suddenly listening to canned music as he was put on hold. It sounded like Dave Koz or David Sanborn, one of those R & B saxes, vamping relentlessly over the same tired chords.

"Hello?"

"Miss Morales? This is Bobby Ware."

"I guess you want to talk to me."

"Well, if it's not convenient I can . . ."

"I have a lunch break at 12:30. There's a coffee place here in the store. We can meet there. This is the big one, on Ventura Boulevard."

"Yeah, okay, that would be fine," Bobby said.

After a pause she said, "This is strange."

"Yes it is."

He got there early and took a cup of coffee to an outside table so he could smoke. Gabriela appeared a few minutes later.

"Oh, there you are," she said. She was dressed in dark slacks and a white blouse with a plastic B&N name tag pinned to her blouse. Her hair was raven black and framed her face. *Very pretty*, Bobby thought as he stood up.

She put her hand on his shoulder. "No, don't get up. I'm just going to grab a sandwich. I'll be right back."

She came back quickly and sat opposite Bobby with a sandwich on a plate and a bottle of water. "Sorry," she said. "I'm on till 6. If I don't eat now, well . . ."

"No problem," Bobby said.

She took small bites of the sandwich and studied him. "You don't remember my brother at all, do you?"

"No," Bobby said. "I'm sorry . . . about what happened."

She nodded and looked down. "He had a lot of problems and it's not so uncommon. Raymond was lost a long time ago," she said, finishing her sandwich. Gabriela looked at Bobby's cigarettes on the table. "Can I have one of those?"

"Sure," Bobby said, offering her one. He lit it for her and watched her take a deep drag and cough a little.

"Wow, it's been awhile. I quit about a year ago."

"Yeah, I've quit a couple of times myself."

"I had quite a crush on you," she said, "after I saw you play at the assembly. I used to see you in the halls, by your locker, and I started going to the games to see you in the marching band."

"That was a long time ago." Bobby looked away, thinking of the early morning practices, the drilling, the music.

"You still play, right?"

"Yes, I'm working a gig not far from here on weekends."

"That's good. You were talented." She paused. "I remember Raymond wanting to be in the band but it wasn't cool, you know that macho shit, so he never pursued it. Maybe if he had he would . . ." Her voice trailed off.

"Look," Bobby said, "I don't want to bother you, I just, I don't know, it's been bothering me. I just had to—"

"See who Raymond was?"

"Yeah, I guess. Since I got the car back, I keep having these visions."

"And there's the horn."

"Well, yes, that too."

She nodded. "I have it in my car. Raymond came home that day, said he'd borrowed the car from a friend. I knew he was lying, but he brought the horn in the house, didn't want anything to happen to it."

"You're kidding."

"No, I think he still thought about playing." She stubbed out her cigarette and glanced at her watch. "I've got to get back to work. C'mon."

He followed her to the parking lot. She opened the trunk of her car. Bobby looked inside and saw the case. He flipped the latches and lifted the lid, and it was like seeing an old friend. He shut the case and took it out of the trunk.

"Thanks, thank you very much."

"Where's your car?"

Bobby hesitated. "Oh, a couple of rows over but you probably need to go and—"

"I want to see it."

They walked over to his car. Bobby unlocked the door and put his horn in the back.

"Do you mind?" She looked inside.

"No."

Bobby watched her run her hand over the seat, her finger tracing the bullet holes. Bobby shivered. She stepped back, her eyes moist now. "It's kind of closure or something," she said. "Thank you."

"I understand."

She managed a smile. "Well, I guess that's it."

"Would you like to come hear me play?" he blurted.

She smiled. "I don't know if that would be such a good idea."

Bobby nodded. "Sure, I understand."

She looked away, then back at him. "But hey, why not. High school crush makes good." She had a beautiful smile and she gave it all to Bobby.

Bobby gave her the address of Gino's and they shook hands. She pressed her hand in his. "Thank you," she said, then turned and walked back to the bookstore.

On the way home, Bobby drove by a deserted warehouse with a huge fenced-in parking area. He slowed, then pulled in the open driveway and drove around to the back of the building. He sat for a moment, the car idling, then slammed his foot on the gas pedal. The car shot ahead. He got up to fifty, then hit the brakes and turned the wheel hard. He threw open the door, stood up, crouched down, stood up again, then threw himself back on the seat, trying to feel the bullet that killed Raymond Morales.

Eyes closed, leaning back, Bobby circled behind the singer on "Lover Man," looking for his openings yet not getting in her way. She finished her chorus and Bobby shuffled toward the microphone and played what he could till the bridge. He stepped aside and saw Gabriela Morales at a table to his left.

She was leaning forward, her chin resting on her hand, gazing at him with what he guessed was memory. Trying to remember that high school assembly? They finished the set with "Just Friends," and Bobby scorched the small audience with two choruses that got him a phony smile from the singer that said, *Hey, I'm the star, remember?*

He sat his horn on its stand and walked over to Gabriela's table. "So, you made it," he said.

She smiled. "You're much better now than in high school."

"Come outside with me," he said. "I need a cigarette."

"Me too." She picked up her purse and put a napkin over her glass.

They walked up Ventura Boulevard a ways, not talking much,

just getting used to each other. Finally, they stopped and she turned to look at him.

"So where do you think this is going?" she asked. Her eyes were so dark and deep.

He moved in closer and kissed her lightly on the lips. She didn't resist, and when he pulled back, she opened her eyes and looked at him again. "That's what I wanted in high school."

"And now?"

She looked away. "What is this? You want to fuck the kid sister of the guy who was killed in your car?"

"What? No, I—"

She waved her hand in front of her as if she was shooing something away. "I'm sorry. I don't know where that came from. Really, I'm sorry. I don't know why I came. It's just, I don't know, a connection with Raymond. Does that sound crazy?"

"No," he said. "I think that's why I came to the service. I wanted to see what your brother was about, what his family was about. I don't know if I can keep the car now."

They turned and started walking back toward Gino's. "Raymond was a gangbanger, a cocaine dealer, and he lost. He got in over his head and couldn't get out, except the way he did. I loved my brother but he gave my mother endless grief and worry. End of story."

"And you?"

"This isn't a good way to start. There must be a girlfriend somewhere, right?"

Bobby nodded. "I live with someone. Two years now."

"Are you in love with her? Are you going to marry her?"

"I don't know," Bobby said. "I thought so."

"I'm not going to be your girlfriend on the side." A glimmer of fire in her eyes now.

"I know," Bobby said.

She got quiet again, but her hand slipped into his. "We're both here for the same reason," she said.

Bobby knew immediately what she meant. They had both been touched by death and they were connected by it in a way only the two of them could understand.

"It's maybe the one good thing Raymond did," Gabriela said.

"Yes," Bobby said. "Maybe it is."

JERVEY TERVALON is the author of *All the Trouble You Need, Understand This,* and the *Los Angeles Times* bestseller *Dead Above Ground.* In 2001, he received the PEN Oakland/Josephine Miles National Literacy Award for Excellence in Multicultural Literature. He is the writer-in-residence at Pitzer College and Occidental College, and is a California Arts Council Fellow. Tervalon was born in New Orleans, raised in Los Angeles, and now lives in the L.A. area with his wife and two daughters.

serving monster
by jervey tervalon

The interview for the position of personal chef for Monster Stiles was going to be at the Trump Plaza at this overblown, over-hyped restaurant that only idiots thought anything of.

Bridget, Asha's girlfriend, was a thin blonde who wore a short skirt, even as the first flurries of snow fell from the gray sky.

"I hate New Jersey," I said.

Bridget laughed. I didn't mean for it to be funny.

"So, you had that cute restaurant in the Village?"

I smiled. "I don't know about it being so cute."

"I loved that place," she said.

"I did too, but not enough."

"Really? How so?"

"When I think about it, maybe I didn't care for it."

Bridget nervously tapped a fork against her water glass.

"Gibson is a fantastic cook," Asha said. She glanced at me and probably could tell I was near tears.

"What happened?" Bridget asked.

I shrugged, and Asha took over. She leaned over and began to whisper to Bridget. Asha wore this loose-fitting, burnished-gold tunic. Her dark skin and hair looked even richer against the paleness of Bridget's skin and hair. As Asha whispered, whatever resistance Bridget had toward me faded. Bridget was totally smitten with Asha and when Asha took her hand, she was transported.

I was almost embarrassed to see how much she was taken with Asha.

"Listen," Bridget said, loud enough for me to hear, "I'll tell you the bottom line. We have a hard time getting quality people up on the mountain."

"Why is that?" I asked.

"It's a tough job, the type of job for a particular person who wants to be in a beautiful place and needs privacy. It's very private there."

"You mean isolated?"

"I call it very private. You can call it what you like."

"Isolated. I don't mind isolation. I don't mind it at all."

"Do you know who Lamont Stiles is?"

I shook my head.

"You've heard of Monster Stiles?" Bridget asked.

"The singer?"

"Yeah. He doesn't do much of that anymore. He's more of a producer with three acts at the top of the charts. Everything he touches is bling; his clothing line made millions last year and this year it's expected to double in sales."

"When you say bling, you mean . . . ?"

"Priceless. You had to have heard of that expression."

"Yeah, but I never used it."

She looked at me like she had already made up her mind.

"So, Mr. Stiles needs a chef?" I asked.

"He prefers to be called Monster. He fancies himself the monster of music, of cutting-edge fashion, of life."

"Monster, it is."

Bridget laughed. "I like how direct you are." Then her face hardened. We were going to get down to it. "You need to understand how this works. If you repeat this to anyone, I'll get fired and you'll get sued."

I laughed. "Listen, I'm on parole. If I don't jump through hoops I go to jail."

She nodded and smiled at me after Asha patted her hand.

"This might be hard to believe, but many people aren't comfortable on the mountain. It takes a special person, someone who really enjoys quiet and their own company. The perfect candidate for this job loves nature, because that's where you are, in the clouds. It's God's most beautiful, pristine country. That's what Monster loves about it, he's above it all, but people get lonely for their families, for life outside of the *Lair*. Plus, well, Monster is demanding. He says that about himself."

"How so?"

Bridget sucked her teeth. "You haven't heard all that rubbish about him?"

"No, I really don't keep up with the music scene."

"He made all those bubble-gum pop songs. You got to wonder about people like that," Asha muttered. "And he had that pet koala hanging around his neck."

"He's gotten rid of the koala, that was a big mistake," Bridget said, with perfect seriousness.

"I'm not sure about this. What do people say about him? Is there any truth to it?"

Bridget laughed. "I'm not going to go into it. People say all kinds of things about him. You'd think he bathes in the blood of little boys. That kind of *National Enquirer* bullshit."

"What do you think of him?"

"Well, it's hard to explain," she said softly, as though she were wary of being overheard. "Monster isn't really someone I see a lot of. He is a great employer in that he's very generous. But mostly he's on the road or holed up in the *Lair*. It's really his encampment, the inner grounds of his mansion and the gardens where most staff aren't allowed. I think that's how those horrible stories of Monster get out. Disgruntled former employees spread rumors when they really don't know what goes on in the *Lair*. Anyway, if you're really interested, I'll fly you out to interview. Asha can come with you. I'll show you Solvang and there's this wonderful little Danish bakery. You'll love the pastries."

"I'm not sure of what he wants. Will I be his personal chef or will I be running the kitchen for everyone there?"

"You know, I couldn't tell you at this point. With Monster you go with the flow. He'll fill in the blanks, he always does."

Bridget shrugged and put her head on Asha's shoulder.

Business was done for the evening.

Asha wore something beautiful. She told me the name, but I immediately forgot. A Jabari? Whatever it was I liked it—a kind of purple pantsuit with fringe around the waist and cuffs. Bridget was in black again, straight leather, suitable for nightlife in the big city but fucking silly on a brilliant day in beautiful Solvang. Bridget was just as schoolgirl giddy to have Asha near as I remembered.

"You are too wedded to that job," I heard Bridget say.

Asha shrugged. "You know, I trained to be a social worker. It's what I wanted to do, and I'm happy with my life," she said to Bridget. It was the same thing she said to me when I asked why she was so content to run a halfway house. I guess Asha was sincere in what she said to people; I admired that, and how rare it was.

At the Dutch bakery that Bridget was so high on, I lingered over stale strudel while the girls stepped outside to admire bachelor buttons and Mexican primrose growing along the road. They held hands, and I saw Bridget lean toward Asha to sneak a kiss. I hoped this Bridget knew what kind of woman she had in Asha, a human being of the first order. But maybe that was too much to hope for. I didn't get a good feeling from Bridget. She probably thought Asha was hot and exotic, the domestic equivalent of an incendiary foreign affair without the bother of having a passport renewed. Maybe I was jealous, but I knew I was right about this Bridget and her bitch nature.

I was supposed to be put up somewhere spectacular, a woodsy resort over in the hills with an amazing restaurant and a wonderful chef I was supposed to know. Bridget mentioned more than a half-dozen times just how excited she was to take us to this slice of paradise. However, something happened to the reservation, or the charge card, and plans had changed.

As we drove downhill, back to the valley, I thought we'd all be staying at Andersen's Split Pea Soup and Hotel—she mentioned that it was campy and fun—but Bridget obviously couldn't wait to drop me off. Even so, she took the time to remind me that Monster liked prospective employees to be an hour early for interviews, expected her to be two hours early, and with unctuous sincerity she mentioned again just how important it was to make a good impression. Oh yes, he'd be there, he wouldn't speak and I wasn't to speak to him, but he'd be highly involved in the process.

Flow.

Monster could flow in any moment and seal the deal, but I couldn't expect that.

Of course, I'd have an in, but really, it was up to me to seize the initiative.

Dragging Asha behind her, Bridget turned her rental around and roared back to the Santa Ynez Inn. Seemed Bridget made sure the Inn had one room available.

I had a bowl of very salty green soup and ate all the crackers in the cracker holder. I thought of ordering a beer, then I wanted a gin and tonic, then decided just a couple of hits off a crack pipe would do the trick. I had another bowl of very salty green soup and found the room Bridget had reserved for me.

I turned on the televison and flipped around. I watched rap videos for a while until it became painful, all that booty shaking and me not having gotten laid in almost a year.

I couldn't help fantasizing about being a third wheel between Asha and Bridget—maybe they would suddenly want to experiment and include me. Yeah, I couldn't sustain that fantasy, too improbable even for a hopeless optimist.

The next morning I got out of bed at 5:00, so nervous about how the day would go that I went for a walk, even though a fog had rolled in, concealing Andersen's Split Pea Soup and Hotel to the point that it was difficult to know what direction to go in. I was lost almost immediately and had to get directions from the surfer dude behind the counter at the 7-Eleven. Then I remembered I needed new razors and shaving cream.

I meandered a bit, eventually finding my way back to the hotel and my room to shave my head with the precision of an anxious man with nothing else to do.

Instinct.

It was obvious what Monster thought of himself. Look at how hard he worked to eradicate the last vestiges of identifiable color from his life and skin.

I wouldn't let him hold that over me. Lack of melanin never held me back; actually, it was a kick, a key to acceptance that never had to be explained. Never deny it, but why let them form the question? Don't make them question their own generosity, don't make them consider the intangibles. What does it mean to hire a black man? Is it the opposite of hiring a white man? The same?

Don't ask and I won't tell you.

I don't know.

I know this, that Monster bolts up from night terrors, chest heaving as he rushes to the mirror to see if that bleach/chemical peel/skin brightener bled off, shed, absorbed away, or simply vanished.

Bet he lives in mortal fear of a stray BB, the living nightmare of the paralyzing threat of a nappy head.

Cool.

Even if he has a nigger detector, he'll never see me coming.

I don't pass, I slip by on the strength of the fact that I can. Maybe it's self-loathing, but I never had the energy for too much of that.

I am what I am—the son of two African-American parents who were light enough to pass as white if they cared to. They didn't because they were proud of who they were and embraced their African-Americanness.

Monster, though, doesn't pass. He thunders by, shouting to the world, "See me! I'm not like them, I'm you!"

He hides in plain sight, and I guess I do, too. Race explains nothing about his insanity, or my blundering into acceptance and not wanting to rock the boat.

Probably, in that sense, we're brothers under the skin.

Bridget showed up two hours late, a woman in desperate need of a toilet, but without a bit of an apology other than a curt, "Monster rescheduled a few hours," before she hauled ass to the bathroom.

"Where's Asha?" I asked, after she returned. I needed to see a friendly face, and Bridget's wasn't it.

"Sleeping in. She needs it," Bridget said, with a hint of a leer, and I disliked her even more. It still ain't polite to hit it and strut. As much as I admired and liked Asha, I couldn't understand her taste in women.

Bridget sped to the 101 and headed east, back toward Santa Barbara. Another stunningly beautiful day. From the freeway, I could see the Pacific lurking behind the hammock of hills, and when we started to climb and banked west, I saw surfers, black stick figures on breaking waves.

Then Bridget turned east and we headed into the Santa Ynez Valley.

At an access road Bridget drove for another twenty minutes or so, until a craftsman bungalow came into view. Near the bungalow was an impressive gate, maybe ten feet high, blocking a well-maintained road.

A man in a gray uniform with a cap like that of a highway patrolman from the forties leaned into the window and took a look at me, then he thrust a clipboard into my hands. On the clipboard was a document which went on for four pages. I hadn't gotten through the first page before Bridget tapped me on the shoulder.

"It's a release. You can't interview without signing it."

"Give me a minute. I like to read before I sign."

She sighed, and watched with narrowed eyes as I hastily flipped through the document.

"Done? Good. Now sign."

I signed, and handed the clipboard back to the security guard.

Bridget burned rubber on the way out, as though she had to make up for lost time, though I thought we were early.

About a mile later she stopped at another bungalow with two very busy men sorting through packages stacked in the driveway. Bridget waved to them and headed inside and pointed to an oversize chair by a window. I sat down as she flipped through more paperwork. The interior of the bungalow resembled the layout of a nicely appointed law office. I remembered wanting to buy those heavy brass lamps with the hand-blown, leaded glass for the restaurant, but I had given up when I couldn't get a reasonable price.

"Wait here. The head of security will be by in a few minutes to begin the interview. Then, afterward, maybe Monster will be ready to ask you a few questions."

A door opened. A tall man entered dressed in the uniform that all these guys sported, as though they could change your oil, carry your luggage, or arrest you. All of them were trim, tall, and white; did Monster hire every washed-out Mormon FBI agent he could find?

Bridget handed him a ream of paper, and then he walked over to me with his hand out and paused, squinting as though he recognized me and wasn't happy about it.

"Mr. Gibson, my name is Timothy Steele. I run security here at the *Lair*. I wonder if you could clarify a few things."

"Sure, I'll do my best."

"You were arrested for attempting to buy a controlled substance. Is that correct?"

"Yes."

"What was the controlled substance?"

"Heroin, to smoke. Usually it was cocaine, but the time I was arrested it was heroin."

He paused for a moment and thumbed through the documentation on the clipboard, then returned his unblinking attention to me.

"You don't have any prior arrests?"

"Nope. I've lived a pretty straight life, other than my recent drug experience. I've received the best treatment and diversiontherapy possible, and I've been clean for a year."

"That's good to hear, but you should know that we do an ongoing security check on all employees. If at some point we discover that you concealed any aspect of your personal history, no matter the relevance, you will be terminated immediately."

I paused for a moment, wanting very much to tell him to fuck himself, that I didn't need this fucking job. However, I did need it. I needed to get back to a life that wasn't embarrassing. Oh yeah, I needed this job in the worst way.

I allowed myself to hope, a threadbare hope I kept in a sock drawer in the hidden closet in the backroom of my confidence, a sad little hope that I could resurrect my career, that I wouldn't fuck up, that I wouldn't make my life a slow suicide. I'd finally shake that fear that I was out to do myself in, that I couldn't trust myself.

I couldn't afford to tell anybody to fuck off, except for maybe myself.

"I told you everything, except for when I got drunk as an undergraduate and wore this coed's panties on my head home. I guess that could be considered a crime."

Mr. Security gave me a look, a look of disdain, of mild disgust. Then, like the sun breaking through the clouds, he smiled.

"I don't think I'll need to make note of that."

That seemed to lighten the ultra-serious moment.

"Good," I said, and stood to leave.

"One more thing," he said.

He handed me a paper bag. I looked inside and saw a plastic cup with a lid.

"We need a urine sample. If you're offered the job, you'll be subject to a random weekly drug test."

My pride sloughed off like a skin I didn't need. I dutifully took the paper bag and went into the restroom.

I was in luck. Someone had pinned the sports page above the urinal, the Giants were on a winning streak. Quite a few of the workers at the *Lair* must have to submit to this weekly ritual. Sheepishly, I came out of the restroom holding the brown bag at arm's length. With a solemn nod, Security took it from me, then he ushered me to another door that led to another room. Inside, Bridget sat behind a very large desk, phone to ear, listening with strained concentration.

"Yes, he just came in. Do you want me to put him on?"

She gestured for me to sit down, her eyes flaring as though she'd toss a book at my head if I delayed for a second.

"Use the speakerphone."

I nodded, confused as to whom I was talking and why.

"Hello?"

I heard raspy breathing. I grinned at how silly this felt.

"This is Monster."

His voice didn't have that ethereal quality I'd heard on those interviews on VH1. He sounded grounded, even a little hard.

"It's an honor to talk with you," I said.

"What's your name again?"

"William Gibson."

"Right, you're the cat who owned the restaurant in New York. You lost it because of drugs."

"Yeah, that's about it."

"It would be cool if we could hire you."

"I would like that very much," I said, wondering what would stop him if he wanted to hire me. Did he need to check with his mother?

"But I need to ask you a question and you need to answer me honestly. Can you do that?"

"Yes, I can do that."

"Good."

I waited for him to ask the question, but he went back to that raspy breathing, as though he had a problem with his sinuses.

"Don'tassumeyoucanplayme."

He blurted it out so fast, at first I couldn't make out what he said.

"Could you repeat that?"

"Do you think you can play me?"

"What?"

"You know what I'm saying."

"I'm not sure what you mean."

Monster paused as though he were ready to drop the bomb on me.

"You gonna play me? That's what I want to know."

"I pride myself on my professionalism. I don't take it lightly."

"I'm not talking about that."

I wanted to ask what was he talking about, but I assumed that wouldn't get me hired.

"I'm a very loyal employee. That's how I've always been. It's second nature to me."

"It's more than loyalty."

"I'm not sure I understand."

"Then that means you're not down. I only hire down cats."

I was beyond confused.

"I'll ask you once more. Are you gonna play me?"

"I don't intend to play you."

Another pause and more raspy breathing.

"I'm supposed to believe you? I think you're lying. Tell me this, are you experienced?"

"What?"

"Are you experienced? Don't bullshit, answer me!"

"Do you mean like in a Jimi Hendrix way?"

"Yeah, exactly. That's exactly what I'm saying. You've got to be down for me."

My stomach sank. If he thought I was going to be getting loaded with him after dinner, that wasn't where my head was at.

"I think I understand," I replied.

"Understand what?"

"What you said about being down."

"Being down? What did I say about that?"

Now *my* breathing was raspy. Was he high? He had to be high. Only people who were fucked up out of their minds, but who thought they were under control, talked like that.

"Long as you down for me, it's all true. You know what I'm saying?" he said, excitedly.

"Yeah," I said, nodding, even though I knew he couldn't see me, unless he had a hidden camera. That, I wouldn't put past him.

"Are you gonna poison me?" he blurted, surprising the hell out of me. Of all the crazy-assed things I've been asked in my life, this surprised me into stupid silence.

"I've never poisoned anyone," I said, with conviction.

More raspy breathing.

"You're not gonna put anything sick into my food?"

"Sick?"

"Yeah."

"I can't say you'll love everything I'll cook, but I can guarantee I'll never poison you or put anything sick into your food."

"Hah, you funny. I'll get back to you."

The speakerphone went silent.

Bridget looked at me with suspicion.

"Did you have any idea what you were saying?"

I nodded without conviction.

"Monster likes people to be straight with him."

"I was being straight. What, I didn't sound straight?"

Bridget snorted. "I don't think you knew what you were saying. You were willing to say anything to get him to hire you."

If it wasn't for Asha I'm sure Bridget would have crossed me off her list. I don't have a problem with that, except for the fact that I did need this job, though it had became obvious that it must be hell to fill if I had gotten to the interview stage.

"I don't see what the problem is. We seemed to have hit it off."

"First of all, that wasn't Monster."

"Huh? Who was it?"

"Monster's assistant."

"Assistant? He sounds like a thug high on something."

"Well, he *is* Thug. He calls himself Thug. That's his name as far as you're concerned."

I felt tricked. It wasn't right and Bridget needed to know how I felt.

"Bridget, you know I need this job, but obviously you don't feel good about me applying for it. Am I wasting my time?"

Bridget looked surprised, like I had just come out of left field with that. She couldn't look me in the eye.

"Is it Asha? You promised her something and now you don't want to deliver?"

Bridget ran her hands through her hair, still avoiding my eyes.

"You might want this job, I know you need it, but once you get out there, it's different. I'm always looking for employees. It's a fucking strain. The lawyers, God, I talk to so many lawyers."

"That's big of you, trying to spare me some grief."

Finally, our eyes met. She looked like a woman who'd had enough.

"I've got my share of problems. I'll admit that. You're right. Asha really wants this for you."

"You don't think I'm capable?"

She shook her head. "It's not that at all. I don't want to have to answer to Asha when it's over."

"What do you mean, when it's over, and what do you have to answer to Asha about?"

"I might be a little jealous about how much she likes you, but it's not all jealousy. I just don't want her blaming me when everything goes to hell."

I stood up to leave. I was through with this shit.

"I finished that diversion program with no problems. You know that."

"Oh, this isn't about you. It's about Monster, and it's about why I want to quit this job. I don't want be responsible for the shit that happens."

"Quit this job? I don't get you at all! You bring me in, then decide I'm not right for the position, and now you tell me you're gonna quit."

"Don't get so pissed off. If I get the call that he wants to offer you the job, I'm not going to disagree. I'm not that kind of bitch. I'm just being up front. You need to know what you're getting into."

"What are you talking about? What am I getting into?"

"You'll see. You'll have to see how this place works. You'll know soon enough if you've got the stomach for it."

The phone rang and she snatched it up with a crisp, "Bridget here."

I walked outside before hearing the verdict; would I live or die? Was I hired or was I flying back to the halfway house to finish probation? But at that moment I just wanted to be outside, feeling the sun on my skin, whatever the hell would happen.

Silence, solitude, and breathable air, that's all I wanted, not exactly a miracle, but I guess this nightmare of a job is what I deserved.

I'm the cook; what goes on beyond the locked door of this bungalow is not my concern. I turn up music, keep lights burning all through the night.

Safe.

No one cares about the cook, that's what I count on. I keep the door locked and I try not to leave, not anymore, after dark.

Cold.

This bungalow is torture, even in the spring. No matter how

many logs I toss into the barely functional woodstove, heat slips through the walls like the mice when I turn on the light. I came with few clothes—two white tunics, a couple of thick sweaters, jeans, and T-shirts. I wear both sweaters to bed, all the socks I can fit on. Coldest I've ever been is spring in the mountains of Santa Ynez. Some nights I can't bring myself to get out of bed to use the toilet, just grit my teeth and endure until I can't stand it.

You'd think somebody as rich as Monster would insulate these bungalows, might have some idea that his employees are suffering. Even so, I should have been better prepared, should have known, paid more attention to what I was getting myself into. A man of Monster's stature probably spends his time plotting world conquest, opening a Planet Monster in Bali or something fantastic, not worrying about the frigid temperature of an employee's bungalow. Maybe that's why the last chef quit, fingers so numb she couldn't dice.

Another glass of a Santa Ynez Cabernet Sauvignon and I'm still feeling the cold, though it's not as sharp. I told myself I was through with twelve-step anything, I can't feel good about getting wasted. Numb is good and warm, but numb turns sour, numb gets you arrested, numb gets you a judge deciding what's best for you, and I can't stand to live through another diversion program. I pour the rest of the wine down the drain. I swore to myself that I would get high on life only and leave killing myself a little each day alone.

I know these extensive, meandering grounds well, but on a moonless night it's almost impossible to stay on the trail. A step in the wrong direction and you're in the middle of scrub brush and blood thorns that rib all sides of Monster's estate. Easily enough you can end up blindly wandering in the wilderness among coyotes, black bears, mountain lions, whatever.

See.

You must walk away from the light into the darkness.

The other direction isn't an option. The closer you get to the big house the more likely the lights will go on, blinding lights that'll make you feel like a frog ready to be scooped into a sack. Then you'll hear the sound of the heavy steps of Security as they converge, shouting commands. It's been worse after some nameless stalker managed, after repeated attempts, to sneak into Monster's *Lair* on some psychotic mission. Someone, maybe even Monster, came up with the *Lair* as the name for this place. Heard it's trademarked, and he's going to use it for his next CD, whenever he gets that done. Clever, I guess, but I don't know. Supposedly, he's been having a hell of a time, the music won't flow at Monster's *Lair*. Maybe it's the name, it's not conducive to creativity. Try telling someone you live and work at Monster's *Lair* and they laugh. *With that lunatic? How is that? What kind of craziness goes on there?*

I can't answer.

They never did catch the trespasser, supposedly a loser from Monster's past who's plagued him since long before he built this playland. I used to enjoy my nightly walks, but that was before enhanced lighting and the dogs. Security lets them run the grounds to get the lay of the land.

Once, I saw Monster walking alone in the middle of a pack of trained attack dogs like he was fucking Saint Francis of Assisi. Security trailed behind him, skulking near the bushes, maintaining that illusion of privacy he demands. The dogs smelled me, and though I was trying to back away from the encounter, too late, they charged forward, frothing and kicking sod.

Monster looked for a moment like he had no idea of who I was, the man he hired to cook for him and his family. I raised my walking stick to bash a dog before the others mauled me, but an impulse of self-preservation kicked in and I shouted my name just as the dogs charged.

"It's me, Gibson! The cook!"

Security shouted something in German, and the dogs stopped in mid-stride.

I heard Monster's voice, high and nasal, a near whine: "Oh, you scared me."

"Sorry," I said, and hurried on in the opposite direction. I caught a glimpse of him in the moonlight—bundled in a parka, though that night the temperature was mild, walking with hands clasped behind his back, serenely in thought. Security caught up and escorted me back to my bungalow, which was more and more a jail cell and less the attractive perk of a rent-free cottage in the beautiful Santa Ynez mountains, the selling point to compensate for a modest salary. Security looked me in the eye and told me to watch it, don't forget who pays the bills.

"Monster does," I said, nodding to show, even if Security wasn't buying it, that I was a team player. It didn't go well. He looked for a second as though I might be jerking his chain, then turned to go, but not before jotting down something in a small gray notebook. I'm sure some notation scheduling another background check.

I didn't mind.

When you work for someone with great wealth you learn quickly that you really do serve them.

You learn to be blind, deaf, and dumb, if that's what they need. Monster needs all that.

Sometimes I see things that don't add up, that make me nervous.

I wanted isolation, but not like this.

The night sky has too many stars; the moon hangs like a gaudy lantern illuminating a path to my bungalow.

I've never felt so alone.

I know what goes on there, behind those hedges, those walls, gates, and sensors.

He's a monster and every day I serve him.

I'm not inclined toward depression, upbeat and all that is how folks describe me, but that was because of the drugs.

Married, living on the Lower East Side in a nice co-op, part owner of Euro Pane, a restaurant with witty angular (the publicist came up with that), Puglia-inspired cuisine that people wanted to spend good hard cash on, you'd think I'd be more than happy, but in truth it was too much for me. Maybe I couldn't stand prosperity, and with things going so well I knew my luck couldn't continue on the upside, something would give and I'd find myself flat on my face. Instead of waiting, I went for it, leaped for the pipe and returned to a long-dormant cocaine habit. If I needed to make an excuse, more so to myself than anyone else, I could offer that the restaurant was overwhelming, and I needed relief from the day-to-day, week-to-week, month-to-month, relentless grind, the kind where you wake yourself with the sound of your teeth grinding. The kind of stress that makes a man long for a hit off a crack pipe.

Ten years ago when I indulged in smoking a little cocaine, I handled it, but now was different. Then it was about staying up to dawn, for the second day, clubbing until I was sick of the whole idea of clubbing. Working and playing, trying to have everything, and it worked until I couldn't stand living like that. I gave it up, put down the pipe and cocaine easily. Proved to myself that cocaine didn't have me by the balls. Suddenly I noticed I had so much more money in my bank account, and I met Elena, fell in love, and that was that. It really was a good thing, and I handled it smoothly so smoothly I had it in the back of my mind that I could do it again. It wouldn't be no thing. But, I guess, shit has a way of catching up with you after a while. My addiction was like a cancer cell, dormant, kicking it until the conditions were right. Probably, the truth is I don't have the same discipline or constitution. I'm not that young man who could do that, keep it going, burning myself out in every direction. Soon enough I lost the restaurant to my partner, and my wife found my fucked-up, vulgar habit reason enough to leave me. I don't blame her. She didn't marry a fiend, I became one, it just took time for me to discover it, my inclination toward self-immolation. I call it that, the suicidal impulse to consume yourself with a Bic lighter. I'd see myself burned out, gone, a neat pile of ashes, but that's more acceptable to my imagination than the vision of myself as a pathetic, cracked-lip panhandler, a martyr to the pipe.

Maybe I wanted to fail, see how far I could fall.

Far and hard.

Lucifer had nothing on me.

Being broke is like having a bloody mouth and loose teeth and there's not a thing you can do about it, except stand it.

How does that song go?

"A knife, a fork, a bottle, and a cork—that's the way we spell New York . . . I got Cocaine running around my brain."

Something like that, but I'm not judging.

I thought I could master my high. I wish I had the courage to have stayed in the city for everyone to see me living in a halfway house, trying to reassemble the remaining shards of self-respect.

What if I ran into her, Elena, my wife?

It's wrong to say that, we're more divorced than married, but far as I'm concerned she still is. Funny how memory works. When you don't fill it with anything new, it replays what maybe you don't want replayed.

My mind replays Elena.

Short, with hair like the blackest ink, strong legs and ass, a delicate face, almost Japanese, like a geisha in a Ukiyo-e print.

Passionate about love and making money and everything else.

Passionate about hating me.

I still love her, though it's hopeless to think she'll ever love me again. I want her back more than the restaurant, a reputation, everything, but it will never happen, not in this life and not the next.

Left with nothing, other than to lie in bed and think about what I've done, hurt the woman I love and lost her, didn't consider the consequences back then, didn't have bouts of guilt, didn't consider anything. It was about me, about what's good for the head. You know, the head. A selfish bitch, that's the truth about me.

About me, that's all it ever was, my love was a fraud, my professionalism a joke, my self-respect, delusion.

And I'll never get it back; you'd think I'd find the courage to do
something dramatic, maybe kill myself or find God. No, I indulged
in self-pity, waiting to be saved from myself.

Elena partied hard, but you know, it didn't get to her. She did it
all—heroin, coke, ecstasy—but when she was through with it, she
was through. Maybe it was yoga or the StairMaster, but mostly it
was because Elena wanted a baby, and she's that type of person, so
directed and focused that she didn't stop to think that the rest of the
world, and by that I mean me, might not be able to live the way she
managed to. It took forever for her to see that I had a weakness.
Never raised an eyebrow when, after a sharing a few lines, I
excused myself to go to the bathroom to do a few more. She even
laughed when she saw me fumbling to put everything away, hastily
brushing white powder from my face, more evidence of my lack of
control.

It was funny in a way. She should have noticed that I was craving, fiending, whatever you want to call it. I had started my downward journey, my decline—in it to win it, a new life consisting of
one long, sustained need to stay high.

My recollection of conversations with Elena replay themselves,
and I listen to myself ruin my marriage.

"We're four months behind on the mortgage?" Elena asked.

"No, I don't think it's that far along. Maybe two months," I
replied.

"What happened to the money? We'll lose the apartment."

"Things got away from me. I'm sure we can put something
together to work this out."

"What are the chances of that happening?"

I shrugged. I didn't want to lie to her.

"Do you know what you're doing to us, the fact that you can't
control yourself? Why don't you admit it, stop being in denial."

She looked at me with smoldering, black eyes.

"You need professional help."

"I don't have that kind of problem."

"You're forcing me—no, you're giving me no choice but to leave you."

"Come on," I said. "We'll work this out."

This time she laughed bitterly.

"Sure we will," she said, but we both knew that was a lie.

After that she moved in with a friend and refused to talk to me, but that particular humiliation didn't sting much because later that week in court I pled guilty and was sentenced to nine months in a minimum-security prison.

In some sense I was content to be going, having done enough damage to my self-esteem that I wanted to crawl away into a corner and wait for the room to stop spinning. And when it did, I woke up to the humiliation of getting processed, prepped, and more to go to the place to do my time. My only regret is that I wasn't high during that humiliation.

The days inside prison weren't totally unpleasant. They had a good enough library, and I spent time lifting weights for the first time in my life. That's it, I thought, do positive things for myself while incarcerated and avoid being raped, but in a minimum-security prison, the only thing I had to worry about was getting athlete's foot in the shower.

I had hoped to hear from Elena at some point, but after months had passed, I began to wonder if I would.

When I was released and moved to the halfway house, she wrote and said she would be coming to visit so I could sign the papers.

Divorce papers.

I tried not to allow those words to rise to the surface. I waited with far too much hope on that moment when she'd appear at the door of the halfway house to be shown inside by one of the work-

246 // THE COCAINE CHRONICLES

ers, who would sign her in and bring me out to sit across from her on the worn couch. Me, smiling stupidly, thinking, feverishly hoping, that her seeing me again would jar something loose and she'd want to forget about the divorce. It was what it was, paperwork.

She wore all black, tight wool skirt and a sweater that looked good on her, but she kept her arms crossed, probably remembering how much I liked her small breasts.

I don't think she ever smiled. Talked to me about some issues, bankruptcy, insurance policy. Nothing I was interested in. I was interested in her, but that was dead.

I was dead to her.

She took it personally, like I had rejected her for cocaine, but it wasn't like that.

How did she ask it?

"How could you be so fucking stupid? Getting yourself arrested buying crack on the subway?"

I shrugged. I guess if it was the first time, she might have been able to excuse it, but it wasn't.

To this day I don't know how stupid I am. I don't think I've plumbed the depths of my stupidity, and when I do, I plan to get back to her. I'll have charts and graphs, a PowerPoint demonstration.

I ruined my life, I know that, last thing I wanted to do was betray her, but I was good at that, too, excelled at it, even.

Asha, the woman who ran the halfway house, realized I could cook South Asian. Being Gujarati she was surprised that I made a better bindi, spiced eggplant, than her mother. She discovered that I could stay in seclusion in a sweltering kitchen cooking up meals for the dozen or so losers that lived at the halfway house. I labored away in silent grief, working with old vegetables, day-old bread, not much meat, which pleased Asha because she didn't like the smell, some chicken, beans, lots of beans. I came up with meal after meal through backbreaking efficiency and invention. When I wasn't cooking, I cleaned. I scoured that kitchen, boiled water, added cupfuls of caustic soap, cleaned the filthy ceiling, cleaned every-thing. Made it spotless, and kept it that way as long as I was there, my six months climbing out of the black hole of my life.

Cooking and cleaning and not thinking was a meditative balm. I hated when thoughts would slither in on their own and have their way with me. Grief caught me slipping, I needed to see her. Thought of leaving, blowing the whole thing off, my contract with the halfway house staff, to make a run to see her, force her to listen to me.

I'd go to prison, and I had sense enough to know I didn't want that. Maybe I might have tried, maybe prison would have been worth it, if I got her to listen to me, but in reality I had no words left to beg with.

I was out of prayers and I was sick of lighting candles to the saint of hopeless causes.

She was gone, maybe here, probably some other city.

"It's for the best," my caseworker said, when I confessed why I wouldn't talk in therapy.

"It's not about the drugs. It's about losing my wife."

"Drugs are why you lost her. You drove her away."

I cried then, in front of that fool. I stopped talking to him after that. Before, I felt like maybe he was okay.

I was wrong.

Up until that moment, I didn't want to do cocaine again. I really was through with it.

Then the cravings started.

I knew she wasn't coming back, but that fiction kept me alive. Kept me thinking it was the drug. The drug did me, and not me the drug.

He ruined that conceit, better than therapy ever could.

Trying to avoid contact with my fellow losers at the halfway house, I took to mincing garlic like garlic would keep everyone at bay, like they were all vampires. I guess we are, vampires that suck smoke instead of blood. It worked, everyone kept their distance, except for Asha. I was her reclamation project and she tried to draw me out. I accepted her good attentions, but I didn't want to be drawn out or in, or anywhere. I wanted to stay lost. Alone would be good, but I couldn't expect that. I had to get with the twelve-step program, show requisite progress to get these people out of my life. Still, Asha was pleasant and charming, with big luminous eyes that were easy to look into. Good thing she didn't go for men, because our friendship would have been much more complicated. Finally, I explained a little about myself, and so when she came into the kitchen with this look on her face, I knew I had probably said too much.

"What's wrong?"

"You. I read about you."

"What? That I'm a fuck-up? You already knew that."

She shook her head.

"Yeah, I made a mess of what most people think was a promising career."

"Don't you miss that life? Running that restaurant, cooking?"

"I don't know. I guess I do."

"My girlfriend works for this famous entertainer. She says he needs a chef."

I raised an eyebrow, in spite of myself.

"I wouldn't get past the interview," I said.

"She's crazy about me and listens to what I have to say. If you're interested, you'd have a shot."

"I'll think about it," I replied, without a hint of enthusiasm. I wondered why she wanted to go out of her way for me, she was smart enough to know I truly was a fuck-up. It had to be her nature, trusting and giving, and maybe a bit naïve, coupled with being smart about people and hard-nosed about the everyday affairs of running the halfway house. I guess that's what you need in order to be in her line of work, skills that contradict each other. Strange how a woman, young and attractive, would choose social work; running a halfway house must be like hanging around unflushed toilets all day, when she could choose so many more attractive occupations. Maybe she wanted to be a Hindu Mother Teresa, and if she could drag me back to respectability, she'd be one giant step closer to sainthood.

Sometimes I think I hear him calling, a sibilant whisper from a satin-lined oak coffin hidden below the sub-basement in a tomb so cold he'd be able to see his rancid breath if he actually had breath. "Living food, that's what I'm feeling," he says.

Because he's feeling it, I'm feeling it, and that's why I'm drinking that Santa Ynez red, and I'm liking it more than I should.

Backsliding.

No more of this drinking after work, getting silly, having flights of fancy that do me no good.

I've still got to deal with living food, no matter how silly it is to consider cooking without fire an earth-shaking invention. Really, you'd think most reasonable people would agree that cooking is a good thing, a good invention, and we should feel good about it. Maybe Monster remembered something about predigestion in high school biology and it confused and disgusted him. Probably, though, it's the influence of a gastronomic guru who put him on the road to bliss through the chewing of fresh bark. Who am I to stand in the way of his path to enlightenment?

Monster is a freak, a freakish freak, maybe a child-molesting freak, but he's not a creature-feature villain, no matter how much red wine might insinuate that.

No.

He's a self-invented American, freakishly fascinating in his attempt at reinvention, and because of it, his self-invention, his desire to live like something out of a cautionary tale of how outrageously famous people go wrong, makes him unique, unique as crazy wealth and an addiction to television can make you. I bet as a kid he rushed home to watch *Dark Shadows* with a chaser of *The Brady Bunch*, which explains some of it—the blond children running around like chickens shooed about by giddy parents. Really, it's not Monster or the kids I wonder about, it's the parents. What must they be like? What do they want for themselves, for their children?

Monster bait.

I'm sure they have lawyers on speed dial, ready and waiting for something actionable. Maybe that's Monster's real value: pulling back the curtain on the banality of human perversity. Give somebody like him enough money and power and what gets revealed?

He's fucking crazy, but it's okay.

Everyone here knows it. It's common knowledge living up here on the mountain. When will the townspeople realize what's up and break out the torches and pitchforks and march on Monster's *Lair*? Isn't it inevitable?

I have another glass of wine and try to return my attention to the task at hand—planning Monster's meals for the week. I figured when I first saw him that the last thing he would be concerned with is eating, figuring him as a man who lived on meth and Twinkies and maybe Diet Coke, because these folks bathe themselves in Diet Coke. For a man over six feet, he must weight 120 pounds, and that's if he hasn't evacuated his bowels.

Considering what he wants to eat, he'd be better served by hiring a botanist than a personal chef.

Living food isn't something a cook makes. No, give a kid mud, wheat, water, and whatever, and let him go at it.

But I'm a professional, and if that's want Monster is into this week, I'll give it to him straight, with a sprig of fresh rosemary on that sunbaked gluten ravioli.

Breakfast: Oatmeal with coconut milk and raisins.

Snack: Cracked-barley porridge with fresh strawberries.

Lunch: Vegan, sunbaked pizza with three kinds of tomato and Mexican salt from Oaxaca.

Snack: Fresh greens in a lemon sauce.

Dinner: Veggie sushi.

Snack: Unsweetened cider.

That's what my life is now; feeding Monster shit he calls food.

If I had more integrity, if I had that kind of character, I'd get my ass off of the mountain, face the consequences, and preserve my dignity.

Fuck yes. The first step on the road to recovery is to know yourself. I'd best start whipping up some sun-baked potato pancakes for Monster's snack, or find a crack pipe; maybe both if I know me, and I do.

Mary Ann Heimann

GARY PHILLIPS writes in several mediums, including comic books, novels, and screenplays, seeking to tap the primal. His published works of fiction include *Bangers, The Perpetrators,* and *Monkology*, a collection of stories featuring private investigator Ivan Monk. Phillips won the Chester Himes Mystery Award, was short-listed for a Shamus Award, and is on the national board of the Mystery Writers of America.

disco zombies
by gary phillips

Wild Willie stumbled backward, knocking against the rickety kitchen table, sending the two plastic bricks of coke somersaulting to the floor.

"Goddammit, Spree, pay up." Wild Willie wrenched hard to get the six-shooter free from the other man's grasp.

"Fuck that, Willie!" Spree Holmes blared. "I did." He had both of his hands clamped around Wild Willie's gun hand, his fingers tugging on the barrel of the revolver, even as Willie beat the shit out of his arm with his free fist. "You fuckin' reneged, man," he added, gritting his teeth.

Holmes sprung from a tiptoe position so as to maximize his weight bearing down on the heavier but flabbier Wild Willie. It worked, and the two went over and down onto the worn linoleum. They slid against one of the lower cabinets, busting off its handle.

"Shit!" McMillan hollered from the doorway, ducking and diving beneath the wind of the Samurai sword Crider swung at the top of his thinning hair. McMillan flopped onto his stomach in his vintage Hawaiian shirt atop the ratty shag carpet. But for once he wasn't worried about keeping his clothes neat. He twisted around onto his back, kicking and flailing his legs like an angry turtle, just as Crider chopped at him with the blade. A piece of the heel of McMillan's two-tone shoe was sliced off and he instinctively shut his eyes as if he'd been gored in the heart.

"Ugh," Holmes grunted after Wild Willie yanked the gun free. He'd been partially straddling him but flung himself sideways as the other man righted the piece. Desperate, Holmes reached out and latched onto anything he could off the counter. With brutal force he slammed alongside Willie's head a glass container used with a blender. Its impact caused Willie's shot to be misdirected and singe past Holmes's head—but not into it.

"Motherfucker," Wild Willie swore. A thick piece of glass was embedded in the meaty part above his eyebrow, and he had no choice but to grab for it to relieve the pain. As he did so, Holmes shoved the heel of his hand into the shard, driving it deeper. Willie's legs twitched in agony as he tore off another blast at Holmes's chest.

In the dining room McMillan keenly registered the shot but was concentrating on throwing a porcelain statuette of a trumpet player he'd plucked off a shelf with as much shoulder as he could put behind it.

"You throw like a little girl," the silver-toothed Crider taunted. A cut had opened up on his face as a result of the miniature musician hitting him. He was on one side of a round dining room table and McMillan opposite. Crider held his gleaming sword in both hands, the bulk of it poised over the table.

"Which you want to lose, man? Hand or ear?" Crider made a quick back-and-forth with the steel, letting it whistle in the stifling air of the little house.

"You ain't man enough to take me without your chop suey prop," McMillan said, inching to his left.

"Come on, I'll make it nice and clean and fast." Crider made a vicious swipe that caused McMillan to tense but not be so stupid as to start running and get the back of his neck severed.

Holmes and Wild Willie tumbled out of the kitchen, entangled. When Willie had shot at him the second time, Holmes was in the process of lowering his upper frame, and as the bullet funneled into the bone of his shoulder blade, his momentum carried him forward and he'd rammed into Wild Willie's chest, stunning him. Battling tears and doing what he could to ignore the stars exploding behind his corneas, Spree Holmes had pressed the fight, knowing if he let up, the next shot from that old Colt would blow his guts out.

Instinctively, Crider bounded over to the wrestling forms to give his homeboy Willie a hand. He turned to refocus on McMillan, who was now pushing the dining room table toward him. Crider dodged to one side but McMillan followed his movement and upended the table onto the swordsman's feet.

"Bastard!" Crider yelped. He got his left foot free but the right, in its snakeskin boot, wasn't so easily extricated. McMillan held onto the edge of the table and lifted it up quickly and then brought it down again on the right's instep. Crider gritted his teeth and wielded the blade toward McMillan's hand. The other man lunged out of the way and the sword sliced into the table's rim and held fast.

McMillan laughed and, putting effort behind it, shoved the table, sending Crider into a wall as he attempted to free his weapon. "I got your girl," McMillan said, and plowed a fist into the opposing man's nose as the sword came loose.

At that same moment, Holmes and Wild Willie were digging into each other's faces with their fingers. Holmes's thumb was gouging into the corner of Willie's mouth. The latter shifted and bit down on that thumb like it was fresh steak.

"That ain't gonna help you, Willie," Holmes said, leveraging forward and causing Willie's head to rattle against the doorjamb. Willie reached for the six-shooter, which was now lying on the kitchen floor, but Holmes wasn't about to allow that to happen. Holmes took hold of what material he could of Wild Willie's T-shirt and, jerking him up, head-butted him, opening the gash wider over Willie's eye.

"Ke-rist!" Wild Willie screamed, and tried to scurry away. Holmes was on his feet and stomped on the escaping man's side like he was a bothersome cockroach. He then pressed the barrel of the gun onto Willie's thigh and shot him.

"That ought to slow you down," Holmes said over Willie's whimpering.

Behind him Crider had his sword but was keeling over from a

rocking blow delivered via the dining room chair hefted by McMillan. The chair was rusted metal tubing and a torn leatherette-covered seat, but it served McMillan well as a shield. Like a lion tamer from an old Saturday morning serial, he had it up and was using it to fend off the blows from Crider's sword.

"Put it the fuck down," Holmes ordered.

Crider and McMillan both turned and stared. McMillan then grinned broadly, stroking his goatee with his long-nailed hand. "Shoot him," he said.

The Colt in Holmes's hand didn't waver, even though the burning in his shoulder intensified.

Crider made a guttural sound and pivoted toward Holmes. The sword was at his side, the blade pointing outward—a Mississippi Samurai in pointy-toed cowboy boots and worn Lee jeans.

"I'm not fuckin' around, Crider."

"Smoke his ass," McMillan repeated. He still held onto the chair.

Crider cocked his head to the side, waiting and wondering. He grasped the sword by two hands on its hilt.

"Get the shit," Holmes said.

"On it." McMillan scooted into the kitchen, not letting go of the chair until he was in the other room. Wild Willie was curled into a fetal position and moaned softly, his leg leaking profusely.

"Something broke?" McMillan teased cruelly, as he scooped up the two keys of flake. "Or is it indigestion from trying to cheat us, you cheap fuck?" Spittle dotted McMillan's graying goatee. "Huh, Willie, that it?" He leaned over, feigning like he was listening for a response.

"You . . ." the man on the floor began.

"You what, you fuckin' Shylock." McMillan planted his two-tone Nunn Bush shoe in Willie's stomach, making him wince and gurgle crimson. "You gonna try and play us, man? After the business we done together, making your own thirty-percent-state-disability-retard-self phatter than you deserve to be?"

Holmes called from the dining room: "Come on, let's hit the road!"

"Yeah, yeah. Can't have no more fun." He kicked Willie in the ribs, a bone giving way. As McMillan started to walk out, Wild Willie suddenly gyrated his body and reached for the exiting man's legs. McMillan reacted but still got tangled up as Willie continued to paw at him, and he fell forward.

Holmes knew better than to be distracted by his partner going timber. The problem was McMillan whirligigged his arms to stay upright, causing Holmes to reposition himself, and Crider took his opening.

There was a flash of silver and the sword swiped downward at McMillan's tilting head. "Oh, fuck me," the goateed man exclaimed and put a hand to the side of his head.

Crider turned on the balls of his feet, bringing the sword level like a batter going for a sliding pitch. Holmes cranked off a round even as he peddled backward to ward off being hacked. The shot blasted into the swordsman's forearm and he dropped his weapon.

McMillan was on his knees, his eyes saucers from fear. "Finish him, shit, finish him, Spree."

"We're done here," the calmer Holmes declared, already heading toward the front door. He carried the Samurai sword, the peacemaker tucked into the hollow of his back. Redness soaked into his shirt and blood dripped onto the carpet.

"You sure?" McMillan stared at Crider, who was crumpled into one of the other chairs where the dining room table had been. He was holding his useless arm by his opposite hand. The .44 slug had entered at such an angle that it exited through his elbow, shattering the joint.

"What's he going to do," Holmes said derisively, "call the cops?"

"Still . . ." McMillan ventured.

"I gotta get patched up. And I'm hungry and I'm hurting." It occurred to him that the money they'd brought wasn't in his hand.

No sense leaving it now, it wasn't like there weren't going to be hard feelings between him and Wild Willie.

He found the small gym bag beside the couch and tucked it under his arm like a football. With that, Holmes made for the front door, not particularly concerned with whether a nosy neighbor or the local law was on the other side. It was getting on toward dusk and he wanted to be out on the highway, away from Wild Willie, Crider, and this shitty town of Greenwood.

"You think this is over, Holmes? You know it's not."

McMillan pointed at Crider. "Shut up."

"Scared, McMillan? Scared I'm going to put my red magic on you?" Crider said, his sunken eyes swallowed up as if his face were caving in on itself.

"I told you to keep your mouth shut." McMillan smacked the wounded man with the plastic Circle K shopping bag he'd placed the coke bricks in. This upended Crider and he crashed to the floor, wailing as he landed on his exposed bone.

McMillan laughed and couldn't resist standing over the hurting man. "You know, Crider, I never did cotton to you."

Holmes called from the vicinity of the front door: "Stop fucking around!" McMillan grinned at him and looked back at Crider. A burst of a sparkling brown cloud engulfed his face.

"Hey," McMillan said, hitting Crider hard, twice in rapid succession, as he lay on the floor. Crider went limp but still wasn't unconscious.

McMillan put his angry face close to the still man. "Why don't I just shoot you?"

"I'm leaving, Mill." Holmes stepped through the door and into the coming darkness.

In the car, plowing across the gravel of the driveway and onto the residential street, each assessed the other's damage.

"How deep is it?" McMillan looked but didn't touch the wound atop Holmes's shoulder blade.

"I can feel the bullet grind when I move my arm." Despite this,

Holmes was at the wheel. He glanced sideways. "How about that chunk Crider took off?"

McMillan blinked and felt along the top, or what had been the top, of his right ear. "Ain't that some shit? I got so excited I forgot that motherfucker chopped this off." He leaned so he could see his lobe in the rearview mirror as he gingerly fingered the flesh. "Can it be sewn back on?"

"Sure, want me to turn around so you can get the piece?"

McMillan gave him a lopsided look. "Shit," he finally said. "So where to, drive across the border to Arkansas? I used to know a cat there in Little Rock who can help us out." McMillan was reaching into his back pocket for his cell phone.

"Too far, and even though we ain't gushing out, I don't want to go that long without attention."

McMillan nodded, understanding his meaning. "You just lookin' to get your dick wet."

"Ain't you? We just scored enough coke that once it's broken down to crack in the 'hood, it will keep us in dead prezs for months."

McMillan indicated the trunk where their cash kept company with the snow. "And the discount we got it at. I still can't believe after we'd already agreed to the price beforehand that Wild Willie tried to jack it up once we got there. What the fuck, huh?"

"Exactly," Holmes said, heading toward Highway 49. "Probably some static from his supplier. But that's his worry, not ours."

McMillan clucked his tongue. "Man didn't want to listen." He sneezed and coughed. "Goddamn ju-ju powder Crider blew on me. What was that about, huh?" He plucked at his nose.

Holmes tried to shrug but his shoulder was already stiffening. "Some kind of Indian thing, I guess."

McMillan looked blank.

"He's part Choctaw," Holmes illuminated. "Crider was always into hoodoo shit, casting spells and chanting and all that to protect him when we were about to do a job."

"You two used to run together?"

"Yeah," Holmes said, but didn't elaborate. He gave a number to McMillan and the other man handed the phone over when the line connected.

"Uh-huh," Holmes said, after saying hi and listening for a bit. "I know I have some nerve, Janey, but I'm hurtin', baby, and I need a safe port in the storm." He didn't dare look over at McMillan or he'd start laughing at how thick he was slathering it on and screw it up for sure. "Baby, I know, but I promise you we'll make it worth your effort."

He listened some more as Jane Corso chewed him out, but he could tell she was softening. What they had once was too strong and too real for either of them to pretend otherwise—and being able to help her with car and utility payments was certainly an added incentive. She was a practical woman, after all.

"And, uh, if it's not too much bother, maybe you could ask what's-her-face, you know, the one with the green flamingo, to help you out."

McMillan brightened and considered just where Corso's friend had that flamingo tattooed.

"Okay," Holmes said, after another minute or so of negotiating. He hung up. And even though his shoulder was starting to burn worse, he winked broadly. "We're set, man."

"Righteous." McMillan settled back, wondering how much reconstructive surgery would cost.

In less than an hour and a half the two reached Jane Corso's modest frame house, inherited from her grandmother, in Clarksdale, not too far from the Sunflower River. It was in a dead-end lush with overgrown shrubs and set down the slope from a small hill. Its location along an unpaved street gave it a semi-rural feel; the nearest house was half a block away.

Corso and her friend with the tattoo, Ella Fernandez, worked at the Diamond Stud Casino over in Tunica. Corso was a dealer and Fernandez a waitress.

"Like old damn times," Corso said, working the probe in Holmes's exposed shoulder area. She'd numbed the wound as best she could using a paste made from some of the coke and Lidoderm, a medicine for cold sores, she found in the medicine cabinet. Holmes sat rigid and gripped the sides of the chair's seat, grinding his teeth.

"You know, I—"

"Hush, Spree," she said, a suggestion of a smile on her face. She kneaded her bottom lip with her teeth while she dug for the slug fragments in him.

It wasn't merely nostalgia or a longing to see her that had brought Holmes to her abode. Jane Corso had been a nursing student at one point—before acquiring a taste for the nose candy and shady men like her current patient. "Ah," she said, removing the probe with part of the bullet. She held the tweezers to the light, examining her find.

"If you could finish up before I pee on myself, doc, I'd appreciate it," Holmes said, sweat moistening his face and chest.

Corso's sometimes pale green eyes lightened with mirth. "Best be cool or I'll really put you under and do a Lorena Bobbitt on you."

"You tell him, girl," Ella Fernandez encouraged. While Corso was in street clothes, Fernandez wore her casino uniform, given her shift had ended after the men had arrived. A short cowgirl skirt barely covered her ample rear and was complemented by a fringed leather vest with a revealing scoop. She and McMillan were sitting on the couch and he was regaling her about his real and exaggerated criminal exploits. They rested against an Afghan comforter spread against the back of the couch.

Fernandez had already snorted up three lines of blow from the glass-topped coffee table. There was a current TV *Guide*, a discount-store 1.75-liter bottle of Jack Daniel's, a few plastic cups, a pack of Kools, and a Zippo on the coffee table, as well. Corso had heated the ends of her tool with the lighter.

262 // THE COCAINE CHRONICLES

More digging and more discomfort and Corso extracted the remaining piece from Holmes. She stitched the gash closed. After that, she handed a grateful Holmes a plastic cup with a dose of Jack Daniel's sloshing in it. McMillan's bloody ear had also been stitched and taped.

"You always gotta do it the hard way, don't you, Spree?" She rubbed the side of his close-cropped graying hair.

He grinned thinly at her. "Bust my balls, why don't you?"

"I intend to." She took his hand and led him toward her bedroom. On the couch, McMillan was busy licking coke from around one of Fernandez's bare nipples. The green flamingo tattoo on the topside of her breast filled his vision.

Near 2:00 in the morning, Holmes and Corso lay awake in each other's arms.

"You heading for New York or L.A.?" Corso put a leg over his.

"L.A."

"Give that heartless city another go, huh?"

He didn't answer right away. "That's where we were going to make it," he finally allowed.

"We almost did, Spree. We sure gave it a good run then."

He pulled her tighter to him and kissed her, lost in what could have been. They soon started to doze off.

"Funny that song would be running through my head," Corso muttered, her head on his chest.

"'I Love the Night Life,'" Holmes remarked. "Alicia Bridges."

"How'd—" she began.

"You're not dreaming it," Holmes said, "I hear it, too."

Suddenly there was a loud blast of wood splintering and the crash of the front door being ripped from its hinges.

"Spree!" McMillan yelled over Fernandez's scream from the front room.

Holmes and Corso had already scooted out of bed. He quickly slipped on his boxers. She tossed the six-shooter to him, which had been resting on the night stand next to a rolled-up dollar bill. He tore into the living room, assuming that somehow muscle sent by Crider and Wild Willie had found them. There was no way he could have anticipated what was waiting for him.

"The fuck?" he breathed.

"Do something, Spree," McMillan pleaded. He was naked and pinned against the wall. Fernandez was clad in her panties and lying half off the couch on her back, her eyelids fluttering. A bruise welled on her jaw.

Holmes extended the gun and shot at one of the things that had invaded the home. The bullet punctured the creature's eye socket, and that should have dropped any man, but as Holmes was rapidly grasping, these were not normal beings.

"*Zombies,*" Corso gasped from behind Holmes.

The one with its hand around McMillan's throat was dressed in tattered clothing of an unmistakable vintage. He had on a dirt-stained silk shirt with billowing sleeves, once-tight bell-bottom slacks, a belt with a huge lettered buckle, and platform shoes. The other creature was wearing what had formerly been a white suit with a matching vest and a blue super-fly collar-point shirt, open and exposing a bony chest crawling with blind earthworms. This one had a raft of gold—now moldy green—chains and medallions draped around its neck, and the remnants of a puffy Afro full of leaves and twigs. He held onto the two bricks of coke.

The feculent odor rising from the two zombies was overpowering and caused Corso to gag. Holmes was more concerned about his dope. Medallion zombie had turned toward the door and Holmes shot him in the knee. The bone popped and the creature stumbled as if it had stepped into a pothole. Holmes ran forward but bell-bottom zombie hurled McMillan, and he had to prone out to avoid being struck.

"Thanks for breaking my fall," McMillan groaned, after colliding with the now broken TV set.

"They're taking our powder!" Holmes yelled, launching himself and tackling the bell-bottomed one. The monster made a guttural sound and hit him so hard behind his neck that Holmes was knocked to the floor, dazed.

"*Coke,*" Afro zombie growled to his buddy.

"*Ughh,*" the other one said, smiling. Dung and beetles spilled out of his maw.

The two shambled out the hole they'd made ripping off the door. Afro zombie walked lopsided due to its decimated kneecap.

"Spree, Spree, get up." Corso shook him.

Holmes rose to a knee like a fighter taking an eight.

"Come on," Corso said, heading out in pajama bottoms, her pump shotgun cradled in her arms. That was the other thing that Holmes liked about her—she always had his back in a scrap.

The two zombies were moving up the hill behind her house and Holmes and Corson went after them, joined by a limping McMillan who'd tied the comforter around his waist.

"Wait a minute," Holmes said to Corso, who was taking aim with the scatter gun. "Bad enough we've been shooting off pistols, but we're not that isolated around here. You start using that sumabitch, somebody's bound to call the law. We've got to follow them."

"To where?" she asked.

"Where they can snort up the shit." He trotted after the pair, clad only in his boxers. The two creatures were nearing the top of the rise.

"Greedy motherfuckin' zombies!" McMillan exclaimed. He looked around and spied a rock about the size of his fist. He picked it up and threw it, hitting the bell-bottom zombie in the back.

The thing turned around, growling and flailing his arms. He charged at them and Holmes grabbed the shotgun out of Corso's hand, swinging the stock at the thing's head. This knocked loose some gray, dry flesh, but it kept coming. Holmes made to swing again and the creature caught the weapon and snatched it out of his hands. He broke it apart by banging it against a thick tree trunk. As this transpired, Afro zombie made it over the top and disappeared.

"Get the coke," Holmes directed McMillan. "We'll take care of this undead shithead."

"Don't have to tell me twice." McMillan went wide when the zombie lunged for him, but as its muscles were atrophied and its joints long since dried out, it couldn't move with the attenuation and speed of a live person. McMillan got past and went up.

Holmes shot the zombie again and it turned toward him, snarling at the continuing irritation of Holmes putting bullets into it. "I need an axe or something to cut the head off or burn it," Holmes said.

"I'm with you, Spree," Corso declared.

They exchanged a quick, meaningful look, then the thing was upon them, clawing and snapping its jaw. Holmes was down on his back and he drove a fist into the creature's rib cage. Some of the brittle bones cracked, but it was taking all of Holmes's effort to keep the monster from biting into his head. He had both hands pressed under what was left of the zombie's clacking jaw, the rancid breath making his eyes water. The stitches on his wound ripped and he pumped red from atop his shoulder blade.

"Get off!" Corso screamed, jumping on the zombie's back and pummeling him.

"*Coke*," the creature intoned. It reached around and pulled Corso off by her hair and flung her away. It got its bony hands around Holmes's neck and squeezed, causing him to gag. The zombie's jaws opened and unhinged, and the thing bent down to eat the man's face off.

"Hey, shit-breath!" Ella Fernandez hollered. She brought the Jack Daniel's bottle down on its head. The thick glass broke apart, causing a dent in the side of the creature's skull. The alcohol spilled over its upper body.

"I got something for you, dead bitch," Fernandez avowed as the zombie started for her. She lit the Zippo and threw it on him, catching his head on fire. The zombie wailed and stomped about.

"I guess it doesn't like fire," Holmes observed in his grass-smeared Fruit of the Looms. The zombie was running around in a circle, screaming. It bumped into a tree and knocked itself down. But it didn't have enough presence of mind—or enough of a brain left—to roll and put out its now totally aflame body. It got back up and screamed some more as it clomped around, continuing to burn.

Corso helped Holmes to his feet. "Or it's the way he died," she said.

Fernandez breathed deeply, her heavy breasts rising and falling, the flamingo contracting and expanding. She was still only dressed in her panties.

"Good work, Ella," Holmes told her. He then asked Corso, "What do you mean?"

She started to run up the hill without answering. "We better get up there."

"The ya-yo," Holmes remembered, as he and Fernandez also took off. At the top it was a regular zombie jamboree. There were eight more of them that had crawled out of their graves, all dressed in disco regalia.

A female zombie milled about in what was left of a miniskirt. She wore torn fishnet stockings over charred legs, and a stretch velour top hugged a worm-infested chest. Another was clad in a spangle-studded safari suit and a broad-brimmed pimp hat. Part of his entrails hung from a gap in his silk shirt. Yet another was in hot pants, thigh-high platform boots, and her angel-sleeve blouse was being ripped off by another zombie in a poncho, gaucho pants, and dingo boots.

The zombies were growling and snarling and tearing at each other to get to the cocaine.

"Holy shit." Holmes held his head, ignoring his freshly opened wound, and marched around in total befuddlement. "What the fuck?"

Corso gulped. "They're the ones who were killed in the fire."

"What are you talking about, Janey?" Fernandez asked.

"New Year's Eve, 1980."

The miniskirted zombie had pulled the arm off the one in the gaucho pants and was beating him with it. *"Coke, coke,"* she repeated, as she drove the other one to the ground.

"Some local talent built a club down here, inspired by Donna Summer, Studio 54, you know, all that," Corso said.

Holmes stopped pacing. "There used to be a disco here?"

"Yeah. It was called, and this would prove to be ironic, the Disco Inferno. From what I understand, it was a popular place from 1976, when it started, to the night it burned down."

"The Bicentennial till the death of disco," Holmes gasped. Not a religious sort, he nonetheless sent a prayer up that the sky would rain gas and the Lord would then add a few lightning bolts to set the zombies ablaze.

Fernandez said, "You must have been a kid then."

"She was old enough," Holmes grinned wanly, grabbing some foliage to light with the recovered Zippo. He had to save his score.

"I'd already run off, wound up in L.A. Got involved with a creep that strung me out and pimped me out to this porn fuck. Even better that I was underage." Despite the humidity, she wrapped her arms around herself. "That's when I met Spree. The man in the white Charger—with a four on the floor."

Holmes gazed at her through the small fire he'd started with his crummy torch. "It was your ass that mesmerized me." With that, he ran into the thatch of zombies, but they were fevered and ignored his pathetic flame as they tore and ate into each other. He found McMillan on the ground, shivering.

"Aghhh," he grimaced when Holmes tugged on him. "Fucking freaks broke my arm." He got up, staring. "We're fucked."

The zombie in the thigh-high boots had jumped on the back of another who wore a torn gold-lamé cape. The cape man had gotten ahold of one of the bricks, or what had been the brick. He dipped his face into the powder, snorting madly like Pacino in *Scarface*. Thigh-high ripped the top of his head off and bit into his pulsing brain. She gobbled up pieces of the matter. The two stumbled about in stoned nirvana.

Holmes's flame petered out. "This ain't right," he lamented. "We gotta save our shit."

"Forget it, Spree," Corso advised, joining him. "These monsters will tear you apart if you get between them and their coke."

"It's not theirs!" he cried.

"It is now," Corso declared.

"'Fraid she's right," McMillan agreed, holding his busted arm. "Crider's spell or mojo or whatever the hell it was has us whupped good."

One of the zombies teetered on its feet, snow powdering its decomposed face. It ran into a tree and started to bang its head against the trunk so fiercely that it broke its face open. It continued hitting its head against the tree, smearing gore over the bark.

"Shit," Holmes swore. "Shit." He stomped about in frustration.

The zombies fought and scratched and snorted and mutilated each other until body parts were littered among the overgrown grass. Even legless zombies crawled their torsos over to any patch of flake on the ground to snort. The moon shone pregnant and brilliantly yellow against the warm night air.

Watching this, the four were soon witness to the actions of the last two zombies left standing. One was the creature with the nasty Afro and the other the ghastly one in the miniskirt. They each pulled on the end of a piece of plastic—a clump of the white stuff clung to the material. They stood among the battered and deformed heads, smashed eyeballs, torn-out tongues, broken teeth, severed fingers, cracked mood rings, ankh and cross ornaments, and knit caps of the walking disco dead.

Several of the disconnected heads mumbled, *"Coke, coke,"* over and over again, as a few of the mutilated hands crept across the ground in search of any fine white crystals left.

Meanwhile, miniskirt had an arm around Afro zombie's neck and was gnawing on his ear as he ignored her and snorted his treasure of blow. He then turned and bit into her face and the two bearhugged each other and rolled down the opposite side of the hill to a tributary of the river. Their bodies broke against a cropping of rocks, yet they continued to claw and rend each other.

Holmes wanted to cry. Corso consoled him as the four trudged back to the house. Each step along the way, all except Holmes grew slowly elated and pumped, having survived a vicious zombie attack.

"Come on, baby," Corso told a brooding Holmes back at the house. "I got something that will make you forget all about those funky zombies." And they made loud, rough love that left them both satisfied and weak, as was the same for McMillan and Fernandez. Fortunately for McMillan, his arm was merely wrenched, and he was able to use both hands to further explore the woman's body.

In the morning they ate well and Holmes and McMillan talked over other sources for some blow, given they still had their cash. Corso had declined any money.

"I'll call you."

"Liar."

"No," Holmes said, as they stood outside her house in the morning. "We connected again."

She kissed him.

Holmes and McMillan had started for their car when they spotted Wild Willie shambling from around a corner of the house. That he was dead was obvious from the hyperextended eyes, gray flesh, and festering leg with flies buzzing around it.

He sprayed bullets from his AK, all the while grunting, *"Coke, coke, give me my coke back,"* as the Tramps could be heard singing, *"Burn that mutha down,"* from their song, "Disco Inferno."

Also available from Akashic Books:

BROOKLYN NOIR edited by Tim McLoughlin
350 pages, a trade paperback original, $15.95, ISBN: 1-888451-58-0

Twenty brand new crime stories from New York's punchiest borough.
Contributors include: Pete Hamill, Arthur Nersesian, Maggie Estep,
Nelson George, Neal Pollack, Sidney Offit, Ken Bruen, and others.

"*Brooklyn Noir* is such a stunningly perfect combination that you
can't believe you haven't read an anthology like this before. But trust
me—you haven't. Story after story is a revelation, filled with the
requisite sense of place, but also the perfect twists that crime stories
demand. The writing is flat-out superb, filled with lines that will sing
in your head for a long time to come."
—Laura Lippman, winner of the Edgar, Agatha, and Shamus awards

SOUTHLAND by Nina Revoyr
348 pages, a trade paperback original, $15.95, ISBN: 1-888451-41-6
*Winner of a LAMBDA LITERARY AWARD
*EDGAR AWARD finalist

"If Oprah still had her book club, this novel likely would be at the top
of her list . . . With prose that is beautiful, precise, but never
pretentious . . ."
—*Booklist*

"*Southland* merges elements of literature and social history with the
propulsive drive of a mystery, while evoking Southern California as a
character, a key player in the tale. Such aesthetics have motivated
other Southland writers, most notably Walter Mosley."
—*Los Angeles Times*

HIGH LIFE by Matthew Stokoe
330 pages, a trade paperback original, $16.95, ISBN: 1-888451-32-7

". . . an elaborately drawn, surgically accurate Hollywood dystopia."
—Ellen Miller, author of *Like Being Killed*

"Stokoe's in-your-face prose and raw, unnerving scenes give way to a
skillfully plotted tale that will keep readers glued to the page . . .
Stokoe's protagonist is as gritty and brutal as they come, which will
frighten away the chaste crowd, but the author's target Bret Easton
Ellis audience could turn this one into a word-of-mouth success."
—*Publishers Weekly*